NIGHT WARDEN

Dark Dreamer

Book Three

Amber R. Duell

For Heather

A sister worth facing the Nightmare Realm for.

Chapter
One

Nora

Rule by fear.

Nightmares respected a ruthless, vicious, unforgiving leader, and it was easy enough to wear those traits as armor. Too easy perhaps. No one knew my decisions were made by asking myself: *what would the Weaver do?* Nor did they know I got the answer right from the horse's mouth.

Rule by fear, I told myself again.

If the nightmares didn't fear me, they were going to make certain I feared *them.* Whatever initial notion I had of making the Nightmare Realm a better place was now a distant memory. Maybe one worth revisiting down the road, one small change at a time, but first I had to bring each and every living thing to heel.

"Nora," Kail said from the corner of his mouth. He stood on my right, arms crossed, gaze ever vigilant. "Sometime today?"

I took a deep breath from where I stood atop the half-completed palace roof. The building was supposed to be finished within a month, not a month and three days. There had to be repercussions. Already, the last two days were more productive thanks to my new form of motivation. It didn't bother me, what I was doing, but it bothered me that it *didn't*. Killing should never be effortless.

"The palace still isn't finished. You know what that means," I called to the nightmares below in my most authoritative voice. It was stern and unyielding, making me feel every bit the villain.

The nightmares building the palace filled the lawn, stretching out in every direction. They were big brutes, mainly. Trolls who doubled as security, a couple giants with ladders grown into their lumpy, jaundiced skin, and a pack of garden gnomes that worked as well and as hard as any colony of ants. Wyverns were outfitted with ropes to carry materials back and forth from wherever they were mined, the digging done by lanky, alien-esc creatures with extendable arms that ended in curved paddles. A smattering of nondescript nightmares helped in whatever way they could, but mostly they just got in the way.

Yesterday, it was one of those that suffered the consequences.

A medium-sized nightmare with black fur, run through with pink scars, hunched and crooked, murdered with a single bullet from my stepfather's liberated gun. The day before it was a gnome in a red hat, and a giant the morning before that. The choices weren't intentional. I simply held the firearm up and sighted the first forehead that came into view. My aim was far from perfect, but the bullets never missed. Not when I wove them on the Weaver's loom to be sure of it.

I didn't bother explaining what would happen next. They knew. All of them knew. I lifted my arm, aimed at the first thing I saw and squeezed the trigger. A troll flew backward from the impact, blood spraying his neighbors. No one moved. Their eyes were trained on me, sharp as daggers.

"Tomorrow, it will be two of you," I promised before I passed the gun to Kail and turned from the crowd.

"Two, huh?" he asked. I leapt through a hole in the roof and into an empty room with him close on my heels. "At this rate, you won't have anyone left to finish the palace."

I leveled a stare at him. His eyes flickered almost lazily, color after color, as he looked at me from beneath his lashes. The white curved beak of his half mask brushed his chest. A sarcastic smile lifted my lips. "Then I'll make more."

That's my girl, the Weaver cooed inside my head.

I blanched at the sound. It was a near constant thing that sponged away my patience and my sanity. Talking, warning, tormenting. Sometimes I woke to him chanting eerie rhymes, old songs twisted and darkened. Other times, it was flashes of emotion that cut through me like a sword, though I didn't think those were intentional. My days were full of commentary. *Criticism.* Praise. Praise that I considered criticism. Having my life narrated by the man who ruined it was a special kind of hell.

"Feeling alright, Lady?" Kail asked. His words dripped with something like concern, something like accusation.

I waved a hand at the construction overhead, focusing my anger on that—*that* I could change. "I will be when there isn't a giant hole over my head big enough for anything or anyone to creep through."

"Yes." Kail pursed his lips and turned his gaze upward. "It's certainly a security risk."

I said nothing. It was easier that way. All the things I couldn't say, the things I wasn't ready to tell, would feel smaller as soon as I reached the art room. With a pencil in my hand and a blank page before me, things felt right again. Normal. A lie, but one I clung to. Because eventually I would have to tell Kail about the voice in my head. The Sandman too—the Sandman *first*. But not yet. Not until he came with news of Mara. I would let myself pretend there was a possibility of getting rid of the Weaver until the very moment one of them told me otherwise.

"Would you like to go out today?" Kail asked. "Explore? Create? Maim? Anything, really, that doesn't involve you holed up in the Keep again."

All excellent ideas. If only leaving didn't make the Weaver more active. "My strength is my thread." The existing coil of black thread, flecked with gold, tightened affectionately around my arm. "If we're going to take down Mara, I'll need as much of it as I can get."

Kail sighed, defeated, and held out Paul's gun. "Where do you want this thing?"

I looked down at the Day World weapon and something inside me wriggled uncomfortably. If the threads were my strength, I should be showing them off. Embracing the power of the Nightmare Realm instead of leaning on what I knew from my old life. "I don't need it anymore," I said carefully. It was time I killed more creatively.

Kail's eyes flicked faster in response.

Rule by fear.

I *was* fear. A Lady made from it as much as controlled by it.

My heart thudded heavily. I hadn't realized before now that acting as the cruel, unmerciful lady would slowly stain my heart. It would burn the edges black, leaving the smallest sliver of red beating at its center. There, Nora lived. *There,* I cared. I loved. In that tiny pocket, I felt pain and regret and even the occasional joy. Mostly, I feared. Feared that one day, I would feel nothing at all.

You will always feel, the Weaver said in a smug voice. *One day, you will feel as I have felt. Then you will understand me as I now understand you.*

New terror seized me. Maybe he was right, and one day I would wake up very much the monster he was, because when I killed those nightmares outside, I felt nothing. No regret, no shame. No *anything.* How long until I was like him? *Truly* like him—the Nightmare Lord that killed my friends and family. *No.* I would never allow myself to be that savage. I was the Lady of Nightmares, but I was also human.

Humanity in an inhumane world, the Weaver mused. *I tried that as well.*

Not hard enough, I thought back, my teeth bared.

Kail waved a hand in front of my face. He tilted his head and eyed me suspiciously. "Is there a problem?"

"No." I jumped away from him, walking quickly into the nearest room. "You're dismissed."

I slammed the door shut in his face and slumped against the heavy wood. Wyverns soared over the open courtyard on the way to pick up their first load of the day. The Keep stood before me, surrounded by a wide circle of grass. I had planted tall, neon-colored flowers around its base to brighten the courtyard, but the fact that they shot poison darts didn't hurt either. If anyone other than Kail and Halven made it into my private sanctuary, it would be the last thing they did.

Rule by fear, I promised myself again and again. Fear would keep my body alive. The rest I needed to protect another way. Bottle it up and keep it safe.

You're wrong, the Weaver said wistfully.

"Shut up," I snarled.

I tried, he said simply. *For him, I did.*

"I will dig you out of there with my bare hands," I threatened. Empty words, we both knew, because I wasn't even able to block him out.

My hands twitched, eager for the relief drawing would bring. I closed my eyes for a moment to center myself. Everything would be fine. Soon, the Sandman would come back, and we would make everything right again. I nodded to myself, and with a deep breath, strode straight for the Keep.

Everything would be fine.

It would.

It won't.

Deep down, I knew my last thought was the most probable.

Chapter Two

The Sandman

One month later

Time was strange.

A second could feel like a lifetime.

A lifetime could feel like a second.

The quiet made it feel as if everything was peaceful and calm in the Dream Realm when that was the furthest thing from the truth. My magic vibrated mercilessly beneath the domed barrier that kept the nightmares out. I felt it in my bones. My breastbone hummed constantly beneath the tattoo of a crescent moon. The navy blue and silver flecks rising from its center flowed down my arms. They had multiplied, become denser, and moved along my skin with an almost frantic edge. It made me want to scream to break the tense silence, but I didn't. Instead, I shoved down the anxiety prowling inside me like a caged beast, so I could channel it later.

Mare had been quiet too. *Too quiet.*

For nearly two weeks now.

That was also a deception. She had spent the majority of the last two months waging mental warfare against both Nora and myself. Her last act toward me was to create a straw man full of nightmare rats, which she then left at the edge of my realm on fire. Mare was fast and deadly, but she was never *quiet.* This long break was simply meant to heighten the anticipation while she schemed. I hated that it was working.

Fingers snapped next to my ear. "Earth to Sandy."

I blinked at the sudden noise and found Katie standing beside me. How long had I stood there, staring blankly ahead? "Sorry." I cleared my throat. "I was…"

"Pining for Nora again?" Katie rolled her eyes. "It's obvious. Really, you have bigger problems, don't you think?"

No.

Yes.

True to my word, I hadn't stepped foot in the Nightmare Realm since Nora defeated Rowan. It was for the best. In a short amount of time, Nora rebuilt the palace entirely, created loyal nightmares of her own, and convinced enough of the others not to cross her. From what I gathered, she was finally able to sleep with both eyes shut.

Halven, being a nightmare of few words, never offered any details when he came to deliver news. In return, I didn't ask how Nora managed to accomplish so much, so fast. I wanted her to tell me herself when we saw each other again. *Soon,* I prayed to the stars. This distance made me feel like a stranger to her despite logic telling me that was absurd.

"No," I finally said to Katie. I hadn't been thinking of her sister *right* then. "I was wondering if the proverbial dam was about to burst."

Katie snorted and plopped down on the edge of my pavilion like she owned the place. "Pretty sure it's been leaking for a while now. At least, it has if your mysterious informant is telling the truth. Rumbling landscapes. Hundreds of nightmares disappearing from the grid. Sounds like time's wearing thin."

I said nothing. Until Halven found Mare, there was nothing to be done. She was an Ancient and there was no rushing into this if we wanted to win. Mare had it all—strength, speed, intelligence. We needed to catch her off guard before she found a way to open the Ever Safe, which was easier said than done, or it wouldn't only be Mare that wanted to crush us. There were fourteen other Ancients, most of them larger, stronger, and undoubtedly more pissed off after so long in captivity. I ran my hands through my hair and blew out a slow breath.

"Bring up the map again." Katie flicked her hand at the sand and leaned back on her elbows, only to fly up with a shriek.

Baku lifted his head from beneath the mound of pillows, blinking sleepy eyes, and I laughed.

"Oh, yeah," Katie snapped. Baku glared at Nora's sister and used his elephant trunk to pull the pillows close again. "*So funny.*"

"Didn't you tell me you were getting used to this place?" I asked, trying not to smile too wide.

"This place. Not…" She pointed to the yawning chimera. "Is he *always* here?"

More often than not these days…

"Nora never got used to him either," I said wistfully. She hadn't gotten the chance, but I was sure they would've gotten along. Before she became the Lady of Nightmares and the ruler of Baku's food supply.

"Cool, cool," Katie said. Queen of sarcasm, as always. "So, the map."

I sighed and lifted my hands, palms up. Sand rose, a million glittering flecks forming an incomplete map of the Nightmare Realm. Every landscape I knew of was represented. The rest were filled in piece by piece when Halven checked in. The outer lines were jagged and uneven. The Dream Realm was at one end, bordered on all sides by nightmares.

"Fewer areas are glowing," Katie contemplated.

I nodded. The places we'd ruled out as Mare's hiding place were faded while the places she might be gave off a faint blue glow. Unfortunately, the closer to the Ever Safe the map went, the more options were left open. The Weaver wouldn't have hidden the key to the safe that close, but—not for the first time—I wished he was here to ask *where*. I clasped my hands together behind my back to keep from fidgeting. Knowing the key's location would put my mind at ease, because if Mare didn't know where the key was, that meant she was going to have to break in. When she broke out all those years ago, Baku following, we sealed that exit with magic and buried it under an icy landscape.

"Halven stopped by while you were awake and cleared an entire sector," I explained before Katie accused me of zoning out again.

"The palace looks safe."

"Yes," I agreed carefully. The building at the center of the Nightmare Realm was surrounded by devoted landscapes, and routinely patrolled by equally loyal nightmares.

"I want to see my sister," Katie said abruptly. She met my gaze, her brown eyes hard and unrelenting. "Take me there."

I barely suppressed a groan. "We've been over this."

"I don't care what awful things I see," she insisted, "and I certainly don't care if Nora *wants* me there. I'm her sister. You don't abandon family."

"I..." I promised Nora. Not only that I would keep Katie away but that I wouldn't go into the Nightmare Realm until we found Mare. We went through enough, Nora and I, and we needed to heal. Not make the wounds deeper. "Please don't ask me to break promises to your sister."

She folded her arms. "Fine. Keep your promises, but I'm *going* to see her."

"Stars." I rubbed a hand over my face. "You're as stubborn as she is."

"You mean, she's as stubborn as I am," Katie said with a satisfied smirk. "I'm older."

Baku groaned from within the pavilion, echoing my own sentiment. Katie had grown on me the last two months, more than I thought she would, but my penchant for humor was drained dry. First Nora inherited the Weaver's power when she killed him, then she snuck back into the Nightmare Realm behind my back. Those two betrayals were enough to dim even the loudest laughter, but it didn't end there. Rowan was taken care of—reunited with her stump amid a now-wailing path of trees—but Mare was very much *not*. The Hours weren't going to wait forever before making good on their threat to dethrone Nora if Mare wasn't dealt with. They probably weren't alone in that mindset either. I turned my attention back to the map.

"Sandman," said a low, rasping voice.

Katie bolted behind me, and I sighed. "Hello, Halven. I thought we agreed you wouldn't come if a certain person was visiting."

"I have important news." He tilted his head, moonlight sneaking beneath his wide hat. The bright red lips painted on his mask were curled in a permanently cold smirk and a red scalloped design circled where the mask's eyeholes should've been. "Hello," he added to Katie as if it would erase any sense of threat from him.

She poked my back with her finger. "Well?"

"Halven is fine," I told her, growing wearier by the second. When had I slept last?

"That has to be the creepiest mask I've ever seen in my life. Can he even see?" she asked as if he weren't standing right in front of her.

Before I could remind her not to offend our ally, Halven spoke, his words forced as always. "I see many things. As for the mask, I believe that was the intent."

"Five stars to the Weaver," she stuttered.

"What's the news?" I asked before the conversation could sink any lower.

Halven was suddenly at the far edge of the map near the Ever Safe, pointing at a landscape full of metal globes. I tapped it with a finger, and it dimmed.

"No." Halven's excitement rippled around him. "She's there."

Baku immediately leapt from the pavilion. He barely spared Halven a glance after his first few visits. I supposed it was because Baku knew that, if the worlds ended, so would he, and that was slightly more important than a full belly. "Stay away from it," I said calmly. "We can't tip Mare off that we know where she is."

"Now what happens? What do we do?" Katie asked, chewing nervously on her thumbnail.

"*We* don't do anything." I took her by the arms and looked her in the eye. "Stay put."

"I—"

"Katherine Gallagher, I swear on my power that if you try to follow us…"

"Fine." She wrenched herself from my grip and threw herself onto the vacant pile of pillows. "I wouldn't want to be a liability or anything. I *am* a weak, pitiful mortal after all."

I raised a brow at Halven in a way that let him know that I knew she was a handful. Apparently, all of the Gallagher women were. I made for the barrier between realms, grabbing my full satchel of sand on the way and throwing its strap across my chest. "Don't walk with me," I said to Halven. "It's too soon to blow your cover."

Halven was already headed toward a different landscape, my magic allowing him—and only him—to pass through.

Chapter Three

Nora

The soft clack of moving loom pieces filled the air. I closed my eyes where I sat beneath the domed half of the Keep and let the sound fill my head too. Magic in. Thread out. Mindlessness was key. The wooden pieces were smooth beneath my hands as I worked. The machine moved flawlessly, drawing from the darkness inside me to create a pile of newly woven nightmares that coiled at my feet. The images I drew a few days ago floated through my mind. A brood of headless chickens gave way to an angry old woman in a cardigan with a forked tongue and then a winged man brandishing an ax.

Magic in.

Thread out.

Magic i—

Are you going to do this little chant every *time you weave? I must tell you, it's extremely irritating,* the Weaver drawled.

I blanched, my hands jerking away from the loom. Two months with a sarcastic, murderous, psychopath in my head and—

I resent that last bit.

"Shut up!" I screamed so loud it echoed off the ceiling.

"I didn't say anything," Kail called back.

My eyes flew open, but there was no sign of my somewhat reluctant right-hand. I scanned the room, knowing he was nearby. Not because I'd heard him—because he was never far. Ever. Which was as infuriating as it was a comfort. Movement caught my eye across the room. Kail's black boots dangled through the hatch that led to the open half of the Keep's roof, and the bottom of his black trench coat hung to one side of his thighs.

"What are you doing up there?" I asked.

He was quiet for a moment. "Enjoying the corpse-free view."

"Go enjoy it somewhere else," I grumbled. Hundreds of human-like nightmares impaled on stakes greeted me from atop the hill yesterday morning, their silhouettes lining the horizon like macabre scarecrows. Mara's choice of creature wasn't lost on me—it was a personal threat. The bodies had barely been gone twenty-four hours now. Not long enough for jokes.

"It's almost as if you don't enjoy my company, Lady Nightmare." He casually propped one foot up on the opposite edge of the hatch. "Though I know that's a lie."

I slipped from the stool as quietly as I could and tip-toed up to the grey light filtering in. With quick movements, I grabbed his still-dangling foot and yanked. Kail tumbled through the opening in a flurry of flapping fabric and curse words.

He landed flat on his back, his embroidered coat pooled out beneath him, and he stared up at me with his ever-changing irises—blue, red, black, yellow, green, and every color in between. A dimple formed on one side of his warm brown cheeks. "I'm beginning to think this is a form of foreplay for you."

"You wish," I snapped. I was still happily in love with the Sandman. Whom I hadn't seen since the day I took the Nightmare Realm. I ached for him every minute, and I had to remind myself that we had, quite literally, forever. In the meantime, it was important to firmly establish my rule over the nightmares. Then, when the Sandman did come with news of Mara, I had news of my own to share. I had to tell him that the Weaver was alive and well inside my head. I cringed at the thought of that conversation.

"You don't have to try quite so hard." Kail's fingers grazed my ankle, and I kicked him in the ribs. "I was kidding," he wheezed. "Totally kidding."

You have so much pent-up anger, the Weaver said with an undercurrent of amusement. *He could relieve some of it.*

"I swear to God if you don't stop—"

"Okay, okay." Kail eyed me curiously and sat up. "I was just trying to lighten the mood."

I spun back to the loom, to my work, so he wouldn't see the pink in my cheeks and think it was caused by his *joke*. Losing my temper and speaking out loud to the Weaver was becoming too common. Exhaustion settled into my bones. How long had I worked? An hour? A day? *Two?* The loom had a way of stealing time from me.

Kail stood and dusted his jacket off. "Lady," he said softly when he was finished. "Please rest."

"Since when is the word '*please*' part of your vocabulary?" I blew out a harsh breath. "Anyway, you know I can't."

"You've been weaving for a very long time." He stepped up to my side and eyed the giant pile of new thread coiled on the floor.

"Mara…" I explained, my voice hollow.

"Where will you put it all?"

I touched my arm where thread already covered so much space that my skin was barely visible. "It's not for wearing."

"You can't keep creating nightmares this fast." His tone was so unlike him. Gentle. Sensible. "There's a balance—"

"*There's a balance,*" I mocked. "I hate to break it to you, but I'm an Aquarius, not a Libra."

"You know I don't understand these references," he said, folding his arms.

"The zodiac sign with a woman holding scales. *Balance.* Nevermind." I waved my hand through the air, brushing the conversation away, and filed the idea away for possible nightmares. The zodiac signs would be interesting to work with. A man-eating crab, a fire-breathing bull. The twins could be interesting to work with…

"Nora." Kail took my chin between his index finger and thumb and lifted my face. When I met his gaze, he lifted a brow. "Do you hear yourself? Not only are you speaking nonsense, but you're extremely distracted."

I swatted his hand away. I thought I was doing a decent job of hiding those facts, but apparently not. "So?"

"You've been off since you defeated Rowan, and it's getting worse."

I approached the pile of thread, giving up on the idea of losing myself in more work, and lifted the weighty material in my arms. With a quick thrum of magic, the part nearest the loom eased away, leaving the rest attached to the loom to finish later. I cradled the humming unborn nightmares as if they were a swaddled newborn baby. "I'm fine, Kail." I strode around him to the spiral staircase leading down to the main floor of the Keep.

Are you? the Weaver teased.

"You are most decidedly *not* fine." Kail stormed after me. "I can't help you if you won't talk to me."

"We don't talk. We bicker." I reached the bottom of the stairs and bumped a door open with my hip. Inside, all the Weaver's charcoal drawings were gone, used up as I learned the loom. Most of his expertly-done sketches existed out there in the Nightmare Realm as physical manifestations, but a few of the more impressive ones I hung onto. It was my own drawings that covered the walls and tables now. Our styles were different—my lines cleaner—but no matter how many new creations I produced and hung, the voice in my head wouldn't allow me to appreciate my art. The process, yes, but the Weaver was a perfectionist. The moment I thought a design was finished, he ripped apart its flaws.

"Nora," Kail practically begged.

I opened the nearest cabinet and carefully set the new thread in beside the last pile I wove. "Leave me alone."

If only I could, the Weaver said wistfully at the same time Kail said, "Just tell me what's wrong and I'll—"

"Get out!" I screamed at the former. Kail paled, and my anger drained, leaving me even more tired than before. "Seriously, I'm fine," I said in a much calmer voice. "Okay?"

His eyes narrowed suspiciously.

"You're right. I should get some rest," I added to appease him. The last thing I needed was him catching on that I wasn't alone in my own head before I could talk to the Sandman about it. Kail was too shrewd—which was helpful when it was directed at the nightmares that came to beg favors, but generally speaking, his mouth was too big and his words too loose. "I'll be better after I sleep."

He stood stiff as a statue when I eased past him and fled from the tower. Outside, the muted sky illuminated my new palace. It was worth waiting an extra ten days for the nightmares to finish. Unless you asked one of the nightmares I killed, though that was worth it too. It struck fear into the masses. Maybe I would get a sign: *No assassination attempts in nineteen days.*

I stood in the circular courtyard, the Keep surrounded by palace walls on all sides. Kail was the only one I allowed into the courtyard or the Keep, and that was mostly due to necessity. Emergencies I needed to be aware of while weaving, rooms swept out. Kail had become quite handy with a broom.

I thought you were going to sleep, the Weaver taunted.

"What do you care?" I growled under my breath and shoved through the door into a vacant room. Most of the rooms were empty since I had nothing to fill them with. I rarely spent time outside of the Keep or my bedroom, so it didn't bother me apart from the annoying echo it created.

I wove through the maze-like corridors of gleaming black stone lit with torches bolted to the walls. No part of the new structure was made from nightmares—I wouldn't risk them spying on me—so I had to get creative with functionality. To keep the palace lit, I created a small, easy-access landscape of cacti that belched flames from purple flowers. It was a rather pretty sight if you ignored the sounds and smells. Luckily the fire itself was odorless.

"Lady Nightmare."

I winced at the voice—child-like, yet prim and proper at the same time. The owner, one of the Weaver's remaining designs, bustled toward me. She was swathed in layers of light pink fabric stained red with blood. The garment hid her figure completely, wrapping her from neck to floor, and her face mirrored the features of whoever looked at her. An extremely unsettling feeling that left me unable to look higher than her waist. Unfortunately, the nightmares didn't always come with names, so I called her Bloody Mary. Not that anyone here appreciated my humor.

"Who let you in here?" I snapped.

"Your guards thought I was the lesser of two evils," she said, bowing low.

My eye twitched as I caught a glimpse of her blonde hair, the same color as mine. "Meaning what?"

Nothing good, the Weaver commented, and I ground my teeth.

"The Hours are requesting an audience," Bloody Mary informed me.

A spark of fear ignited in my chest. The last time I saw them, they threatened my life if I didn't take care of Mara. Threatened me with a hail of arrows. But they weren't pushing their way inside, though I knew they were capable of it if they wanted to badly enough. Where was Kail? We needed to double—no, triple—security.

Your arm is about to break beneath the weight of all those threads, and you're worried? the Weaver scoffed.

"Of course I am." I stretched my right arm out until my elbow popped. The long thread was heavier than I expected it would be when I put it on.

Bloody Mary shifted. "You are what, Lady Nightmare?"

The Hours should be afraid of you, not the other way around.

Easy for him to say. If the twelve of them thought they could do better, they'd kill me and take over as the new Weaver.

False. I put myself here on purpose.

"What?" I shrieked. The shock of his statement made the room blur around me. That couldn't be true.

"Lady?" Bloody Mary asked, her curious tone fading to concern.

"Get out!" I shouted at her, then spun on my heel, heart hammering.

Two months. The Weaver made his grand appearance two months ago and *now* he'd dropped another bomb. Assuming it wasn't a lie. The Sandman would know. I winced. *No.* He clearly thought it was an automatic transfer of magic because he said to kill the Weaver was to become the Weaver. No one had ever killed a Lord of the Night World before. No one would know what really happened—no one except the Weaver. *Oh, God.* He did this to me on purpose.

It was less doing this to you, and more doing it for me.

Six of one, half a dozen of the other. Either way, the Weaver chose to invade my body, and the room tilted. It would've been nice to know so I could've passed the information along to the nightmares that wanted to butcher me.

Then how would we know who the enemies were?

"Call me crazy, but I'd rather not find out by them shoving a blade in my gut."

That only happened once.

Once was enough. It took two days for my stomach to stop hurting even though it only took a handful of hours to heal the wound. That was the last time I saw a nightmare without a thorough body search, and even then, they didn't need a weapon. They *were* weapons. I put a hand on the wall to stay myself.

"Anything else you feel like sharing?" I asked, feeling breathless.

Not at the moment, no.

That didn't mean *no*. My vision blurred again, a combination of pure exhaustion and, quite possibly, shock. I had to lay down—to think, process. I hurried blindly through empty hallways until I reached my private chambers. A soft gold rug took up the center of the room—a gift from the Doll Maker as was my entire wardrobe minus the few items I had originally brought with me—and a soft mattress piled high with pillows filled a canopied frame. The only other piece of furniture in the windowless room was a giant wardrobe Kail found…somewhere.

Are we really going to rest? the Weaver asked, contradicting himself. *With so much to do.*

I slammed my door. "Stop saying *we*! I'm *me* and you're a *soul-sucking parasite.*"

It wouldn't kill you to say thank you.

"Thank you?" I pried off my boots, my socks sticking inside, and stumbled across the room. "There's nothing to thank you for."

No? The grin glimmered faintly. *If I hadn't fused my essence with the magic before it was too late, your Sandman would be dead, and both our worlds would be imploding.*

My mind exploded with events of my reign, starting with the moment I woke up in the Doll Maker's forest. I stared down at my hands. It still wasn't clear how much of what I'd done was me and how much was the Weaver. Though, either way, I'd brought this situation on myself. But now…*now* it was the Weaver's choice. Sure, I had killed him, but it was to save the Day World. He did this to me to save himself.

Actually, I saved two worlds *with my actions,* the Weaver said. *I only hid because I was letting you gain confidence without me.*

"What do I have to be confident in? That you'll keep me alive until you find a better host?" I said through my teeth. "You destroyed my entire life."

It's called supply and demand, but, trust me, Keeper, being in your head isn't fun for me either. Oh, woe-is-me, it's been so long since I stared into the Sandman's eyes. And, gasp, what does my family think about me being gone all this time? I trust Kail. I don't trust Kail. I hate being the Lady of Nightmares. I love being the Lady of Nightmares. I—

"Yes, yes," I hissed. "You're privy to my every thought. I get it. Your eternal commentary is equally thrilling."

He let out a low, disgusted sound. *Go meet the Hours.*

"They can wait." I peeled back the covers of my bed and climbed under them fully clothed. It didn't take long for sleep to find me. It swept me under like a riptide, and I tossed and turned against the echoing screams of the Weaver trying to get me to remain conscious. My body won in the end, and all resistance faded.

***

Wake up, Keeper. Wake up, wake up, wake—

A hand slammed over my mouth, another gripping my thread covered arm. My eyes flew open to find two silver masks staring down at me with the Roman numerals for one and two embossed from forehead to chin. My body grew hot with fear.

I hate to say I told you so, the Weaver said with resignation. *But I told you so.*

I tried to scream, but One's metal gauntlet bit into my lips, muffling any sound. My fingers dug uselessly into the chain mail around her wrist. Two's bare hand gripped my throat and, with expertly placed fingers, ushered me into oblivion.

Chapter Four

Nora

Any time now.

The Weaver's words cut through my unconscious state, and a small groan built in the back of my throat. I scrambled to piece my current surroundings together and find my footing, but I couldn't because I wasn't in control of my body. The Weaver was driving, and he wouldn't so much as let me open my eyes.

Don't, the Weaver warned. *They don't need to know you're awake yet.*

Awake. Was I awake? It felt as if I were just dragged over a bed of nails by…whoever *they* were. This had to be a bad dream, but I didn't dream anymore. Working constantly for days on end must've stressed me out so much I was hallucinating as I slept.

A few seconds of pressure to your jugular doesn't wipe your memory. Snap out of it, Keeper.

Jugular. Right. The Hours. New Hours—One and Two—had burst into my bedroom and attacked me. All fogginess fled, leaving me acutely aware of my precarious state. Judging by the hard surface beneath me, I was no longer in my bed which meant they kidnapped me. *Bastards.* Mara or no Mara, this was unacceptable.

Bingo.

I swallowed a retort to the Weaver and listened hard to see if I could determine whether I was alone.

You know you don't have to say it for me to hear it, he purred.

Can you truly feel a death threat if I don't scream it at you? I thought back.

Oh, indeed. It's delicious either way. He released the vice grip on my bodily functions. *Stay still and don't open your eyes yet.*

I huffed. A mistake.

"I see you're coming around," someone said a few feet to my left.

That was the end of my ruse. I steeled myself and sat up. My muscles cried at the movement, but I didn't allow myself to voice any complaints. *Power. Authority. Be the Weaver.*

Before me, Six perched on a chair in an otherwise empty room made of dulled brass. Her elbows rested on her knees as she leaned forward, spinning an arrow between her fingers. Her dark braid hung nearly to her lap, and I could see a blurry reflection of myself in the flat, shiny metal mask covering her face. The last time we met, when Kail and I were on our way back to the Blood Tower, she shot a ring of arrows around us. Then she and two other Hours forced me to heal their comrade after a run-in with Mara.

"You," I growled.

"I had nothing to do with this," she said casually. "Those who brought you here are with the Chime now."

"The Chime?"

Six leaned back in the chair and crossed her arms. "Thirteen."

Before you say that everyone told you there were twelve Hours, Thirteen isn't an Hour, the Weaver supplied. *The Chime has final say over the clock. Now try to stop making yourself look incompetent. You need to gain the upper hand and let them know just how unacceptable this is.*

If you're not going to work some of your mojo, stop talking, I thought back, then to Six, "what am I doing here?"

"Mara is still a problem," she said simply. "I'm sure you haven't forgotten."

Mara was more of a problem than even *she* knew. Entire landscapes were razed to the ground, nightmares slaughtered, all by the Ancient's hand. The problem was that she waited until just before she moved on to disturb anything, so it was difficult to track her. She left me presents, too. Unnecessary reminders that she was out there. The impaled corpses that greeted me when I left the palace were only the latest in a string of gifts.

Considering that the Sandman and I hadn't made a single move in two months, the Hours probably thought we weren't going to hold up our end of the bargain. I was willing to bet they thought I was stupid enough to brush it off in favor of my other mounting responsibilities, but I had to be smart about it and trust the Sandman's judgment.

I lifted my hands to brush the hair from my face and found them bound, wrapped from the wrist all the way to the tips of my fingers with smooth rope. "What the—"

Six cocked her head. "We couldn't let you create anything new inside the clock."

Things kept getting better and better. Without the ability to create nightmares or use the existing ones around me, all I had were my own innate skills. Which were basically nonexistent even though I was getting better thanks to my continued training with Kail. *Kail.* Had he noticed I was gone yet? It was only a matter of time, but even he wouldn't think to look for me here.

"Kail will find me," I said in a rush of faked confidence.

Shut up.

Finally, some sound advice.

"He could call upon his brother to find you, but Halven can only find *where* someone is. Not when."

I couldn't see her face behind her mask—if there was a face there at all—but still, I felt the smug smile. *Shut up, shut up, shut up*, the Weaver urged.

"Make me," I growled under my breath.

"What?" Six asked, confused.

Again, I can hear you without speaking.

I thought the loudest shriek I could and leveled my gaze at Six. Two months of killing nightmares without mercy gave me a decent chunk of respect. Or fear. But if anyone found out the Hours kidnapped me, *poof.* All of it a waste. Not only did I need to escape, but I had to do it quietly and without any additional notice. Then punish an entire group of powerful nightmares because nothing ever stayed a secret here.

"Do you think I need Kail or Halven to rescue me?" I asked Six.

You're backtracking. Why would you say Kail would find you if you didn't need him to? If you're going to play tough, at least do it right.

Ignore him. I had to ignore him.

Six laughed. "If you could escape alone, you wouldn't be sitting here right now."

She has a point. All talk, no action.

For someone that depended on my life to keep himself alive, the Weaver was awfully quick to side with the enemy.

I *am your enemy*, he snarled.

All talk, no action, I said, throwing his own words back at him. The Weaver was absolutely my enemy, but until we figured out how to get him out of me, we were forced to accept a truce. Or, at least, to press pause on killing each other.

I cleared my throat and raised my chin. "Take me to the Chime so we can get this taken care of."

"You don't get *taken* to the Chime. The Chime summons you."

It was my turn to laugh. "I'm the Lady of Nightmares. No one *summons* me." I stood, poking at the internal grin that was the Weaver. His sigh breathed through me as he let the darkness swirl violently. A decent trick we came up with to our mutual benefit. The air darkened around me, pulling in energy from surrounding nightmares, feeding me like a banquet for one. The magic took from Six until she visibly struggled to stay upright. I shoved at the grin until the Weaver reluctantly cut off the surge of power.

"The Chime," I demanded. *"Now."*

Six straightened, her shoulders stiff. She said nothing as she stood with a chorus of clinking chainmail and spun a cogwheel set in the wall, hidden behind her chair. That wheel set off another, then two more, then four. A panel of wall slid away to reveal the inner workings with each new piece that turned until the entire wall spun. A weight dropped from the middle of the ceiling and dangled there, waiting. With a terrible grinding sound, a slab shifted overhead, and with another few grinding clicks, stairs popped from the far wall.

"We have to go up," Six said when I didn't move.

I took a deep breath and tread carefully into the brighter chamber above. The walls glowed faintly, illuminating more moving pieces. The floor was a blanket of nuts and bolts, and the pieces pressed into my bare feet. A window served as the roof with an inverted Roman numeral six painted black across the surface. I stepped around the shadow it cast and followed the curve of the room. *The clock face.* I knew it without the Weaver's input. Six said Halven wouldn't know *when* I was…did that mean I time traveled to six o'clock? What time was it really? There was no sign of the clock hands.

No one can time travel, the Weaver said rather blandly. *She was messing with you. Honestly, you make it too easy.*

"After you," Six said, and spun another cog.

I held my breath and waited for the next opening to appear. It took longer this time. More sliding pieces. More clacking mechanics. When the door finally slid up, my heart rammed into my chest. The other eleven hours stood around the perimeter of the circular room. On the floor, black lines marked white marble, forming the blank face of a clock. But it was what was in the middle that drew my attention.

Standing at the center of the clock face was a man swathed in layers of glimmering bronze material. His robe flowed around him like water. A heavy matching chain ran down from the ceiling, attaching itself to the nightmare's back. True to his name, each slight movement sent a musical tinkling through the chamber.

When the door clanged to a stop over my head, every eye found me, and I struggled to keep my composure. "What's wrong?" My voice miraculously sounded commanding and sure. "Not expecting me just yet?"

"Six," one of the Hours snapped. I refused to look away from the Chime to see which one spoke.

The Weaver lashed out unbidden, sucking away what little energy Six had left. She fell to the floor just inside the room, unconscious. "You." I held my bound arms out to the nearest Hour, guided partially by the true Nightmare Lord, and glared at the knife on Seven's hip. "Free my hands."

When he hesitated, I poked at the darkness again, letting it dim the bright room. Slowly, Seven pulled the knife free and carefully sliced through my bindings without harming my threat. I rubbed my wrists, glancing at each Hour in turn, before meeting the Chime's gaze.

Say nothing, the Weaver said quietly as if he were talking to a spooked animal. *Just turn and walk out.*

Ha! Like that was happening. Not only because I wanted revenge first. They didn't go through all of this to let me waltz out the door.

You showed your strength, Keeper. Leave now before they see a weakness. "Lady Nightmare—" the Chime began.

"First, I was brutally attacked by Three in the Barren, then threatened by her again along with two others. Now, you've stolen me from my bed." It flowed off my tongue so fast, I couldn't have stopped it if I wanted to.

"Lady—"

My eyebrows rose, and I glared pointedly at the glimmering figure. "Be glad I gave you so many chances. Others weren't so lucky." I backed out of the room, setting off a flurry of motion from the Hours. "This better work," I mumbled both to myself and the Weaver.

The Weaver didn't bother to hide his disdain as I pressed my hand against the same cog wheel Six used to open the chamber, but he lent me his power anyway. I didn't always need his help—I was learning to harness it on my own—but right now, speed was a major factor, especially since the Hours were already lunging after me. With a lightning-fast bolt of energy, the door slammed down between us. Bodies rammed into the other side, armor clattered against armor. Another brush of power melted the moving pieces, effectively sealing them inside. At least from this entrance.

There, I thought at the Weaver, and practically felt his eyes roll.

You could've maimed them a smidge.

You literally told me to get out of there two seconds ago.

The Weaver settled, his magic relaxing, and said nothing because he knew that would get under my skin the most. His back-and-forth instructions were one thing, but his indifference when I called him on it set my nerves on edge.

A shadow passed over the floor, drawing my attention to the glass ceiling just in time to see a figure vanish. That was quick. Another exit had to lead directly to the exterior of the clock face for the Hours to be there already.

That wasn't an Hour.

My stomach twisted with unease. "Great. Let's get out of here before—"

A loud crash reverberated through the tower. I covered my head, biting back a scream, but when nothing fell down around me, I dared to look up. Cracks webbed across the ceiling, stemming from the room I just sealed.

"Please tell me that's one of their buddies," I said softly.

Shouts rose up on the other side of the door.

Doesn't sound like it, the Weaver said. *You'll want to take a right up ahead.*

I took one step and paused. My fingers twitched at my sides. The Hours threatened me, beat me, and broke into my palace to kidnap me. They were probably planning to kill me like they said they would—I still had no plan to deal with Mara, after all.

And yet...

Leave them.

I should. It would be the smart thing to do. Leave and let something else kill the Hours for me. They had a fighting chance. Thirteen against one, a home turf advantage, undoubtedly more exits if they wanted to run.

Don't get soft now, Keeper.

Don't get soft? I winced. Did he think I had hardened *that* much? So soon after picking up the mantle of Lady Nightmare?

Not completely, the Weaver said. *Or you wouldn't hesitate to leave them to their fate.*

That was true. He certainly wouldn't have cared—not unless it served a purpose for him. But I didn't want to be like the Weaver. Whatever scraps of humanity I had left needed to be guarded, so I put my hand back on the wall and reopened the door.

Inside, chaos reigned.

Hours ran and leapt, swung weapons and fired arrows, all with carefully executed precision. The Chime shouted orders and dodged projectiles. But only one thing sent my pulse roaring.

Mara.

She stood taller than I remembered, her legs at ninety-degree angles instead of bent up to her ears. A hump bubbled between her shoulder blades, but it didn't slow her movements as she sliced at the Hours. Her nails—once jagged—now shone like blades on the tips of each finger.

"Summon the Hands!" the Chime shouted above the melee.

One of the Hours jumped over the Chime's head and scurried up the chain to the ceiling. She ripped open an overhead chamber and two black blobs fell to the floor with a splat.

If you're just going to stand here, it's better to leave, the Weaver commented.

I jolted at his words. Right. *Do something.*

This was your idea.

My nostrils flared. I pulled a thread from my wrist at the same time a loud gong blasted everyone in the room backward. We froze in the air, moving ever-so slightly, as two enormous figures rose from the black blobs. They took the shape of humans dunked in tar with unnaturally long limbs and featureless faces. With lightning-fast movements, they each grabbed onto the Chime's throat with one hand and opposing walls with the other.

Another gong sounded, low and impossibly drawn out. I was still flying back, almost as if frozen in time, but Mara wasn't. She fought her way forward with seemingly forced steps and dug her nails into the nearest Hour: Four—the same one I healed near the river two months ago.

You might want to snap out of it if you want to save them.

Why the hell would they slow down time and put themselves at risk? *You do the snapping,* I told the Weaver. *I'll do the stopping.*

I'd rather do it all, he said casually.

The next moment, my body wasn't my own—it was the Weaver's. He pushed against the invisible force holding us in place so hard that I swore my bones would break. I cried out, but he was the only one to hear my internal scream.

The Weaver used the thread I pulled to create a molted grey scorpion with two tails, both tipped with three stingers. On the inside of its claws were hundreds of smaller ones pinching at the air. It took off straight for Mara.

The black figures—the Hands—began moving in unison, spinning the clock face, and the Hours shimmered in and out. It only lasted a handful of seconds before they flashed out of the room altogether.

Are you serious? I screeched inside my head.

The Weaver smirked using my mouth. *I told you that we should've left them.*

Mara stumbled forward with Four gone and spun to face the scorpion. Her thick tongue darted out with a low *tsk*. She launched herself forward without missing another beat and spun through the air like a torpedo.

One moment, the scorpion stood there.

The next, it split down the middle and black blood splashed all around us.

"We meet again, Lady," Mara crooned. She stood in the middle of the carnage, covered in nearly as much black as the two figures that fell from the ceiling. It trailed down her face and mixed with chunks of scorpion flesh that clung to her skin. "You look well."

Do something, do something, do something, I chanted at the Weaver.

Before he could, Mara scuttled across the floor, hunched as she was in the Day World, and sliced the backs of my ankles. Stars burst before my eyes and the Weaver's control slipped in and out.

Don't you dare give my body back now, I warned.

The Weaver's grip tightened, but Mara was already sitting on my back, her breath hot on my ear. "I'd love to see what you look like on the inside." Her fingernail cut a line down my cheek and hot blood raced toward my chin. "Such a pretty color. Sadly, I haven't decided if you'll be useful to me yet. Until then, I must leave you alive."

The Weaver rolled us, and Mara leapt off, fleeing through the hole she made in the ceiling. *Your body has more limits than mine,* he thought bitterly. *The least you could do is not let pain get in the way.*

Excuse me? How was I supposed to react when my tendons were severed?

You're not supposed to react at all. Then the Weaver receded, leaving me to figure out how to move on my own.

Don't react at all? As if that were possible.

Chimes tinkled softly, drawing my attention back to the center of the room. The black figures were blobs again, and they inched up the Chime's chains to the hatch they fell from.

"As you see," the Chime said in a stern voice. "Mara needs to be eliminated."

I glowered at him and sat up the best I could. Blood pooled around my feet—mine and the scorpion's. "You fared well enough," I accused.

"She wasn't controlled by the slowing of time," he said as if that should've meant something.

It means she isn't affected by us. Why do you think it took both the Sandman and me to get rid of her the first time?

If this was some sort of set up to show me how dangerous Mara was, I was seriously going to lose it. It felt like too much of a coincidence to be anything else, but seeing Mara again blew on the fire raging inside me. "I'll deal with Mara," I warned him. "Just stay out of my way." *We should leave before the Hours return.*

Finally, a suggestion I couldn't argue with. The problem was actually moving. I bit my lip and snagged someone's bow from the floor. Slowly and with blinding pain, I used it to pull myself onto my feet. The wall was the only thing keeping me up, the bow the only thing helping me shuffle back into the corridor. How the hell was I supposed to walk like this?

Turn right, the Weaver instructed. Heat burst through my legs, almost too hot for comfort, but it stole away the pain. *Don't say I never helped you out.*

I look a tentative step and nearly fell flat on my face. The pain was dulled, but tendons were rather important if one expected to use their limbs. Thankfully they would heal thanks to my Nightmare magic. I leaned on the bow again and shuffled from the room the best I could.

After a few more guided turns, I found myself outside a giant grandfather clock. And I wasn't alone.

"Lady Nightmare," Halven said, bowing.

I gasped for breath, sweat dripping down my face. The sight of him with his ridiculously frivolous outfit and cruel mask brought tears to my eyes. Never had I been so glad to see a nightmare in all my life. "What are you doing here?" I asked, allowing every ounce of relief to leak into the question.

"You called to me," he said in his rough voice.

"I did?" I asked, mostly to myself.

You're welcome.

"Of course," I snapped back. "I thought you said I didn't need them."

No. I said you shouldn't let the Hours know you needed help.

"You're hurt?" Halven asked, his head cocked.

"I'll live." I turned my gaze up to the face of the massive clock, half expecting to see figures through the broken glass racing after me. Hobbling as I was, I couldn't chance that happening, so I touched the outer wall. Heat flowed between my palm and the bronze panel as I fixed the damage Mara caused. Then I sealed every door that led outside.

"Let's get back to the palace before your brother ends up with an ulcer." I took a step toward Halven and tumbled to the ground. "Actually, we're making a stop somewhere else first. I'm going to need a little help though."

Halven lifted me from the ground without another word and began walking without my having to tell him the destination. A perk of having the nightmare of lost things come to your aide. "Thanks," I breathed.

It wasn't just his help I was grateful for. Around Halven, I didn't have to worry about judgment if I showed everything wasn't okay. He gave me a small squeeze as if to say *you're welcome,* and I rested my head on his shoulder. Weakness didn't feel so wrong around the right people.

Chapter Five

The pain in my ankles faded to a sharp prickle by the time Halven carried me into the Doll Maker's clearing. Forest animals made of buttons trekked behind us with curious gazes. Soft clicks surrounded us as they moved among the trees while the carpet of green buttons crunched beneath Halven's feet. I liked to imagine the button trees smelled like pine, but they honestly smelled like nothing at all.

"Put me down," I told Halven. It was bad enough I was going to ask the Doll Maker for stitches again—I could at least look as if I got there on my own two feet.

Halven immediately set me on my feet but stood close, arm at the ready in case I needed it. I wasn't entirely sure I wouldn't. Dropping that bow awhile back wasn't my best move.

"Lady Nightmare!" The Doll Maker rounded one of her gigantic mounds of color-coded buttons in the clearing. A tiny top hat sat crooked on her head and a basket hung off one arm. Around her neck clicked a necklace of more buttons, and her skirt was the brightest tulle, making her look like an eccentric middle-aged woman. "Do you need another garment?"

I shook my head and fought off a wave of nausea the action sent through me. Suddenly, sitting down seemed more than ideal. "You told me to come back next time I needed to be stitched up."

"Oh." She dropped her basket with wide eyes. Ribbons and buttons spilled across the ground. "Of course, of course. Come to the table."

The table where she tied Dreamers down to sew buttons over their eyes, adorn them with frills, and paint their skin as if they were her personal toys. *Great.* Beggars couldn't be choosers, and the surface was blissfully empty tonight. All traces of blood were scrubbed away, though the red ribbons she used to hold down the Dreamers' limbs dangled like entrails.

Ugh. I've spent way too much time in the Nightmare Realm.

The Weaver chuckled, but otherwise remained silent. A shock, honestly. I was showing multiple weaknesses to the Doll Maker when Halven could've simply whisked me back to the palace and let the cuts heal naturally over the next day or two. It was my residual human side that wanted medical attention because my nightmare side certainly didn't *need* it. Sure, it helped, but it wasn't necessary. I'd given up so much of my former life though that I felt no regret.

"What are we patching today?" The Doll Maker patted the tabletop.

I sighed and allowed Halven to hold my elbow while I stumbled up to the table. Once there, I brushed him off and hoisted myself onto the cool surface. "My ankles."

"Rather important, those are." The Doll Maker rummaged through her braided hair until she found a needle. "Nothing will topple a Dreamer faster than putting them in shoes that their ankles can't support. The older they are, the lower the heel has to be. More than once I've had them just *pop* right out of place and no one wants a broken doll. They're never the same if you try to fix them either. Limping around and such."

"I'm sure you do your best," I said without conviction.

"Always, my lady. Now, let's see." She bent over, threading the needle without looking, and let out a low whistle. "The tendons are nearly cut through. What happened?"

I peered at Halven where he stood a foot away and wondered if I should tell the Doll Maker the truth. It wouldn't do any good for the nightmares to know I couldn't handle Mara, but the Hours would escape eventually. Plus, with all the trouble the Ancient stirred up, it was no secret she was on the loose. Still…

"I'd rather not talk about it," I hedged. "Can you fix it?"

The Doll Maker smiled brightly. "I can fix anything, though, if you don't mind me saying, you shouldn't be walking on it."

"It would take months to heal in the Day World if I were still human, so I think I can handle a day or two off," I reassured her.

Can we though? the Weaver asked.

Of course we couldn't. *What else do you want me to say?*

He grunted. *Let her sew you up if it settles your mind. I'll work on internal repairs so we can put this whole ordeal behind us.*

You could've been doing that since I walked out of the clock tower, I thought harshly. It was as if he enjoyed withholding help just to torture me.

One must get their thrills where they can. Be happy I assisted with the pain.

I sucked in a breath, but the Doll Maker's needle pierced my skin, erasing the scathing reply from my mind. It was strange how I could force myself to walk around like this, albeit with the Weaver's help, but the Doll Maker's stitches sent my head spinning. I laid back on the table and bit my lip.

"I hear Mara decorated your hill a few days ago," the Doll Maker said conversationally. "Though, clearly she stole the idea from one of the Weaver's landscapes. Ivan the Impactor? No, that doesn't sound right."

"Vlad the Impaler?" *Original,* I tacked on in my head for the Weaver's benefit.

The classics never go out of style, Keeper.

"That's it!"

The Doll Maker chattered happily as she worked. Something about one of her dolls escaping and ending up on one of Vlad's pikes decades ago. It was such a waste of her hard work, blah, blah, blah. I focused on her cheerful voice to take the edge off the pain, but the words blurred together. At least, until she brought Mara up again.

"What?" I bolted up onto my elbows.

"Stay still, Lady."

"Repeat what you just said."

"Mara." The Doll Maker brought the needle up with a gentle tug. "She collapsed a nearby landscape. From what I hear, she burrowed into the ground without realizing a system of caves was beneath."

Or she did *know.* My skin prickled with goosebumps. It would really help if someone remembered the exact location of the Ever Safe door or the key to open it, but no. The Weaver made it disappear, even from himself. Apparently, that was a Night Lord trait, but unlike the Sandman, there was no Dream Keeper to retrieve the information from.

Halven did what he does best, he said, sounding slightly offended. *The less I knew about its location, the better.*

"The whole thing crumbled into itself, killing everyone down there. I don't know who or where it was, mind you, as I only heard second hand. A real shame though."

"Yes. A shame," I agreed and looked to Halven. Did he know about this? He was spying for the Sandman, but that didn't make him any less a nightmare. I needed to be kept in the loop.

Wait. Halven hid the key?

The Weaver didn't bother to reply with words—he didn't need to. I felt his withering glare as clearly as I felt each stitch slide through my skin. Of course Halven hid it. Who else?

The sharp snap of metal scissors signaled the end of the Doll Maker's work. "Good as new."

"I appreciate it."

The Doll Maker waved off the words. "I'm working on something new for you. I'll send it to the palace when I've finished."

"I have enough clothes," I promised her.

"That isn't possible. Besides, your pants aren't any good like this. Look at the holes!"

A small smile spread on my lips. There was no arguing with her. "Thank you."

"Off you go now." She tucked the still-bloody needle back into her braid and wiped her hands on her skirt.

I held a hand out to Halven again, but instead of taking it, he wordlessly lifted me in his arms. *Right.* I wasn't supposed to walk on my own yet.

I only need a little while to make the tendons functional, the Weaver said. *Not that it won't still hurt.*

"Such a good boy," the Doll Maker said with a pat to Halven's arm.

He bobbed his head to the Doll Maker and carried me back to the palace. Part of me wanted him to slow down so I could avoid Kail's hissy fit a little longer, but I wanted to be back in my own space more. Mostly, I wanted to sleep. For a very, very long time.

Chapter Six

The Sandman

Nora's new palace was impressive. Her security, on the other hand, was not. Sentries lined the walls and manned the entrances, but there were no built-in defenses that I could detect. I strode straight for the front door where a rather gruesome nightmare sat on a bench, one hand hovering over my satchel. A multitude of nightmare eyes burned through the layers of my clothes, and I swept my gaze from one end of the wall to the other. No one moved to stop me which made the hair on my arms stand on end. Nora couldn't think this was enough, and if she did, Kail should've known otherwise.

I stopped in front of the nightmare just outside the main entrance. Pink, blood-stained fabric swallowed her shapeless body. When I looked up from the clothing, I startled. My face stared back at me, curly ash brown hair, violet eyes…it was like staring in a mirror, except where I knew my jaw hung open, the nightmare smiled coyly.

"Where is the Lady of Nightmares?" I asked.

The nightmare scrambled to her feet, stumbling on the hem of her outfit to give a minute bow. "Dream Lord."

I glared expectantly. "Well?"

"Kail said to wait," she fumbled. "That I had to wait."

"Sandman." Kail burst through the massive doors and glanced at the waiting nightmare. "What are you doing here?"

"Waiting," she said again.

He shook his head, eyes rolling. "There's no time today. Leave."

"But you said—"

"I said your problems could wait, not that you should." Kail grabbed her by the upper arms and shoved her unceremoniously away from the building before dragging me inside. The slam of the door echoed through the empty entryway. With a quick look down the hallway, Kail looked me straight in the eyes, his irises flashing wildly. "Nora's gone."

"Gone." I tested the word. "As in out taking a stroll?"

"Damned if I know." Kail stormed down the hallway with sure, angry steps. "She said she was going to sleep, but her room is empty. As well as the Keep and the interior courtyard."

I rubbed my forehead. Everyone had to be somewhere. Gone didn't mean *gone*, especially when Nora was Lady of this realm. She knew better than to disappear without telling someone when things hadn't fully settled yet. The way Kail acted, I knew this wasn't commonplace. "Where would she go?"

"There's a movie she's been wanting to see at the theater. Oh, and Suzie from down the street has become her new bestie. Maybe they're painting each other's nails and talking about boys." His sarcastic tirade ended with him sucking in a deep breath and holding it while his fingers curled in and out of fists at his side.

I waited two beats for him to gain some semblance of sobriety before remembering who I was dealing with. "Don't test me, Kail."

He paced the patchwork of shadows in the windowless hall, dim torches burning every few feet. "She spends most of her time in the Keep. Occasionally meets with nightmares when they show up if she's feeling restless. That doesn't happen much," he added, then paused. "The meetings usually end with her killing one of the nightmares."

"The Keep…" I started, ignoring the last part. How bad had Nora gotten since we parted? It took the Weaver a few years after banishing Mara to enjoy killing, but Kail hadn't said Nora *liked* it. Just that she did it. I took a moment to center my thoughts in an attempt to ward off an avalanche of fear.

"The Keep!" he shouted in mock surprise. "Why didn't I think to look there? Thank goodness you showed up when you did."

"Kail," I warned in a low voice.

"What are you doing here?" Kail whirled on me as if he were angry at himself for not asking before. "Maybe I should be asking *you* where she is?"

"What?" A flash of anger cracked the word.

"You show up here the same day Nora disappears." He looked me up and down. "That's what I like to call suspicious."

What did he think I'd done? Whisked her away to the Dream Realm where she would taint my sand? Forced her back to the Day World where she would wither? More importantly, *why* would I? I inhaled slowly, forcing myself to calm down. "Halven found Mare. I came so Nora and I could take care of her before she disappears again." A thought hit me like a lightning bolt, and my body went cold. "Mare…you don't think she—"

"No. Mara wouldn't bother to take her anywhere. If she did get in here, Nora would already be dead." The certainty in Kail's voice was enough to make me believe it. He picked at his bottom lip and fidgeted nervously. "Something's wrong with her."

"Everything is wrong with her. Which is why we need to send her back to the Day World where she isn't a threat."

"Not Mara," he said so softly that I barely heard. The front door slammed open before I could ask for clarification and Halven swept in. Kail brushed past me to greet him.

Halven reached out to take Kail's hand. "Sorry we're late," he croaked.

"*Please.*" Nora's voice barreled through the entrance like a battering ram. "Your Lady is always on time."

Kail practically shoved his brother out of the way to reveal Nora in the doorway. His shoulders visibly relaxed, but his sarcasm hid any hint of relief. "Nice of you to join the party."

Nora snorted. "Yeah. This place is a real rager."

Her eyes landed on me, and she froze, her lips parting. I didn't dare move though my heart was beating so fast I was sure she could see it pounding against my chest. Her hair framed her face, her freckles stark against already pale skin, made only paler by her black sweater and dark pants. A line of dried blood marked her cheek, though the wound had already healed. The gold of her eyes burned bright, but beneath them, a familiar haunted expression lurked.

"…you been?" Kail's voice drifted to my ears, interrupting my thoughts.

"Visiting the Hours," Nora said off-handedly.

Silence.

Nora kicked the front door shut. "Don't give me that look, Kail. It wasn't *my* idea."

Kail whirled on Halven.

"It wasn't his either." Nora tucked a piece of hair behind her ear and let out a slow breath. "I'm not really in the mood to explain, but they won't be giving us any more trouble." She wrinkled her nose in the way I loved best. "I think. Not for a while anyway."

I stepped forward and Kail tossed an arm out to bar my way. "Not in the mood? I just spent half the day—"

"I'm fine." She stared at him hard, then turned on her heel. There was a slight limp in her steps and, at the back of her ankles, torn, bloody fabric that said otherwise.

"Where are you going?" he asked frantically.

"To bed." She flicked a quick look at me and bobbed her head as if telling me to follow.

I did, of course, as quickly as my feet would carry me. When I got to Nora's side, she took my hand. Her fingers were freezing, trembling, but they sent jolts of fire straight to my core. Kail called after us, but we didn't stop until we were in another set of rooms deep inside the palace. Thick black curtains hung around a massive wooden bed frame. The four posts were sculpted with care, each long swirl brushed lightly with gold, and a rich, brocade fabric covered the mattress. A large matching wardrobe and plush golden carpet were the only other items of note in the otherwise nondescript chamber. Nora's bedroom, I guessed, noticing the bookbag thrown haphazardly in the corner. A far cry from her old room with its sheer curtains, white mini lights, and pastel color palette.

I turned to ask if she wanted me to bring her anything from home, but before I could get the question out, her lips were on mine. They were warm and pliant, almost reverent. My fingers tangled in her hair, and I pulled her close, hands against her lower back. I breathed her in, and a low noise caught in my throat. That sound was a key twisting open a lock.

Our kisses became more frantic, more eager to make up for lost time. I shuffled back, pulling her along with me, but misjudged the bed's location. Her lips quirked into a smile without leaving mine as my back hit the wall. We kissed until I was drunk on the taste, and my hands burned with the desire to touch every inch of her.

Just when I thought I would combust, her lips trailed along my jaw and down my neck. My grip on her hips tightened. "I missed you," she breathed against my skin.

"I see that," I teased, and she nipped at my ear. "I missed you too."

"Let's never stay away from each other this long again?" she asked lightly, though I could tell she meant it.

If only we could promise that. "Mare—"

"Can wait until tomorrow," she interjected. "I've been awake for days, more or less, and there's something more important to talk about."

The lingering heat from our kiss cooled. *Days?* Even I got regular rest to keep my mind clear and decisions judicious. "No," I said, though I was dying to ask what happened to her ankles. "Now, you sleep. We can talk when you wake up."

She glanced longingly at her bed and shuddered. "You need to know."

"All I need to know—" I gave her another quick kiss, "is that you're okay."

I guided Nora to the bed, and she eased down onto the rumpled blankets. When she looked up at me, every ounce of exhaustion showed on her face. There was a sadness there, too. *Something is wrong with her.* I shook Kail's words away. Of course there was something wrong. A strong, dark power surged through her, twisting her into something she was never meant to be, and she was dealing with it the best she could. Nora was good at that, at adjusting, but she was also good at hiding things. It was one thing for her to let me see her struggle because she'd always allowed me in, but for Kail to notice…

"Close your eyes," I said softly and bent to remove her pants. There was nothing worse than prying fabric away from a wound after blood cemented them together.

"I thought you wanted me to sleep," she said with a tiny smirk.

I smiled back and kissed her bare stomach just above the ties on her pants. "You are going to sleep, but not in bloody clothes."

She made a soft sound of consent.

"What happened?" I asked when the fabric peeled free. There were black stitches over jagged, semi-healed cuts. I ran my thumb over the skin near it, careful not to touch too close.

"Mara needs a manicure."

My eyes shot up to Nora's. Halven found Mare, and it wasn't anywhere near the clock tower. "Excuse me?"

"I suppose there are two things I need to tell you." Her eyelids shut. She took a deep breath, then shimmied under the covers. "Tomorrow?"

The exhaustion and stress hardening her features injected me with a dull ache. "Tomorrow," I reluctantly agreed.

Nora relaxed slightly and held open the blankets. "Will you stay with me?"

She didn't have to ask. I would've sat outside her door just to listen to her breathe, outside the palace even, just to be in the same realm, anything to be allowed near her again. But, as I crawled into the bed beside her and she snuggled against my side, I was glad she had invited me to stay. I took my first easy breath in two months and ran my fingers through her hair until she finally fell into a deep slumber.

Chapter Seven

Nora

Fire danced. It swayed and spread, crackled and popped. An entire town became an instrument, the screams of its residents an orchestra. Smoke billowed into the sky and blotted out the sunrise. Perhaps the orange glow coming from behind was another fire. Another town.

The image moved, my view through another's eyes: through the Weaver's. This was another memory, a fissure in the dark of sleep. I usually had to approach the glowing fissures to see inside—or ignore them, if it suited me, but this time it sucked me in without warning. If I had seen it from a distance, I would've ignored it this once instead of approaching to peek inside, but as it was, I was too weary to fight my way out. Even my strange, false sense of a body ached at the thought of forcing my mind away.

The Weaver coughed as he walked straight into the burning streets, boots sloshing in the mud. Judging by the curved roofs, he appeared to be somewhere in the far east. A man with a long braid of hair stumbled away from the inferno, his arm around a woman. Their white silk clothing was stained black with soot.

The Weaver passed by them without hesitation, and they didn't appear to see him at all. He moved with purpose. Steps steady. Focus locked. It took a moment before I realized what exactly he was staring at.

A dark figure stood atop a building. Despite the smoke swirling, I knew it was Mara. Her posture was the same as it was in the clock tower—partially hunched—but when she leapt from her perch in front of the Weaver, it was with a pained expression.

Mara stood slowly, wincing, limbs bending at crooked angles, but her head…that was held high. She hissed like an animal at the Weaver, then bound around him to slit the couple's throats. They fell right there in the muck without knowing they were in danger.

"Come to take me home, Lord?" Mara taunted.

"Stop this," he replied, arms held out to imply the destruction.

She feigned surprise with a hand going to her chest. "Lord, you've given me a new home. I only seek to change it to my liking."

The Weaver looked down at the threads on his arm but made no move to touch them. They were useless to him in the Day World. "The worlds have already changed, Mare."

"Because *you* changed them," she spat.

"No." He stepped toward her carefully. "Men did. They chased the magic from this world, but they've breathed their own sort into it. You and I are the ones out of place here. You can't make this place something it isn't."

"This is a means to an end." She leaned over the corpses, jabbed her finger in the man's open throat, then sucked the blood off like it was brownie batter. "If I have to destroy this world first, so be it, but I will live again in chaos. Darkness is my home, Nightmare Lord. Ashes and dust and bone. My brethren and I will have it as such again."

"Then who will be left for you to kill?" the Weaver tried to reason.

Mara smiled, her teeth tinged red. "That's the point—to be rid of the vermin."

Kindly step away from my memory. The Weaver's thought broke through the scene and everything froze.

If you don't want me to see something, don't show it to me.

He huffed. *No one can have control of their thoughts a hundred percent of the time.*

I've seen this much. Might as well let me see how it ends.

It ends with my burying her a thousand feet in the ground, he said simply. *I had to stop her from destroying the Day World—my nightmares need Dreamers to survive.*

I would've loved to see that. Served her right. Too bad she didn't stay buried. Though, it was probably less about his nightmares and more about him not wanting to die along with everything else.

How exactly did you manage that feat by yourself?

Do you underestimate me, Keeper? the Weaver asked, feigning offense. *Mara was wreaking havoc in your world for a long time by then. She was weaker than she was when the Sandman and I banished her.*

Still, to dig so far down, get Mara inside the hole, and fill the dirt back in over her? Not to mention that he had no nightmares to help—threads yes, but not actual nightmares. The next thought I sent his way was less of a thought and more of a wordless annoyance.

You should've seen what she did before that, he said, indignant. *Moving entire landmasses, hurling fiery comets—*

Okay, okay. Evil. Got it. Not in the mood for a complete recap. I was exhausted. Was one night too much to ask for? One night free of being reminded of my mistake in accidentally letting Mara back in? Just one night?

The paused memory vanished, and I loosened a breath. Distantly, I heard the steady *thump thump thump* of a heartbeat and felt the Sandman's warmth against me. I held onto that instead of the gnawing fear and let my mind rest.

***

My fingers danced over the gleaming crescent moon on the Sandman's chest while he slept beside me. I had no idea when he removed his shirt, but his skin was hot beneath my touch. Almost too hot, just like mine, which I suspected was the reason I couldn't fall back asleep. Still, I didn't have the heart to get up yet. I would have to crawl over him to leave the bed and I hated to wake him. The Sandman looked peaceful, so at ease. I missed the days when sleep brought me the same sensation. I tried—I really had—but even when the Weaver was quiet, his magic buzzed in my head like a swarm of bees.

There were also the memories to deal with—but last night was different. Silly me for thinking nightmares were impossible for me to have anymore. The Weaver in my head was like having a night terror every moment of my life, asleep or otherwise.

Pity party for one.

I will kill you one day, I vowed to the Weaver, counting it a miracle I managed not to say the threat out loud.

You promise that a lot, Keeper, but what will happen to you if I'm dead?

I didn't want to know. Only part of me cared at this point. Maybe I would go back to being human, or maybe I would die along with him, but a literal eternity with the Weaver lodged in my brain was nothing short of torture. I had to do *something* because there was no living like this forever.

Tell him about me, the Weaver suggested. *See what happens. See how he looks at you once he knows.*

I bit my bottom lip. My killing the Weaver was enough of a disappointment to both of us, but this…this was another ball game. The Sandman had to know—I would've told him last night if I weren't so exhausted. When he woke up, I'd try harder.

If you wanted, this could be a symbiotic relationship. I'll keep you strong.

I am *strong*, I shot back. And I was. The Weaver lent me his strength when I needed it, but it was me who built this new life. The palace. Me that spread new fear through the Nightmare Realm. Besides, however the Weaver expected to benefit in return was sure to be too steep a price.

"Morning," the Sandman said in a husky, sleep-filled voice.

I jerked my hand away from his tattoo and looked up to find his violet eyes cracked open. "Morning," I replied, almost shy.

"What's wrong?" he asked and skimmed my cheekbone with his thumb.

"Nothing." I shook my head. No—he wouldn't believe that. "Mara," I amended. "Facing her yesterday was a wakeup call. She's been taunting me for weeks but seeing her was different."

A flash of fear crossed his face, disappearing as fast as it came, replaced by a playful smirk. "You know, there's a way to make you less afraid for a little while."

"How?"

He was on top of me so fast that I'd barely realized he'd moved. Then his grin widened, and he buried his face in my neck, tickling me with play bites. I squealed with laughter and shoved him away. "You don't play fair."

"Not always," he admitted.

Staring at his bright, smiling face, my gut twisted. No more lies. No more stalling. But the Weaver's ever-so-sure warning that the Sandman would look at me differently sent a wave of prickling shame down my back. It didn't matter—the truth had to come out before he learned it another way. "There's still something else I need to tell you."

A hard knock shook the door. "Are we going to deal with Mara or not?" Kail droned from the other side.

"Go away," I called.

"No rest for the wicked," he replied.

I rolled onto my back and stared at the bunched fabric hanging above the bed. Wasn't he *just* telling me that I needed to rest? A throbbing ache began in my jaw, and I forced myself to unclench it. "That explains why you're constantly around like a tiny, yappy dog."

The sound of the Sandman's quiet laugh warmed me from the inside out and chased away my irritation. A small smirk lifted my lips.

"Woof," Kail deadpanned.

Fine. There was no ignoring Kail. I'd tried. Almost every day. He only became more and more annoying, as if that were possible. I climbed reluctantly from bed and hurried into a clean pair of soft black pants, a green shirt of the same mystery material, and a long black jacket with a stiff winged collar of gold, all gifts from the Doll Maker.

With a resigned huff, I yanked the door open to face Kail. "What?"

He mimicked knocking again before raising a quizzical brow. "I already said what I wanted."

"We're coming," the Sandman told him, then, to me, "we need a place to practice."

"Practice what?" Kail asked before I could.

The Sandman met my eyes. "Day Walking."

***

The basement of the Keep provided both the privacy we wanted and the caution we needed. I'd only been down here a few times, once to check it out, a handful more to scream where no one could hear. It was spacious, nearly four times bigger than the Keep above, with massive support beams running down the center. The floor was made of large stones, artfully placed in a jagged circle, while the walls were the same black and gold marble as above. Pieces of straw littered the floor, though I wasn't sure why, and any nightmares the Weaver or Rowan kept here were long gone.

The Sandman stood at the bottom of the stairs, whispering to Halven. Halven nodded once, then caught me watching. "Lady," he said with a bob of his head.

"Ready?" the Sandman asked, walking to my side.

Halven strode back up the stairs, leaving us alone with Kail who stood, brooding, in the corner.

I waved a hand toward the empty staircase. "What was the about?"

"I asked him to make sure Mare didn't move again after yesterday's attack."

That made sense. I stared at where Halven just was, unsure what answer I wanted him to return with. If she was still there, we could make our move. If she wasn't, well… It bought a little more time for my ankles to stop feeling weak.

"Nora? Are you ready?" the Sandman asked again.

"I don't want to do this," I whispered, my voice cracking. Day Walking was at the bottom of my to-do list, right under being boiled in hot oil. The pain of the Day World was still fresh—both the physical and mental. It ached down to my very bones, the air grating my skin, but my family…they were there. Thinking I ran away with *Ben*. Except Katie, anyway, because it took her until I was gone to realize I'd always spoken the truth about the Sandman. What if I suddenly popped up in my living room? I wasn't ready to deal with that particular confrontation.

"We won't go to your house," the Sandman promised with a smile that let me know he understood my worries without voicing them.

Perceptive, isn't he? the Weaver pondered.

The Sandman brushed a kiss over my knuckles. "Mare can't cross into the Day World without our combined power to carry her, and now that you don't have the dream …"

I nodded. Mara could only hitch a ride back to the Night World with me because I had carried a small sliver of the Sandman's power. Now that the dream was gone, the barrier wouldn't let the Ancient back through unless we worked together. Putting her back in the Day World wasn't my first choice though. I wanted her dead and buried, but clearly that was more difficult than it sounded. So the Day World it was. Sure, it would keep Mara from opening the Ever Safe and destroying everything and everyone, but there would still be a cost. The people who had no idea of the danger of this world would be the ones paying it.

I knew that should bother me. It didn't.

Much.

But I *wanted* it to which had to count for something.

"I follow Dreamers' cords to get to the Day World," the Sandman continued. He looked between Kail and me and shifted uncomfortably.

"I don't have that ability." My voice was hard-edged with frustration.

"Is there a place inside you that feels like it would help?" he asked, eager.

If he only knew, the Weaver taunted.

"Not really." Kail's presence burned at my back. No way was I spilling the beans about the Weaver in front of him, so I shut my eyes instead. "I'll try."

Okay. What's the secret to this whole Day Walking business? I demanded from the Weaver.

Why don't I do it for you?

My stomach twisted at the thought of him taking control of my body like he had when I found Rowan and when I woke up in the clock tower. The helplessness, the fear. *No—*

"Nora!" The Sandman's voice cut through the silent conversation, and my eyes flew open. A crease formed between his brows. "We have to go together."

"Right. Sorry." Had I almost gone somewhere? I flicked my gaze over to Kail. He eyed me suspiciously, and I squeezed the Sandman's hand. The Weaver's near-giddy laugh lingered in the back of my head, his claws sunk in deep. It was a miracle I was able to speak at all. To hold onto the Sandman. It was almost a certainty that I wouldn't be able to move without setting off something terrible. A domino effect, starting with the Weaver's talons slicing through my brain and ending with me dangling off a cliff somewhere in the Day World. *He needs me alive*, I reminded myself. "On the count of three?"

The Sandman nodded and began the count. Time seemed to slow, his words blurring, and my body felt fuzzy. Weightless. I focused on the Sandman's eyes and let them ground me as the Weaver's manic energy fizzled through my veins.

"That wasn't so bad, was it?" the Sandman asked.

I blinked and the hair on my arms rose. Not because I was unnerved—I was—but because it was freezing. Wind whipped around us, pelting us with hard bits of snow. It blew in sheets that seemed to erase the world beyond. I winced and huddled closer to the Sandman.

"Snow isn't supposed to hurt," I cried as it stung my face.

Snow was supposed to be fluffy. Pretty. It wasn't supposed to attack you. It was everywhere, as far as the eye could see, endless blankets of white. "What is this place?"

"You've never seen snow, so I thought I'd show you." He cringed when a particularly large piece landed in his left eye. "Sleet is admittedly less exciting."

"I think I've seen enough," I said, unamused. "Can we go back, or do we have to do something first?"

He scanned the area through slitted eyes. "This will be a good place to bring Mare, don't you think?"

I tensed at the reminder. But yes, this was a good place. Frigid, which would hopefully take a toll on her, and not a building in sight. Not that we could see far in this weather.

Maybe by the time she found anyone, she would be too weak to do much damage.

Don't lie to yourself.

I pursed my lips. The Weaver was right—it was a lie. Mara survived centuries—

More than centuries, the Weaver corrected.

—without losing her touch. Why would a little cold weather change that?

"We can't bring her here." I met his eyes. Curse my stupid desire to be empathetic. "She'll eventually find a way to kill people."

The truth of it flickered across his face. "Losing some lives is better than losing them all, which is what will happen if Mare opens the Ever Safe."

"I don't accept that." I stepped away from him, shaking my head against the buzz of power. I *couldn't* accept that. My family was here, my friends' families. I owed it to Natalie and Emery to protect their kin. Even if their loved ones weren't a factor, even if this was happening a hundred years from now when everyone I knew was dead, I couldn't willingly allow people to be killed. Everyone was important to someone, even if they didn't know it. Like I hadn't known how important I was to my mother. It was still hard to reconcile that fact with the way she treated me.

The darkness in me pulsed. It wrapped itself around the thoughts of loved ones and grief and squeezed. And squeezed. And squeezed some more. *Stop it,* I hissed mentally.

I'm not doing that, the Weaver said, his voice honest, intrigued.

Panic boiled, but as each bubble popped, it left behind resignation. Tranquility. A void. Maybe the Sandman was right. Mara could kill a handful of people to keep the rest of our worlds alive. Thousands, even, which was more likely. But what did I care? I wouldn't die.

That last thought tore through the suffocating darkness. "I'm going back," I managed to say in a crackling voice.

And I did.

I sacrificed the thread nearest my wrist and used it to go home the same way I had used the one in my pencil box, not trusting the Weaver to help. Not trusting the power to not grow into something worse.

"You're missing something," Kail said carefully when I reappeared in the basement alone.

I took deep breaths to situate myself and flung the melting sleet from my hands. It hit the ground with a splat. "Don't start."

"You didn't toss the Sandman into some deep, dark abyss or anything, did you?"

More snow and ice melted from my hair, running down my face, and I glared at him. "Shut. Up. Kail."

He pushed away from the wall and straightened. "You aren't denying it."

My patience plunged into the negatives, and I snapped. I lunged at him, knocking him back into the wall. My fists balled into the front of his jacket. "I said, *shut up.*"

With one slow, confident swipe of his arm, Kail knocked my hands away. "Thou doth protest too much. Did it cross your mind, then?"

"Can you tell what's crossing my mind right now?"

Kail's eyes flashed in beats—three quick changes, a slower one, and then back to their usual steady pace. He gripped my chin between his thumb and forefinger, then blocked the slap I brought up to remove his hand. "You may think I'm a fool, Nora, but I'm nothing if not observant."

Oh, I knew he was no fool.

"I'll find out what's going on with you," he vowed.

The Sandman stepped up to us. "What's going on?"

I jerked away from Kail with my heart in my throat. Why did he insist on silently popping up out of nowhere all the time?

"Someone needs to get you a bell," Kail said.

A wonderful idea for Christmas. "He thought I tried to hurt you."

The Sandman glared at each of us in turn with no expression to give away his thoughts. That in itself told me he was utterly confused. "Right," he said carefully after a long, strained silence. "Can you do that again? At a moment's notice?"

I opened my mouth to say no, but the Weaver gripped my head and nodded for me. *We have to take care of Mara, dear Keeper. Deal with your personal demons later.*

You *are my personal demon*, I shot back.

Maybe the Weaver was right. Maybe it was something else, something *me*. The darkness left a stain, because now very little felt truly heinous. It felt almost justified that the Day World should make a few sacrifices of its own. Just like killing all those nightmares had, but people weren't nightmares. I scowled. That should matter. Why didn't it matter?

"Halven's waiting outside," Kail said with measured words. "Are we doing this?"

I sighed, resigned. "Yes."

We walked single file out of the Keep's basement and back into the palace. Melted snow and ice dripped around my shoulders from where it had crusted my hair. I gathered the ends and squeezed the excess water out.

"Lady Nightmare?" I winced at the sound of Bloody Mary's voice. The slap of her footsteps filled the hallway as she rushed toward us. "I've been waiting so long to speak with you."

"Not now," Kail told her impatiently.

"It will only take one moment." The nightmare turned to me and clasped her hands in front of her chest. "Please, Lady?"

I ran a hand down my face, careful not to look at hers. Seeing my features on her was unnerving, and she'd been lurking for days. If hearing her out got rid of her, then by all means. "Fine. What?"

"Can I have the meat?" she squeaked, as if she suddenly lost her nerve. "It's old now and you haven't touched it."

I shot Kail a questioning look, only to find his brows lowered in equal confusion. The Sandman tensed beside me. "What meat?" I asked, half-certain I didn't want the answer.

"I...I wasn't snooping around," Blood Mary assured me quickly. "I came to ask you to fix the damage to my territory and smelled it."

"What meat?" I repeated, with growing irritation. We had things to do, an Ancient to see.

Blood Mary pointed to a set of double doors. They led to a room with a long dining room table—no chairs, because no one actually ate there—that spanned the length of the room and ended with an identical set of doors. The other set opened almost directly across from the main palace entrance. Had one of the nightmares come in to ask a favor and died inside, waiting? I hadn't been slacking *that* badly, had I?

"Sure." I spoke slowly, regretting the words as they left my mouth. "Take it and leave."

"Thank you, Lady!" Blood Mary wasted no time tugging on the doorknob.

The heavy wood barely budged, but it didn't seem to faze her. She simply kept pulling, making progress one centimeter at a time. If she knew there was meat inside, she had managed to open them before. How long had it taken then and why hadn't we noticed?

I looked to Kail again and bobbed my head, signaling him to follow her.

"I'd really rather not," he glowered.

"If there's something dead in there, I want to know what it is," I said from the corner of my mouth. Bloody Mary didn't need to know it worried me, and Kail was better than me at hiding emotions.

"Well, then. By all means, after you, Lady." He held an arm out to usher me forward.

The Sandman exhaled heavily and eased between us to follow the nightmare. Bloody Mary looked up at him and cringed away. "Shortcut out of here," he said as an excuse to help, and pulled the doors open with one yank.

The smell was immediate, overwhelming, and utterly fatal. Fatal for me. Not for whatever creature was decaying in my would-be dining room. They had already perished—clearly—though if they hadn't, this odor would've surely done them in. There was no possible way these doors could trap every trace of this catastrophe.

Quality craftsmanship, the Weaver said with a touch of admiration.

What? Oh, dear lord. I was going to throw up everything I'd eaten in the last eighteen years.

It's air tight, he mused.

Not now, Weaver.

"Do you want the note?" Bloody Mary asked before entering the room.

"Note?" I wheezed, and stifled a gag as best I could, bile burning my throat. The Sandman stepped away from the doors, his face white, a hand clamped over his nose and mouth. I desperately wanted to follow him away from the source. We were going to have to burn the palace down and start over if I was ever going to be rid of this stench.

"What does it say?" Kail asked calmly. As if we hadn't entered the devil's lower intestine.

"I didn't read it. Only saw there was one," Bloody Mary replied.

Ah, hell. The sooner I went in there, the faster it would be over. "Yes, I want it."

With watery eyes and a hand firmly clasped over my nose, I followed Bloody Mary inside. A mound of carefully cut meat was stacked at the center of the table in a semicircle. Each piece resembled a pork chop, except the two center pieces that looked more like a roast. It was as if they were waiting to be packaged and sold at the grocery store, minus the huge rotten black spots.

"It's there," Bloody Mary practically sang as she pulled the front of her dress out to create a pouch.

I struggled not to inhale and approached the table. A butcher knife stuck out of the wood at an angle, pinning a piece of parchment down. My pulse beat erratically. Every piece of me screamed not to look at the words scrawled across the page. In rusty colored ink.

Blood, the Weaver interjected.

My stomach roiled. *Yes, I got that.*

Read it, he urged.

"I can still have it?" Blood Mary asked, eying me with one hand hovering above the top cuts. "The meat?"

I scowled at her, disgusted. "Why do you want this?"

"It's a delicacy, even if it's spoiled." She slopped the round pieces of meat into the pouch she made from her dress. "Dreamer meat is nearly impossible to come by."

My body jerked to attention. Dreamer meat? She couldn't mean…

The note, the Weaver reminded me. *Read the note.*

I stumbled up to the table, doing my best not to vomit all over it as Bloody Mary hummed happily beside me, and snatched the paper up. It slid free of the knife with a soft rip. Blocky letters stared up at me.

Humans say not to play with their food. If they only knew how much fun it could be…don't you agree?

I crumpled the message in both hands. *Mara.* She didn't sign it, but she didn't have to. No one else would be brazen enough to cut up a Dreamer and leave them here. In my palace. With a note that taunted my human side.

"Get it out of here," I said breathlessly to Bloody Mary. "All of it. Now."

In that moment, it didn't matter that it was a Dreamer. A person. Chopped up. I needed it out of my sight and out of my palace, along with anything that could link me to it. If nightmares thought I forbid them from killing Dreamers while I feasted on them, there would be trouble. And I had enough of that already.

Get Kail, the Weaver ordered.

As if on cue, he waltzed into the room with a large wooden crate. "Here," he said to Bloody Mary. "Hurry up." His eyes fell to the meat on the table and, for the first time, he paled. His throat bobbed with a hard swallow.

"It's a Dreamer," I supplied.

He looked at me from the corners of his eyes. "You don't say."

"It's very recognizable," Bloody Mary commented as if it backed him up. She then dumped the pile of meat from her dress into the crate with a *squick*.

The sound sent me reeling, and I chucked the balled-up note at Kail's feet. "Another gift from Mara."

"Someone really needs to redefine the word *gift* to her. Get her to send a nice fruit basket, perhaps."

"How did she get in here?"

She got in, the Weaver said matter-of-factly, *because you built yourself a house of stone instead of a palace of nightmares.*

My stomach dropped. He was right—this wasn't an impenetrable sanctuary. The Hours waltzed in and kidnapped me, so why had I expected Mara not to get in? I stormed from the room without letting Kail answer.

"Let's go kill her," I called when he didn't follow me out.

Kail moved then, barking orders at not only Bloody Mary, but every nightmare within hearing distance. Inspect every inch of the palace. Destroy anyone unauthorized. Clean the dining room until they could see their reflections in every surface.

I joined the Sandman and Halven just outside the main doors while Kail set everyone into motion, my jaw clenched. When we returned, if there was a single cell from an unwanted nightmare within a five-mile radius, it would die a slow, painful death.

"Lady?" Halven croaked.

"Not now." Not until we were far away, and the scent of rancid Dreamer meat was gone from my nostrils. Not until I knew exactly what features I would add to the palace walls for security purposes. "Where's Mara?"

"Halven just confirmed her current hiding place." The Sandman opened his mouth to say something else, but Kail bustled up to the group, out of breath, and his focus shifted. "What happened in there?"

"What happened?" Kail scoffed, glancing quickly at me, then followed Bloody Mary with his gaze as she dragged a full crate of meat out the front doors. "Ask me again when I feel less like saying *I told you so.*"

Chapter Eight

Nora

I knew I wasn't the only one thinking it was too easy to toss Mara back into the Day World, but they acted like it was as simple as dragging the garbage out to the side of the road. Our *trash* had no intention of going anywhere though. We had to get close, had to touch her. A chill crawled up my spine at the thought of grabbing her dry skin, of her coarse hair and sharp nails. She would undoubtedly use her teeth too, if it came to that, and her knees were big enough to act as sledgehammers.

But here I was, making my way through the Nightmare Realm with the Sandman, Halven, and Kail. The Sandman assured me Day Walking would be as effortless as when we practiced. The hard work was done already. He and the Weaver erected the barrier between worlds, and it had proven effective at keeping her out. But what they considered effortless, I considered dangerous. The dark coil that tarnished my conscience earlier sat poised to strike again. Was that the price I had to pay for the Weaver's power? Was it becoming more like him and less like me?

I feel the same as always, the Weaver chimed in.

My eyes twitched with the effort not to respond. If the magic was turning me into something else, why had it waited the better part of a year? Maybe the Day World kept it at bay. If I had come back sooner, maybe this would've happened a long time ago. And speaking of coming back, how did the Sandman Day Walk alone if the barrier needed both Dream and Nightmare magic? The Weaver had to have the same ability too.

Before I was bound, the Weaver added, grumpy.

I sighed. *Are you ever going to let that go?*

Unlikely.

If that wasn't the truth, I didn't know what was.

We can pass through the barrier to Day Walk because we're made of pure magic. There was a way around it for my nightmares before the Sandman stole the information and hid it in your head, but the Ancients are made of something else.

Super.

For the record… The Weaver hesitated. *No one here thinks this will be easy, but it has to be done either way. Why splash around in a puddle of fear and doubt when it solves nothing? A brave face can go a long way, and you of all people should know that.*

I made a low, contemplative sound, and Kail whipped around to stare at me. The Sandman and Halven were too deep in a hushed conversation about our destination to notice—something about a map and symbols and the clock in the Blood Tower.

"What?" I snapped.

"Nothing," he replied, every syllable full of sarcasm.

I bristled. The least he could do was voice his thoughts if he insisted on being so obvious, and not the same *what's wrong* spiel. "Liar."

A blur of black and orange zipped past me, and I jumped, my heart in my throat. When the creature skidded to a halt at the Sandman's side, my pulse only beat faster. Baku, your friendly neighborhood nightmare eater and all-around sketchy chimera. I tried to convince myself the increasingly bad vibe I got from him was because he looked at me like a juicy burger fresh off the grill. With his elephant trunk and tusks large enough to skewer me, tiger paws to shred me, and the same watchful eyes as a rhinoceros, I would be a fool not to be wary, but it was something else. The watchfulness was tinged with a sense of anger. Of resentment.

"Hello," the Sandman greeted cheerfully. "Where did you run off to yesterday?"

Baku gave no reply, of course, as he couldn't speak. It was just as well because I doubted I could stomach hearing about his hunts.

Kail gripped my wrist and slowly tried to pry my clenched hand from his forearm. When had I grabbed him? "Sorry," I whispered and relinquished my death grip.

"Relax. He won't eat you in front of us," he said, impassive.

"I wouldn't be so sure." What could they do to stop him? If a few nightmares were all it took to bring Baku down, he wouldn't currently be a thorn in the side of my realm, but I kept my mouth shut for the Sandman's sake. He was alone in the Dream Realm with the chimera as his only steady companion now that I couldn't visit the beach.

Kail let out a small breath. "I'm sure of nothing."

"Except maybe yourself." I shot him a knowing smile, but his eyes were glued ahead on Baku.

"True. But him… even I can't figure him out."

The statement was lacking, as if a whole story needed to follow. And I would hear it, just not with Baku three feet away. My guess was the chimera's presence put Kail on edge too because he wasn't one to hold his tongue. And with the Sandman's proximity, we couldn't exactly speak freely about his friend without putting him on the defense. Plus, we were on the way to fry a bigger fish. A whale, really.

"You won't need Halven to spy after today." Kail's voice wavered. "Mara will be gone."

My guard melted away, replaced by the familiar tang of guilt. I was almost relieved that I could still feel that way, but it was hard to be glad when it hurt so much. Not as painful as Kail and Halven must have felt being torn in two…

"I'm sorry it's taking so long to make good on my promise," I told him sincerely. I hadn't wanted to wait at all, but we needed them apart to keep up our ruse.

He shrugged, glib. "What's an extra two months when I'm withering away on the inside?"

I held back a wince. They were apart for a long while now, and the side-effect was constant pain. Though they both hid it extremely well, I knew first-hand how exhausting it was. Day after day. Week after week. For them, decade after decade. Maybe even longer as I actually had no idea how old they were or when the split happened. I hated delaying their reunion, but it wouldn't matter if they were in one body or two if Mara opened the Ever Safe.

"You're easily the most irritating thing in my life but—"

"The *most* irritating? I can think of a dozen other problems that should come before me. The Doll Maker's constant gifting of ridiculous clothes—" He ticked off a finger, staring pointedly at my collar. "That bloody creature hanging around the palace—really, I don't know why you didn't kill her." He ticked off another finger. "The Hours."

"Some of those clothes are cool," I shot back. The jacket I had on made me feel like I belonged in an action movie, kicking butts and taking names, which I happened to be doing. Well, the butt kicking anyway. I didn't care about their names. "Bloody Mary probably won't come back for a while now that she took off with the Dreamer…" I couldn't bring myself to say *meat* out loud. "And the Hours are locked up at the moment, so, you win."

"Those are all temporary fixes. Mine would be permanent."

"If you had let me finish." I purposely cleared my throat. "You're the most annoying thing in my life, but you deserve this. Tonight, after Mara is gone, I'll put you and your brother back together."

"Tonight?" he asked skeptically. "You won't be too tired?"

I lifted a brow. "Do you want to wait until tomorrow?"

"I'm just saying, the Sandman stayed over last night and—"

"Kail." I elbowed him hard in the ribs. "Quit while you're ahead."

"Right." He stood a little straighter and sniffed. "Tonight is fine, I suppose."

"That's what I thought."

He rewarded me with an extremely rare true smile, then quickly tried to hide it. Maybe he would be freer with his feelings once he was back with Halven. His brother was kind and empathetic, so with any luck, some of it would rub off on him, if only to give me a break from his constant attitude. It would be nice to have someone I could hold an actual conversation with.

In front of us, Halven and the Sandman slowed. "This is the place?" the Sandman asked him.

Halven nodded.

Braided metal, knotted and tarnished, stretched high above our heads. Hundreds of spires, maybe more, in groups of four and five, held up globes. Some of the spires were misshapen, others tilted, the shine gone, and each sporting holes rimmed with crumbling rust, while the spheres ranged from colossal to minuscule and everywhere between. A decaying city in the sky. Occasional sprinkles of dust fell like autumn leaves. Metal creaked around us, sounding as if the slightest breeze would knock everything over, and a chill ran over my skin.

"You're sure about this?" I felt less brave than ever as we hid behind half of a rusted globe that had fallen to the ground. "Because it *sounds* easy and all, but I've seen how agile she is now."

The Sandman tucked a piece of errant hair behind my ear. "It's not easy to kill an Ancient. This is the fastest and most effective way to stop Mare. We can monitor her in the Day World and, if she's out of control, we can kill her there, where she's weaker."

If. The Weaver laughed. *Might as well stay when you get to the other side and finish the job.*

You're awfully sure we'll get her there without her ripping us to shreds.

Oh, she most certainly will. Especially with you *in charge of* us.

"Stop." It was almost as if I could feel the smoke from his memory snuffing the air from my lungs. Those people… She killed them without reason. What would she do now that she had a personal vendetta and my home address? At the first whisper of the Weaver's breath, I rushed to stop him from telling me *exactly* what Mara would do. "Just stop!"

The Sandman cocked his head. "Stop what?"

"Not you." I squeezed my eyes shut. Right. *That* conversation still had to happen, but not right before we faced the big bad. I flicked a hand casually through the air. "Myself. Doubts or whatever. Mara knows what we'll try to do, and she'll never let us get to her at the same time."

Kail glowered around the Sandman at me, the suspicious look returning. "On what planet did you expect her to *let* you?"

"It's okay, Nora," the Sandman said calmly. Though it was obvious he wasn't convinced . "You know the plan. We both need to have a good grip on her, then Day Walk. The second we're there, we let go and come back."

He forgot to add 'and hope she lets go too'. Remember how well she latched onto your back? It's not often a lord—sorry, lady—*requires stitches. Twice now. Not that I'm keeping count, but I'd really love to stop wasting energy fixing you for stupid mistakes.*

"That's not much of a plan," I said softly. There were too many holes. Too many things that could go wrong.

"Try, try again," Kail said in a flat voice. "And again, and again, and—"

"You're not helping," I hissed.

Fallen crumbs of rust *crunched* behind us, and I whirled to see Baku trotting straight into the landscape. He wove expertly between pillars with his trunk straight out in front of him. "What is he doing?"

"Besides giving us away?" Kail pressed his lips together and shrugged.

The Sandman's eyes widened. "He must be staking it out for us."

Halven made a choked sound, then, "Stop him."

"What do you want me to do?" the Sandman asked helplessly.

Because there was nothing he *could* do. If any of us ran after him, it would only create a bigger scene. Any microscopic hope that Mara didn't hear Baku's paws hitting the ground would be lost.

"He hunts in the Nightmare Realm all the time," the Sandman added without conviction. "It wouldn't be out of the question for him to be here."

Kail glared openly at him. "It took Halven weeks to find Mara, but your most well-known associate just *happens* to stumble through her camp? Did you forget to tell us someone knocked the sense out of you recently?"

Indeed, the Weaver said skeptically. *Keeper, what do you say to a little field trip after this?*

"We should probably…" I said, motioning forward and ignoring the voice in my head. Pain flared hot in my shoulder, the Weaver's not-so-subtle reminder of Mara's welcome home gift. It healed quickly thanks to my magic, not even leaving a scar, but I *had* needed stitches. *Knock it off*, I warned. *I need to focus.*

I stared at Kail for a moment, meeting his wariness with brash determination. Not that I felt anywhere close to determined, but I learned quickly what showing weakness could cost.

"We have plans later," he reminded me. "Don't go dying just yet."

I rolled my eyes. "Wait here."

"I'm certainly not going in *there*," he said, horrified.

I wanted to punch him for making me more nervous, but it wasn't possible for my anxiety to get any worse. Plus, I needed to save my energy. "Stay put and watch him," I told Halven, and gave his forearm a squeeze. "Only come out if there's no other choice."

Kail folded his arms over his chest. "I don't need a babysitter."

"Don't you?" I shot him a quick smile that I was positive looked as fake as it felt and left both brothers there to lie in wait. If anything went wrong, at least there was a chance for them to step in with the element of surprise.

The Sandman and I walked side-by-side, our arms brushing. I wasn't sure if it was because he needed physical touch as much as I did, or because he thought it would help me. Either way, I was glad for the contact as we entered the landscape. The groaning was louder close up. Each pillar creaked with its own tune, in its own time, as if the landscape was meant to play like a symphony.

"How do we know where to find Mara?" I asked quietly. The Sandman flicked a look at his satchel. A thin line of sand trailed out, running down his leg, spreading when it hit the ground. "Ah."

Before his sand could tell us anything, a different sound rattled the air. A drawn-out scratch like the needle my father's broken record player used to make. I waited to see if it would happen again. If it were simply a wrong note or a broken piece of the landscape. Echoes came instead, one right after the other. *Footsteps.*

My mouth ran dry. "Do you hear that?"

Another scratch like the first.

The Sandman and I stopped in our tracks. My hand went for the thread around my arm while his dove deep into his satchel of sand. Whatever it was, it was close, but it wasn't necessarily

Mara. Other nightmares had to live here—the globes were too perfect a habitat to pass up. My heart hammered, the sound filling my ears. I flexed my fingers. Maybe I should alter the landscape. Make it silent just until this was over so we could hear where—

A figure launched itself from the globe in front of us. A flurry of white fabric and wild brown hair. *Mara.* She landed on her feet, crouched and ready to pounce. Her long shins stretched up to knobby knees that bent near her head. Deep black veins covered her pale skin. She smiled viciously.

No words were exchanged. No quips or threats. They weren't necessary when Mara's next attack said everything. She lunged at me faster than a whip. Her nails were longer now, sharper than they were in the clock tower, her teeth filed to points. Spittle sprayed from her mouth on a hiss.

I froze.

Move! the Weaver screeched.

A net made of glimmering sand shot in from the side. Mara leapt over it and gouged my arm on her way past me. Her nails dug in hard as she swung herself around my torso and landed a few yards away. The pain jarred something in me. Darkness swirled rapidly. Its energy rose up around me, and my vision tunneled to the hideous ancient creature. It was as if someone flipped a switch inside me. Nora off, Lady Nightmare on. Any sense of self evaporated, and I plucked a thread from my wrist. Gave it life. Heard its first vicious roar. A great beast with a head of horns and sparse red feathers decorating its thick hide leaned back on its haunches in front of me.

Mara made the most inhuman of sounds and skittered backwards. A hail of dream-made weapons flew through the air—knives and grenades and throwing stars. My nightmare chose that moment to charge, and my chest tightened.

"No!" But my cry was too late. The nightmare took nearly every one of the weapons meant for Mara.

You have more, the Weaver reminded me.

Yes. I had more nightmares woven than I could count, but it wasn't about the nightmare. It was about all those lost chances for a weapon to strike Mara. To slow her down. But it was done, so I loosened threads from my wrist, one after another. A floating saber-tooth shark and monsters made of muck. Human-like fodder beside things that would never pass as such. Thorns and teeth. Archers and mountain men with picks.

"Nora." The Sandman stopped me from pulling another thread. "It's too many. She'll run, and we'll never catch her."

"They'll slow her down," I disagreed. Mara would cut every nightmare down—I knew that—but they weren't meant to do my job. They were meant to make my job easier.

He winced and pointed the long spear in his hand at the worn pillar holding the sphere above our heads. "Look."

Mara scrambled up the knotted metal as easily as a monkey climbed a tree, and my nightmares attempted to follow. Tried and failed. The corroded, weakened post disintegrated beneath their weight and the whole construction groaned against the pressure. Rust rained down around us, and I shielded my eyes. Panic flashed through me, hot and tingling.

"Enough," I screamed at them. They would bring the entire thing down and the close, confined quarters of the sphere would make it easier to get our hands on Mara. "Stop!"

The nightmares eased away reluctantly. Mara was a bone to chew, and I had taken it away from a pack of loyal dogs. They surrounded the base, immobile yet waiting. Waiting for Mara to fall. Waiting for me to let them attack again. They wanted an order from their lady, but my brain scrambled to think of a purpose for them on the ground. The archers could still shoot, and if any of them had aerial abilities—

Screw the nightmares right now, the Weaver practically roared in my head.

The Sandman pulled me to him with an arm around my waist and shot a grappling hook straight at the top of the globe. "Hang on."

Handy, that sand of his… I was beginning to see why the Weaver was jealous.

I'm not jealous.

The next moment, my feet were off the ground. The Sandman and I hurtled toward the globe at an alarming speed, and my stomach churned. How did you stop these things? Mara squeezed up through a small hole at the base of the globe. *Perfect.* Now, if we could only get—

The Sandman let go of the hook.

I would've screamed if I remembered how. Or if I was able to breathe. Or do anything except cling to the Sandman for dear life. Which was exactly was I did. Why would he let go? He just told me to hang on. My hands balled into the fabric of his shirt, and I fought the urge to close my eyes as we free-fell straight down.

The sphere was getting closer and closer, and a scream stuck in my throat. A moment later, we hit a large rusted area near the top. The Sandman twisted so his back broke through the metal instead of mine, and the thin material crumbled like dust. We continued to fall. And fall. And fall. Shards of muted light pierced the interior of the globe. The entire thing was hollow save for the pillar that went from the north pole to the south pole.

Mara scurried around the center post, eyes fixed on us. She wouldn't have to wait long at the speed we were going.

Oh, this was going to hurt…

The Sandman produced a short scythe and drove it into the pole. It sliced through the metal with a loud screech, tearing a jagged line behind us. "Hang on," he said again in my ear.

Not a problem. My eyes tracked Mara's every movement until she disappeared into our blind spot. *Nightmares.* I needed to make more in here. Two or three… They could pin her down and we could—

Something hard slammed into me from behind, causing the Sandman to lose his grip on the scythe handle. We broke apart and we careened the rest of the way down. His sand shot out to catch me, but while he loved me, his magic didn't. I fell straight through the sand and hit the bottom of the sphere with a resounding *thwak*. It echoed through the metal interior and through my ears. My head. My bones. Did I still have bones that weren't broken?

Shake it off.

The sound of fighting filled the globe. Mara screeching. The Sandman calling my name. Metal striking metal. A loud thud.

Help him! The Weaver's shout bounced through me alongside the pain.

He was right. I had to get up. Help. Move. Make a nightmare. Something. Anything. But my body refused to listen to commands.

Worthless, the Weaver snarled.

Darkness swooped in. My vision faded, returning only in brief flashes. The ceiling. Mara sitting on the Sandman's chest, digging her nails into his face. A wall of sand rising.

My shoulder exploded into fiery agony. Mara was beneath me, said shoulder rammed into her ridiculously hard sternum.

"Quickly," I said to the Sandman. Only it wasn't *me*.

I scrambled to regain control of myself, but everything spun violently. Turned black and suffocating.

The next instant, Mara's face lit up with a victorious smile.

Metal creaked.

Metal crumbled.

Metal gave way.

The Weaver clenched my jaw. *We'll be fine, Keeper. The Sandman is safe.*

But all I knew was the ground outside quickly rising to greet us. The déjà vu didn't escape me in that very brief moment. I fell into this life with Mara clinging to me, and now I was falling out of it with a single difference. She wasn't going to break my fall— I was going to break hers. And, likely, my neck.

Chapter Nine

Nora

A fissure glowed bright in the darkness. I stared at it for a long time, struggling to connect the dots. The only time I saw these was when I was asleep, but we were just fighting Mara…

Look, Keeper, the Weaver's voice urged quietly.

At what? I asked, the thought feeling far away.

He didn't answer, but there was a deep knowing inside me. At the memory. He wanted me to see this one. I crept closer, steeling myself against the unknown. The other memories I had seen of him and the Sandman weren't exactly informative. Insightful, maybe, but not in a way that helped me rule. *Here goes nothing…* I swallowed hard and peeked inside.

A knife sat in the Weaver's palm. His threads throbbed weakly over the pulse point in his wrist. There weren't many left—a single long strand that housed maybe a dozen nightmares. He turned the blade over carefully, and I jerked forward. It was *the* knife. The one I used to kill him. Only the handle wasn't glowing with magic.

"This will likely have dire effects," the Sandman warned.

The image shifted up as the Weaver looked at him. He was covered in filth, his violet eyes dull. "What choice do we have?"

"It's not too late. We could still find a way to put Mare back into the Ever Safe."

The Weaver shook his head. "Baku can't remember how she lured him out, and there's no time left. If we don't stop her now, she'll let more Ancients out. We both know there are worse things still locked up."

"The balance…"

"Will compensate," the Weaver said. "We've been over this. It's decided."

His gaze went back to the knife, and I felt his sigh as if it were my own. The thread slithered away from his wrist and toward the heel of his hand where it reached up to circle the handle. A piece of it separated and wrapped itself around the hollow hilt in the same pattern it had when I held it.

"Your turn," he said.

The Sandman held out his hand, sand cupped at its center, and the Weaver set the handle down on top of it. A slight sizzling filled the air as the sand coated the spaces between the thread. The two lords looked at each other and a sense of foreboding swelled within me—within the Weaver. The same feeling was written all over the Sandman's face.

Without looking away, the Sandman sliced his forearm with the tip of the blade. His blood ran down the center chamber of the gleaming metal, and the Weaver held his own arm out. "Be quick about it," he said.

A moment after the Weaver's blood mixed with the Sandman's and reached the interior of the hilt, the knife glowed brightly. The space around them rippled with magic so strong that the hair on my neck stood straight up. The Sandman handed the knife back to the Weaver and pulled out a handful of sand.

"We'll be fine, right?" he asked.

The Weaver tightened his grip on the knife. "Hurry before Mara finds a door back to the Night World."

The Sandman pursed his lips and tossed the sand into the air above them. It clung to an invisible sheet riddled with holes. *The fabric between worlds.* The Weaver stepped up to it. With a single swipe of his arm, he sliced it open. The tear released hurricane level winds, ripping a line down its entire length. The Weaver stumbled back. He shouted to the Sandman, but it was impossible to hear him. Dark hair whipped across his face, obstructing his vision. The rest of the scene became an erratic flash of images as strands were blown from his eyes and back again.

The Sandman hurried in front of him, struggling to control his sand. There were barrels worth of it in the air. It spun and spun, half of it blowing away. The Sandman's arms were raised, his head angled against the wind, knees bent in a struggle to stay on his feet.

After what felt like an eternity, some of the sand reached the cut, flashing bright blue on contact. The rest of the Weaver's final thread flew off his arm. Together, their combined magic stitched the fabric between the worlds back together. The ground grumbled, tilted, groaned—

The fissure slammed shut.

Wait! I called.

You've seen what you needed to see, the Weaver said. *A knife powerful enough to split worlds will surely be powerful enough to kill Mara.*

We couldn't even touch *her at the same time*, I cried. If we couldn't manage to grab two random body parts, how did he expect us to be precise enough to deliver a fatal blow?

The Sandman's plan failed. Now it's your turn.

My turn. The words sunk in. As the Lady of Nightmares, it was only natural that I should get equal say.

Don't forget, Keeper, we need to take a little side trip. Send the Sandman and Halven out to find Mara again, but bring Kail along with us. He might prove useful.

Care to expand on that?

He paused before answering. *Not yet, but it needs to be done whether or not you comply.*

Anger rose hot as his words reminded me of my last few conscious moments before he took control again to attack Mara. *He* was the reason the plan failed. The Sandman had direct contact—all I had to do was lay a hand on Mara and it would've been over.

I saved him, the Weaver said, *and you know it's true.*

It wasn't true. Yes, I was having trouble moving, but he didn't have to tackle Mara off the Sandman. All he had to do was touch her, then we could've warped to the Day World and ended this. We had her. *We had her.*

If the Sandman was hurt further, he would've gone back to the Dream Realm, leaving you all alone.

"I hate you," I screamed, and the action yanked me fully back into consciousness.

Three familiar faces greeted me along with the smell of burning pine. I sat up with a start. The sudden movement set my head spinning, and I groaned, digging the heels of my hands into my forehead. *Deep breaths.* There would be no sorting things out until I calmed down. Until I shifted through all the new information. Even if the Sandman was too hurt to continue with the original plan, which I immensely doubted, there was time. A split second more and—

"Take it easy," the Sandman said softly. His hand landed, feather-light, on my back.

I nodded stiffly and cracked my eyes open. We were surrounded by a forest of black and white. Greying leaves coated the ground, each balanced upright on their narrow tips, and white flames licked a pile of black sticks inside a freshly dug pit. "Where are we?"

"Did you expect us to carry you all the way back to the Keep?" Kail poked at the fire with a long stick. "You're not as light as you look."

I dabbed at the lingering ache at the back of my head. A knot rose beneath my hair, but not so big that one would think I fell dozens of feet to the ground. Hooray for magic healing. I was lucky my neck wasn't broken. At least, not any more. Who knew what state I was in when they had dragged me here? Judging by how dark the muted sky was, I had been out nearly all day.

"It wouldn't be a good idea to let the nightmares see you weak," the Sandman explained. "They shouldn't see you as something they can defeat."

"Mara isn't exactly the same caliber as nightmares." Not to mention that we were surrounded by nightmares at that very moment, even if it seemed like an empty forest. Other things surely lurked nearby, and Rowan proved that even trees weren't to be trusted. I stretched my back and groaned. "Besides, Halven could've whisked me back to the Keep unseen."

"Forgive me, Lady," Halven said in his usual raspy voice. "That would be difficult."

I opened my mouth to ask why when I saw the answer. Blood flowed freely from his arm and bones jabbed through his skin in two places. "What happened?" I demanded.

"*That* happened," Kail growled, pointing a finger into the wooded area behind me.

I twisted around to see Baku prowling among the trees. "Baku did that?" I asked with raised brows and leveled a look at the Sandman. "Why didn't you stop him?"

"Don't look at me," he said, staring into the flames. "He's his own creature."

"Perhaps he misread my intentions," Halven suggested painfully.

Kail and I snorted in disbelief at the same time. "He tried to attack me before," I said. "He'd eat me if he could."

"Hunger?" Halven proposed.

"Hunger," Kail echoed. "After he gorges himself almost nightly? Is that why he bit *you*?"

"Wait. Let's focus." I scowled at the shadow moving around us in giant, predatory circles. "Give me your arm."

Halven held out the mangled limb, and I took his hand. Closing my eyes, I quickly found his knot of thread and stitched the injured part together. When it was finished seconds later, I let go, and Halven flexed his arm. "Thank you, Lady."

"Sorry I couldn't do more." I looked between him and Kail. They should've been back together by now, like I promised Kail this morning. Bitterness coated my tongue.

"So," I began carefully. "What's next?"

"I was thinking about our next move." The Sandman paused and stared into the flames for a long stretch of time.

"Oh? It seems as if this new plan upsets you. I like it already. Tell us. What offends your morals so?" Kail leaned back on his elbows, smug.

The Sandman's jaw twitched. "We should gather forces and lay a trap. Mare was able to run off because there was no second line."

"That sounds like it would take too long," I said.

"You have enough thread to pack the Nightmare Realm full of nightmares," Kail reminded me.

"Fine." I had to pick my battles. The truth was, I wasn't worried about making the necessary nightmares. I was worried that it was going to take time to find Mara again and sneak this second line into position without her realizing it. There was almost no chance she wouldn't see us coming if we traveled with an entourage. "I'll make whatever you think we need, but this time, we're doing it my way."

Kail looked me over. "We're to pace back and forth through the Keep and avoid the problem?"

"No. We're getting the knife I used on the Weaver." I met the Sandman's eyes and held his troubled gaze. He knew where I was going with this without my voicing it, but the others didn't. "We're putting it in Mara's heart."

That's not quite what I had in mind, but it'll do.

What else could you possibly have meant? I snapped. *You literally said the knife could kill her.*

"Why not all of the above?" Kail offered. "Trap her in the Day World. Stab her with the knife. Deposit her somewhere far from civilization. If she's not completely dead, she'll still be weak. And not to mention, *gone.*"

It felt like overkill, but with Mara, was *anything* overkill? The Sandman and I held each other's stare for an entire minute. He knew he was fighting a losing battle—I could see it in his expression—but I could also see his hesitation. That knife was responsible for changing so many things. Now it was time for it to do some good.

"We have a plan then," I said finally.

"Right." The Sandman gnawed on the inside of his cheek. "I'll travel back to the Keep with you, then get the knife by myself."

By himself. The Weaver sounded as bitter as a grapefruit. *Always doing things alone. Always thinking he knows better than everyone else. Watch out, Keeper. You might be next.*

"I won't," I hissed.

The Sandman's eyes narrowed. "Won't what?"

Kail flew up straight, staring at me as if the Sandman sharing his suspicions somehow validated everything. "Yes, Lady," he added in a cynical voice. "Won't what?"

"Let you go alone," I said quickly, panicking. "Halven will find Mara's location while the rest of us retrieve the knife."

"It won't take three of us to—"

Kail cleared his throat, and the Sandman cocked his head. A curious look passed over his face as he looked at me. He might as well have been Medusa the way I froze under the scrutiny. If the two of them were going to team up on me, I was in trouble.

"If you insist," he finally said.

I stood and wiped my hands on my pants. "You have no idea where the knife is or what you'll have to do to get it, so yes. I do insist."

Chapter Ten

The Sandman

Kail was right. Something was wrong with Nora.

She came up with an alternative plan to deal with Mare rather quickly. A very *specific* alternative including the knife. There were the strange things Nora said, the comments that had nothing to do with the conversation. Something was off, but I couldn't place my finger on the cause. So, if Nora wanted to come with me to get the knife, fine. Hopefully it would give me a chance to ask her for the truth.

"Yo," Katie called. She floated in the water at the edge of the beach, letting the luminescent waves push and pull her gently. Her arms were flung out wide as if she were in her own private swimming pool, complete with bathing suit and foam noodle. My nostrils flared in annoyance, though I knew it was uncalled for. We were out there risking everything while she was taking a dip, but what was Katie supposed to do? We had banned her from entering the Nightmare Realm.

"Enjoying yourself?" I asked neutrally.

The knife. I had to find the location of the knife. Too much was going on right after Nora became the Weaver to give it much thought so I hid the blade as well as I could on short notice.

First stop, the second Dream Keeper. Katie could only hold one dream, so I had to use another. The problem was that I didn't bother keeping an eye on whoever it was. Nora, Kail, and Halven were the only ones who knew I took the knife, and none of them would go looking. *Yet.* Not when we had to get rid of Mare, and the brothers still needed Nora. It was safe for the moment, but the plan was to move it somewhere more secure as soon as I had the chance.

"I am, in fact," Katie answered, gliding her arms through the water.

"You do know there are sharks in there, right?"

Katie bolted upright and swam frantically toward shore. When she hit sand again, huffing and puffing, I couldn't help but laugh.

"I was kidding."

She glared up at me. "I liked you for a hot second there."

I crouched in the sand and shoveled some into my satchel. "Do you want me to whip up an inflatable chair before I go?"

"You just got here." There was a slight whine in her voice, but she hid it well as she shook glowing water from her hair.

"Yes, well…" I rubbed the back of my neck and stood. "Things with Mare didn't exactly go according to plan so we're busy putting together a new one."

Katie's eyes widened. "That was today? What happened? Where's Nora?"

"She's okay." There was no reason to mention the ten-story fall, Nora's temporarily broken back, or the way her skull had cracked open like an egg. The magic healed her, aided by the fear siphoned off from nearby nightmares, but I wasn't ready to relive it. I probably never would be. There's something about seeing the brain matter of the person you love…I shivered. "She's at her palace now."

Katie pursed her lips like she did whenever I said a word like *palace, Lady,* or *ruler.* "No one got hurt?"

"Nothing we won't recover from," I hedged.

She crossed her arms. "Your face is literally covered in blood."

I scrubbed at my cheek with the back of my hand. "Just some scratches, but as you see, no lasting damage."

"You strike such confidence in a gal."

"Don't take this the wrong way, but I'm in a hurry." Retrieving the weapon required at least two steps—finding the Dream Keeper and fetching the knife—but it was possible I threw in a couple side tasks to get to the final hiding place. We had to be ready to go as soon as Halven found Mare's new hideout.

I strode back toward the barrier, and Katie followed at my heels. "What are you going to do that you didn't do last time?"

"Bring a weapon."

"That sounds suspiciously like you didn't bring one this time." She hurried in front of me and walked backward. "But that would've been dumb, so I know that's not the case."

"We did." Nora and I were technically weapons, if used as such.

Katie made a low disbelieving sound and tied her hair back with a band from her wrist.

"Alright, well, you have fun." I slipped the satchel across my chest.

"Wait!" She grabbed my wrist before I could I turn away. "How was she?"

Somehow, it was an entirely different question than when she asked where Nora was and what happened. It was also a loaded inquiry that I had no idea how to answer so I didn't, which was undoubtedly worse.

"Did she…" Katie winced. "Did she ask about me? Or Mom? Paul, even?"

I shook my head slowly. "We didn't have much time to talk."

She quickly shuttered the splash of hurt on her face. "So, where are we going?"

"*I'm* going to get a knife. You're staying here."

"Like hell!"

I pinched the bridge of my nose. "I can't take you into another person's dream."

"Nice try. You were heading toward the Nightmare Realm."

Touché. My impatience to be near Nora again got the better of me. "I can do it from anywhere."

"Safely?" She quirked an eyebrow and paused for my answer. I stayed silent. "I didn't think so. You never know what's waiting in the shadows, eh?"

"Katie, listen. Please," I begged. "I really can't take you into someone else's dreams. *Can't*, not won't."

"Fine." She plopped down on the beach. "You go do whatever you've got to do inside someone's head, and I'll sit right here until you get back. Then we'll go back to Nora together."

I lifted my satchel off and dropped it to the ground. There wasn't time to argue but…our first attempt to get rid of Mare failed. Worst case scenario, if I took Katie with me, she would get a chance to say goodbye before Mare wrestled the knife from us and destroyed both worlds. Best case, Katie would see Nora and give some insight into what was wrong. I always thought I was the closest person to Nora—I *was* at one point. Now…was anyone? Not even Kail knew, and he was beside her nearly every second of every day.

"Wait here." I gave in. How could I not? There was no way I'd let anything hurt Katie, and it would put her at ease to see her sister alive. Nora though, that was another story.

She stretched her arms over her head. "As I said."

I bit my tongue and shut my eyes. The cords stretched out before me, a tapestry of glowing strings mingled among duller counterparts. I mentally ran a hand over them, sending out a spark of power and waiting for the dream to answer in kind. Like with Nora, it would be an ache, almost a cry, begging to come home. All I had to do was let it. The trick was getting the Dreamer to relinquish the information, and for that, I needed to spin a dream that would make them happy enough—*distracted* enough—to say yes.

There.

A wobble down a dull cord. Of course the Dreamer would be awake right now. I gripped the connection anyway and followed it to a quiet cobblestone street, letting sand cloak my presence. The scent of freshly baked bread filled the air, and a middle-aged woman hummed while watering a potted shrub beside a sign reading *kleintierpraxis*. The sun wasn't completely over the terracotta roofs, yet which meant this early bird would be up for quite a while. I groaned impatiently as I hovered beside the woman.

The veterinarian took her time—another two minutes admiring the flowers followed by ten minutes plucking dead leaves from a range of potted shrubs—before heading inside. I followed on her heels, waiting until I could safely put her to sleep. A dog barked from somewhere in the back of the house-turned-animal clinic. She cooed reassuringly that their mama would be there to pick them up that afternoon and slid behind her desk, humming again.

I took the smallest pinch of sand from the pouch around my neck. She had to be awake for her job, after all, and it would only take a moment to get what I needed. The vet opened an appointment book and skimmed a finger down the page. *Now or never.* I tossed it in her eyes and whispered, "sleep."

A second later, her head flew toward the desk. I flung my palm out, catching her forehead before it slammed into the wood, and brought her arm up to cradle her cheek.

I pulled on the magic inside her, and it dragged me inside the vet's dream. We sat at a fire at the foot of snowcapped mountains with three other people. Stars hung in the sky as the group laughed and passed a flask to each other. I eased onto the log beside the vet.

"May I please have the dream back?" I whispered in German. The woman jerked out of the scenario to stare at me with wide, frightened eyes. I exhaled quickly and dumped more sand into my palm. It swirled into an elderly man that immediately drew her attention.

"Klara?" he asked in an awed voice.

She stood with tears in her eyes. "Papa?"

"The dream?" I prodded. "Will you give it to me?"

"Papa?" she asked again.

I let the image of her father fall back into its original form. "He will come back, but first, the dream. Please allow me to take it," I urged in a gentle voice. It was an awful thing to do, using her dead father to blackmail her into cooperation, but time was short. I would make it up to her when I could, just like I had with the children I'd stolen dreams from. A years' worth of dreams with her entire family, dead and alive.

"*Ja.*" She blinked at the sand scattered at her feet and repeated her consent. Three times. Four.

I willed the sand into her father again just as the dream flew from nowhere and slammed into my chest. The location of the knife flooded through me along with images following my steps as I hid it. I was a little disappointed in myself for the lack of tasks required to get to it. I knew it was a possibility, but still…two stops and a weapon capable of killing Nora could've ended up in enemy hands. Though the final resting place made it fairly improbable…I shook my head. Next time I hid it, after Mare was dead, there would be more time to think it through.

***

When I returned, Katie was dressed in jeans and a faded yellow t-shirt with a setting sun printed across the chest. "We good to go?" she asked without preamble.

"Not yet." I stared at the sea. Somewhere out there was the only token capable of calling to The Spectral, which we could use to sail to the knife. There were two options—swimming down to the bottom of the very deep water or letting my sand do the work—and I wasn't in the mood for a dip. With a flick of my wrist, a thin veil of sand shot across the water like a pool cover, and I sat down beside Katie to wait. "Did you wake up to change?" I asked to fill the silence.

"The power of the dream is mine." A proud smile stretched her lips, and her t-shirt darkened to orange.

"Nora never figured that out." I chuckled, but reality wiped away the sliver of amusement. Nora asked me to keep her sister out of the Nightmare Realm, yet here I was, preparing to do the exact opposite. "I should probably fill you in on a few things while we wait."

Katie raised her brows. "I'm all ears."

Chapter Eleven

Nora

My hand flew furiously over the paper, creating a rough human figure. Anything to distract myself while we waited for the Sandman to come back. Anything to stay busy.

You know what would keep you busy? the Weaver asked, though it wasn't really a question.

"We are not going to the Blood Tower," I retorted.

I need to see if I'm right about something.

"We have more important things to do."

It could be related.

I stood, flinging a stack of half-completed sketches at the wall of my studio. They fluttered to the ground when what I needed them to do was slam into the marble. Shatter. Crack. Break. Then I could pretend it was the Weaver I was hurting. Anxiety swelled, reaching peak levels, and I knew that, given another chance—if the Weaver stood in front of me now—I would kill him all over again.

My breath came too fast, my heart like a hummingbird. My stomach rose up, up, up amid remembered flashes of falling from the globe. The Weaver practically threw me out of that sphere to save the Sandman. In his warped little mind, he did it to save me from fighting Mara on my own. If it were true, I should've felt grateful, but I didn't. The Weaver didn't try another option first. The resulting wounds would've been worth it if we had completed our goal.

You like the kill plan better, he said matter-of-factly.

"Yes, I like it better!" I screamed. "Only a fool would want—" The rest of the sentence stuck in my throat as I turned to find Kail leaning against the door frame. How long had he been standing there? "Kail," I breathed, ignoring the growing tightness in my chest. "What do you want?"

"That's hardly relevant at the moment." He stared at me as if he knew. As if I had just confirmed something. The slow, thoughtful shift in his eye color held me frozen as he stalked toward me. "Hello, Weaver."

A nervous laugh bubbled from me. "What are you talking about?"

"It took me a long time to put the pieces together." Kail tilted his head. "You used your power expertly at times, but two minutes later struggled with the easiest problems. You've been distracted, troubled, and talking to yourself. I don't claim to know your every side, Nora, but it wasn't hard to pick up on the fact that something wasn't right."

"It's been a learning curve. How would you know what's *easy* for me to do? You don't have this magic inside you," I snapped.

There was no way he could come up with the truth on his own. *No way.* "In case you haven't noticed, I'm stressed."

He made a low sound of assent and stared into my eyes. "I'm sure you are. Being held hostage is no walk in the park. I would know."

"I'm—"

"Tell me." Kail leaned in until his mask skimmed my nose. "Are you working yourself so hard because *he's* making you or because *you* want to?"

"I don't do anything I don't want to." I lifted my chin, my hands balled into fists. "I'm the Lady of Nightmares."

Kail jumped up to sit on the long table, his knees bumping into my hip. Paper, pencils, and charcoal scattered. He stared at his lap, and his long beak skimmed his chest. "Don't lie. You're not good at it."

"I'm not—"

You're a terrible liar, the Weaver agreed. *The Sandman only believes your untruths because he loves you and wants to believe you're speaking honestly.*

Shut up, Weaver.

This is getting ridiculous, the Weaver said, impatient and cutting. *Why deny it? Kail knows.*

I haven't told the Sandman yet.

"You're talking to him now, aren't you?" Kail smirked knowingly and watched me from beneath his lashes. "You can admit it any time now. Just say the words, *Kail, your observant ways paid off once again.*"

The world shifted, pushing me down, burying me. Flashes of color broke through the darkness as it grew. My knuckles throbbed. The Weaver's low growl filled my head, and my muscles strained to hold him back. To stay *me.*

Did you not train with the Sandman to build your strength? he quipped. He knew very well I had. Apparently, he was there the entire time. *A lot…of good…it did,* he strained.

Weight bore down on my chest. I struggled to breathe as memories of Mara sitting on me in my bedroom intensified the pressure. Mental warfare on top of physical assault. The Weaver's specialty. Then my vision cleared in an instant, though the weight remained, and I found myself held against the floor. My arms were pinned behind me, fists digging into my lower back, with Kail's thighs firmly securing my own to the ground. This close, I could almost taste the pinch of fear mixed with the light scent of cinnamon that he'd smelled like for nearly two days now. The beak of his mask pressed roughly into my cheek.

"Kail," I managed to squeak. "I can't breathe."

He shifted his weight slightly, lifting his head to meet my gaze, but kept me trapped. "Explain."

"You first," I wheezed.

His eyes narrowed. "Lady or no lady, I'm not going to let you attack me without cause."

"There's always cause with you."

"You're in no position for jokes." A small flicker of enjoyment crossed his face.

I wriggled beneath him. "As much as you love knocking me down a peg or two, would you mind?"

"That depends. Would you mind terribly *not* lunging at me like a maniac?"

"Get up. I'm not going to do anything." *Probably* not going to do anything. If my hands ever regained feeling, I might use one to punch him for this.

"Are sure about that?" His voice rose an octave at the end.

"It was him," I admitted. "The Weaver. Are you happy now? Let me up, and I'll explain."

Kail lifted himself slowly, one limb at a time. As if he didn't quite believe me. If I were being honest, I wouldn't have either if our roles were reversed. I would probably chain him to a chair and make him talk to me from behind a concrete wall. But Kail was too curious a creature not to get all the juicy details of my possession.

I'm not a demon, the Weaver said. *But if you want to see a real possession, I can tell you which landscape to visit.*

I ignored him as best I could. Kail crouched in front of me, his expression blank. Waiting. This could be my practice run for telling the Sandman. Get an outsider's opinion. Test out reactions. I sighed and pulled my hair back into a ponytail. "Ever since I killed the Weaver, a grin has haunted me. Only that grin turned out to be your friendly neighborhood serial killer." Then I launched into the shortest version of events possible, starting with the day I beat Rowan.

When I finished, the exposed bottom half of Kail's face was drained of color. The hollows of his cheeks seemed to deepen as his flashing irises studied my face. "He's really in there?"

"I thought you figured that out on your own?" I accused.

"I'm usually only ever ninety percent sure about my theories."

My eyes widened. "Considering the risks you have me take, those are terrible odds."

Kail shrugged, unbothered, and continued to stare. It was more of a curious study than a judgment, but still I fidgeted under the scrutiny.

"Trust me," I grumbled after a long minute. "It's worse for me than it is for you."

"There are…options…" He grimaced. "I'm sure there are."

The only way to get me out of your head is if you're dead, the Weaver said to me. *Though, seeing as their whole theory is wrong about what would happen next, it would only create bigger problems for everyone.*

"Oddly enough, I like living," I said to them both.

Kail offered a lopsided grin that didn't reach the rest of his face and eased back until he sat against one of the cupboards. "You should've told me," he said. "If he can take over like that, it was a dangerous truth to keep to yourself."

"He's only done it a couple times." More than a couple, but not more times than I could count on my fingers. It felt almost shameful. A stupid sentiment, but one I couldn't shake.

Kail glared at me like that wasn't an excuse. Because it wasn't. "Has he said anything about what you promised me?" he asked. "He won't try to stop it, will he?"

I have bigger problems than you and Halven, he said dismissively.

"No," I said. "Even if he did have a problem with it, I'll keep my word."

Kail stared at my forehead with a crease in his brow.

"You can't see him," I said, my voice flat.

His eyes darted away. "Thank goodness for small miracles."

Tell him that I want to go to the Blood Tower.

Why?

I practically felt his eyes roll. *Just do it.*

Fine, I'll play along. If out of my own growing curiosity than anything else. The Weaver was this insistent about very few things. I think he enjoyed watching me fail too much. "He wants us to go to the Blood Tower."

Kail licked his lips. "Why?"

I don't know yet.

"You don't know?" I half-shouted.

Trust me.

Never going to happen. He killed my boss, slaughtered a girl with a glitter pen, tortured my friends to death, and gave my father a heart attack. Not to mention kidnapping my sister and making Detective Bell turn his sole focus on me because apparently there wasn't enough pressure already without adding possible murder charges to the mix.

There was never enough to actually charge you, the Weaver said in his defense.

"This is creepy," Kail said, watching me through narrowed eyes. "And, coming from me, that says a lot."

"You have no idea."

***

The Blood Tower was exactly how we left it. Blood flowed in place of mortar and the new front doors stood intimidatingly tall. Unlike before, it was somewhat comforting to see the stone tower before me. It felt almost like a childhood home. In a way, I supposed, it was. I became the Lady of Nightmares within these walls alongside what some might consider a new family. One corner of my mouth twitched into a smile, and I stole a quick peek at Kail. I thought of him as a brother of sorts, so yes. A weird, dysfunctional, messed up family.

Not such a different family then, the Weaver said, not unkindly.

I snorted. My family was messed up—there was no denying it—but I couldn't help wondering if I would feel this calm walking up to my mother's house. Odd that Kail's domain would be the one I felt most connected to when it was where Rowan instigated my demise. I told Kail the tower was his to do with as he pleased, though I wasn't sure what his plans were. Or if he even wanted it. There was an unspoken rule that I did not ask specifics about his time with Rowan, but it was obviously unpleasant for him. Just because I liked the tower didn't mean he did. To my knowledge, he hadn't come back since before we dealt with Rowan, but I hoped, for selfish reasons, he had set something up to keep scavengers out.

You actually have to go inside, the Weaver said when I simply stared at the exterior.

"We came this far." I looked to Kail, completely aware of how awkward this was. The two of us…doing something because the Weaver wanted. When he was supposed to be dead by my hand. Because of something Kail helped orchestrate, willingly or not. I grimaced. "Might as well do this."

He pushed the door open with his shoulder, eying me. "If only we knew what *this* was."

Rowan was very detail-oriented. She liked lists. I think it had something to do with the tree line being so perfectly spaced and orderly. Even the berries—

I don't care, I hissed. Rowan was back as her perfectly-spaced self, suffering eternally. Exactly where she belonged.

You'll care if she kept notes from her spies.

My brows lifted. "Rowan had spies?"

"Of course," Kail answered. I startled at the realization that I had spoken out loud. "Many."

"You didn't think that might be important information to share?"

"I thought it was obvious," he said with an edge. "Did you think she had some sort of all-seeing eye? Really, Lady. Where's your head?"

I chewed on the idea as we entered the tower. It *was* obvious—as obvious as the tarantulas on the wallpaper.

Medallions, at first sight. Furry, eight-legged horrors, at the second. Rowan knew a lot. Too much. I thought she was following me that day she and Kail found me in the Barren, but maybe not. She also knew which people the Weaver personally killed, and which murders he delegated to other nightmares. *Why he delegated to other nightmares. He was busy with the Sandman at the time*, Rowan told me. How was it that she knew what the Weaver was doing at the exact time my friends died? Unless someone told her…

Yes, yes. Spies, the Weaver said, impatient. *Now that you're caught up, pay attention.*

Oh, I was going to pay attention, alright. To who these spies were, where I could find them, and how best to kill them. "Kail." I paused when I noticed he was no longer beside me, but halfway down the hall. I raced after him. "These spies—"

"Don't know." He didn't slow or stop.

"I didn't—"

"You were going to ask me who they are. Why would Rowan tell me her secrets when she could use them against me instead?" He shot me a sarcastic smile over his shoulder and paused at the bottom of the stairs. "I don't know who spied for her because they probably spied on me too."

My mouth opened, but no words came out. I knew Kail didn't want to follow Rowan, knew they didn't exactly see eye-to-eye, but if she didn't trust him, why keep him around? She had the Blood Army and a single brush of her skin was enough to bring down an elephant while Kail was just good at…being Kail. He was smart, sure, but so was Rowan.

Nightmares have the same emotions as humans, the Weaver said. *The intelligent ones anyway. Just because something delights in the dark doesn't mean they're incapable of love.*

Love? I thought a bit too loudly.

Perhaps not your version of it, he conceded.

I would say not, though Rowan did seem to love herself. Did she have feelings for Kail too? The idea of that gave me a squicky feeling.

No. Rowan loved power. Kail did too, though not quite as much. She kept him because he was able to convince *other nightmares to see things her way, and he stayed because she had leverage.*

Leverage?

"You're talking to him again," Kail stated with a flicker of hatred. "About me?"

I wanted to deny it but couldn't. Instead, I would ask Kail the questions I wanted answers to. It was the fair thing to do, and I would accept if he chose to keep something to himself. The Weaver had no right telling personal secrets.

"Why did you stay when Rowan was so awful to you?" It felt much *too* personal the second the words left my mouth, so I quickly added, "You don't need to tell me if you don't want to."

"Better the enemy you know than the enemy you don't." His voice was dreary, his irises yellow for nearly fifteen seconds—the longest I'd ever seen them stay one color—before he spoke again. "I'm going to get a few things while we're here. I'll find you when I'm finished."

He climbed the staircase with stiff shoulders, and a part of me—a part that felt far away and almost wrong now—wanted to comfort him. Even if that feeling wasn't faint, buried deep inside, I would never have followed. Not when I knew Kail wouldn't want me to. I could only imagine his reaction if I tried to hug him.

Halven.

"What?" I turned away from the stairs.

The leverage. It was Halven.

"What happened to paying attention?" I asked, steering the conversation away from things I had no right knowing. "We're here for the notes, not a history lesson."

He's a little like you, you know. Halven may not be his brother in the literal sense, but they care for each other the same way you care for Katie.

"Focus," I insisted. "We're short on time. What am I looking for?"

The Weaver was silent for so long I thought he wasn't going to answer. *Her room. Go there.* I tensed at the command. *Just do it, Keeper, before I make this easier on all of us and take over.*

I shivered. He was in my head; he knew how much I loathed him controlling my every move. It made it even easier to hate him when he used my emotions against me. "You should really learn to keep your mouth shut."

Oh, I deserve an award for that after five months.

I groaned and reluctantly turned toward Rowan's room, the hidden door familiar to me after my temporary stay. Inside, the bed was nestled in the trunk of a thick tree that grew from the ground, twisting upward until it hit the ceiling where vine-like branches hung down. Red ribbons were knotted on the thinner areas, intermingled with small dried flowers.

"You know I already tore this place apart," I reminded him.

The obvious places, yes. Be more inventive this time.

"I hope you didn't bring me here on some stupid whim," I warned.

None of my whims are stupid.

I begged to differ, but that was a fight he'd never concede. So, I opened Rowan's closet and kicked aside the pile of her clothes where I had left them crumpled on the floor. With a long exhale, I ran my fingers along the wall, looking for the smallest inconsistency.

***

"There's nothing here." I flopped onto Rowan's bed nearly an hour later. Kail shuffled around the room, having joined me almost fifteen minutes ago. Why it took him forty-five minutes to *get a few things* was beyond me, especially since he returned empty handed. If I didn't know any better, I would've said it was a ploy to keep from helping me with this wild goose chase. "Maybe she hid them somewhere else." *If the notes existed at all.*

"No. She would've kept them here." Kail picked at the bark of the tree, listless, and completely unhelpful.

"Why?" I asked. "This place has more unused space than the palace."

"That's hardly true. And where would *you* keep top secret records?" He looked me over as if entertaining the idea that I might, in fact, have a cache of files squirreled away somewhere.

"I wouldn't."

"If you did. And if I were living with you," he pried. "Would you keep them anywhere except close?"

I rolled onto my back. "First off, you do live with me. Second, I wouldn't keep evidence around for anyone to find."

Kail made a loud beeping sound. "Wrong answer."

I wasn't sure why I bothered to question him—Kail knew Rowan. Her habits. Her daily routine. Plus, he never gave me real answers. The whole search seemed like a waste of time, which was what got under my skin. That, and allowing the Weaver to talk me into something, even if it was something as stupid as hunting down—

113

There.

I flinched at the Weaver's sudden exclamation after a long stretch of blissful silence. *What?*

There. The ribbons.

I zeroed in on the red knotted strips of satin. Some were brighter than others, a handful fraying, as if they were a collection Rowan gathered over time. I flew up from the bed and jumped, snagging the nearest vine. It strained as I held it down low enough to pick at the knot.

"What are you doing now?"

"They've been in front of us the whole time," I breathed.

The first ribbon fell away. My hands shook as I straightened the length of cloth to reveal a message written in fading black ink: Kail seen in the spaceship. Elkmar.

"Spaceship?" I held the note out to Kail, my pulse thumping. Seeing Elkmar's name sent a shiver down my spine, almost as if the shadowy nightmare were standing right behind me. Watching. Waiting. Standing too close on legs that bent backward with his ribbed horns and webbed feet. I rolled my shoulders against the sensation, knowing it was just my imagination. My magic would tell me if it were true.

Kail pulled the ribbon slowly from my fingers and scanned it. "One of my first safe houses." His gaze traveled to the hundreds of ribbons overhead. "Compromised, obviously, hence the others."

"So Elkmar was her spy?" It made sense. Rowan trusted him to deliver me to the Weaver, but she also didn't tell him that I wasn't meant to make it there. Did that mean Elkmar was loyal to the Weaver or to Rowan? Was he under the impression Rowan was working as the Weaver's hand?

You give him too much credit, Keeper. Elkmar simply likes to shadow things, and she gave him cause.

I jumped for another ribbon at the same time Kail snapped a vine clean off. Note after note. Secret after secret. There were names written that I didn't recognize, ones the Weaver assured me were no longer a problem, but there was one that appeared over and over that left me speechless.

Baku.

Each new note naming him as spy crushed me a little more. My soul floundered, a predator dragging it down into a murky grave. The Sandman…this was going to destroy him. They were friends. *How could he…?* I tore down each and every ribbon with shaking hands.

"He's been spying on the Sandman this whole time?" The words were hard to say. Harder to believe. How did he even communicate with Rowan?

"And you," Kail added.

Things made sense now. So many things. "We have to tell the Sandman."

Do we?

"Are you kidding me?" I said in a single breath. Kail watched me carefully as if I were a grenade ready to blow. "The Weaver doesn't think we should tell him," I clarified.

"Maybe we shouldn't," he agreed reluctantly.

My jaw dropped. "Okay. Both of you have clearly lost your minds."

"Better the enemy you know," Kail echoed his words from earlier.

I flung the latest unfurled note to the ground and whirled on him. "Rowan's gone. This isn't the same thing."

Meaning Baku is still hanging around because he found someone else to spy for.

"We *are* telling him. That's final." I met Kail's stare and held it. There was already enough the Sandman didn't know. When he found out about the Weaver, it would be a hard blow, but knowing I kept it to myself would be worse. I wouldn't repeat the mistake. "What we do after, we decide together. All of us."

Kail ran a tongue over his front teeth. "Can we hold hands and skip merrily into this fantasyland you've imagined?"

"What?"

"Nothing." He bowed with a flourish, making it perfectly clear he didn't mean the action. "You're the Lady."

"Damn right I am." I kicked at the pile of red ribbons. "Now find something to carry those back home in."

Chapter Twelve

The Sandman

Nora's palace stretched out before us with its harsh, intimidating lines and numerous watchful nightmares. I tried to see it through Katie's eyes, as something new and frightening, instead of the simple building it was. For her, this wasn't reality like it was for Nora. It certainly wasn't something Nora wanted her to see. I winced at the imagined potential tirade I would receive the second I crossed the threshold with Katie in tow.

"I can't believe I let you talk me into this." I snapped my hood up, hiding. "Your sister is going to kill me."

"I'll take the blame," Katie said, unconcerned, as her gaze traveled from one end of the palace to the other. "It's not like I gave you much choice anyway."

"You gave me *no* choice," I clarified.

She smacked my upper arm lightly with the back of her hand. "Then you have nothing to worry about."

Katie took off down the narrow path worn through the grass like the surrounding area wasn't crawling with nightmares. Two mangled trolls with crooked swords stood on either side of the path, and a woman with four eyes and skin a rainbow of color splotches trailed our movements from behind the easel she held. The massive dog I saw that day at the Rowan trees lounged against the outer wall. Yet, Katie's expression remained a blank slate the entire way up to the massive main doors. I almost had to wonder if she saw them at all. They were rather hard to miss, especially when the trolls grunted with each exhale and the artist reeked of paint and turpentine.

The dog lifted his head, ears perked, as Katie flew by him and flung open the doors. "Nora!"

A stunned Kail leapt back, arms flying out to catch the heavy wood before it smashed him in the face. "The hell…?" His eyes flicked over Katie's shoulder to me. "She's some sort of sand illusion, right? Or did the door actually hit me and I'm hallucinating Nora's sister? Because we can fix brain damage."

"She's real," Halven whispered from further inside.

Kail's irises flashed faster, his hands sliding higher up the door to bar the entrance. "Oh, no. No, no. You can't be here."

Katie's laugh was sharp. "Try and stop me, Tweety."

His brow lowered in obvious confusion, and I stepped forward to diffuse the situation. "It's fine," I assured him.

"That's rather hard to believe," he shot as Katie shoved her way past him. "Nora is going skin you alive."

Kail wasn't wrong, but here we were. There was no changing my mind now.

"There's an emergency back in the Day World?" Kail asked hopefully.

"No." I sighed.

A muscle jumped in his jaw. "Halven, don't let her find Nora. And keep her quiet." To his credit, Halven hesitated before obeying Kail's orders. Katie deserved at least that much fear with her stubborn temper. "In case you've forgotten, we *do* have an emergency here," Kail said under his breath the moment we were alone.

"I'm well aware of the threat Mare—"

"Not Mara, you idiot," he hissed. "Nora. I *told you* something was wrong with her."

My brows lowered. "She was fine when I left a few hours ago."

"Was she?" He dragged out the words.

It wasn't really a question. We both knew she was keeping something from us, but objectively speaking, Nora was okay. She was alive, and the Nightmare Realm accepted her. She would never be safe just as the Weaver never truly was, but there was a solution to every problem. Katie was hopefully the key to figuring out what was bothering her.

"Sandman!" Nora's voice bounced down the bare hallways. It was still echoing down the far end of the palace when she flew into view. Rage colored her pale cheeks red. "What were you thinking?"

Katie ran at her heels. "I was coming whether he brought me or not."

"Did you tell her to say that?" Nora asked.

The accusation grated. "Did I tell her to use the same reasoning you used to sneak back here? No. She just happens to be as stubborn as you are."

"Don't turn this around on me." Nora narrowed her eyes. "I specifically asked you *not* to let Katie come. What if something took her? There are still nightmares that want me dead. The Hours won't stay locked up forever, and Mara's running around."

"Mara is in the ice caves," Halven said calmly.

Nora shot him an angry glare before turning her fury back to me. "Now is not the time for a family reunion."

"You're just embarrassed," Katie snapped. "You don't want me to see you like this. Like one of *them*."

She spat the last word. I couldn't blame her—the Weaver had strapped her down inside a cave with an enormous serpent and a crazed clown as her babysitters—but I knew the hatred stung Nora. I felt the hurt as if it were my own. But Nora knew how her sister would react, which was another reason she asked me to keep Katie away. Seeing it in action only intensified my regret at bringing the two of them together.

"I'm not one of them," Nora snarled.

"Your eyes are glowing, Nora, and look at your arm. Look at this *place*." Katie flung her arms out toward the walls. "You left home for this? Mom has been inconsolable."

Nora balled her hands. "Detective Bell gave her my alibi."

"That you ran away with Ben?" She laughed bitterly. "Why would that make her feel better? You could be living in a cardboard box for all she knows."

"She never liked me anyway!" Nora shouted. A vein throbbed in her temple. "She should be happy I'm gone. No more *'crazy Nora'* to worry about."

Katie's face turned a deep shade of magenta. "You know that isn't true."

"Isn't it?"

"Alright," I said calmly. "Let's take a breath. Katie hasn't seen you in months and wanted to make sure you were okay before we went after Mare again."

"Why? To say goodbye?" Nora gave me a scathing look. "I don't intend on dying, Sandman."

"No one ever *intends* to die," Katie said in a hard voice.

Nora's laugh was hollow and unamused. "You want to make sure I'm okay? Well, I'm not, but I won't die. Ever."

"You can't know that," I said gently. "The Weaver never expected to die either." Our magic kept us alive, kept him alive, until it killed him.

She scoffed. "The Weaver isn't going to die a second time."

One Weaver wasn't more powerful than the last. In fact, I would say Nora was much weaker. That didn't mean she wouldn't grow to be as strong as her predecessor, but she was still learning. It wasn't possible to gain the kind of experience she needed to be considered his equal in so little time. She had the same amount of magic, yes, but the ability to wield it? The knowledge of when to go all out and when to hold back? She needed longer to master those skills.

"Your magic won't protect you from the knife if Mare gets hold of it," I said.

"That's not what she means." Kail's demeanor shifted, half fearful, half reverent. *"The Weaver* won't die again."

The Weaver, yes—Nora. But that didn't seem to be what he was hinting at. I scowled. "I don't understand."

Katie gripped Nora's arms and regained her sister's attention. "You're not indestructible."

Nora shot daggers at Kail as she replied to her sister, "I'm as close to it as someone can be."

Katie took a steadying breath. "Come home. This Mara chick can't get you there, right?"

Nora brushed her sister's hands off, her expression tight. "I *am* home, and if we don't stop Mara, you won't have a home to go back to."

"Then come see Mom first," Katie begged.

Kail groaned. "There isn't time for this. Really, Sandman? This is what you brought her here for? Now? It couldn't have waited a few more nights?"

"It should've waited until I was ready to go to her," Nora said to the empty space between us. "We all know this place isn't safe for Dreamers."

A sense of foreboding hung in the hallway. Words not yet spoken seemed to drip from the ceiling like heavy condensation. In a moment, I knew Nora would open her mouth to say something—perhaps *the* something—and I also knew I no longer wanted to know. Needed to, maybe, but wanted to? No.

"The Weaver didn't die," she said.

I couldn't tell if she whispered it or not over the roaring in my ears. "I saw his body."

"That doesn't mean he died."

I held my hands out at my sides. "That's exactly what seeing a body means."

"He attached himself to the magic that day in the Keep," Nora explained. "His body is dead, but he's inside my head. Talking. Constantly, constantly talking." She winced. "It's getting harder to know where he starts and I end. Or if there are ends at all anymore."

Breathing became impossible. My hands tingled. The Weaver was inside her head, filling her mind with his poison this whole time? "Since the day in the Keep?" I forced out. "That was almost ten months ago."

Nora blanched, and her eyes shifted almost unwillingly to Kail. "I didn't know," she said after a long moment. "That he was there. I didn't know. Not until the night we defeated Rowan, but I've only seen you once since then. I was going to tell you."

"When?" I demanded.

Nora gripped the sides of her head, her features twisting. "Knock it off," she said through clenched teeth.

"Nora?" Katie touched her shoulder. "Are you okay? What's going on?" Silence. Nora drew in a deep breath and clenched her jaw, lips tightly pursed, as if holding back a scream. "I don't understand what's going on. Do something!" Katie yelled at me.

Nora straightened before I could move. Her head tilted, chin up, shoulders square, and the look she leveled at me wasn't Nora at all. The world slowed. Nora—the Weaver—drew every drop of oxygen from the palace. To see him so boldly looking out from the face of the woman I loved was a new sort of torment.

Kail swore under his breath and slipped behind me. "As entertaining as this has been, may I suggest immobilizing her now?"

"Don't even try it," Katie warned.

The person before me ignored them both, eyes only for me. "Always taking things so personally, old friend."

It was Nora's voice, but it wasn't Nora speaking. An icy death crept up my spine.

"You." Kail hurried toward Katie when no one else spoke. "It would be a good time to wake up."

"Fat chance."

Kail took another step toward her, and Nora grabbed his arm. "Touch my sister, and you can forget about our deal."

"You can't leverage that," he breathed.

Her gold eyes shifted to his. "You can forget about it because you will be dead."

"Get out," I boomed, my voice hoarse. Katie wasn't the Weaver's sister and for him to call her that was a slap in Nora's face. If it had been up to him, Katie would be long dead by now. "Get out of her right now."

Nora winced and stumbled back. "Bastard," she said between heavy breaths.

"What the ever-loving hell was *that?*" Katie's demand was a boulder crashing into an otherwise silent ravine.

Nora launched into a detailed timeline of the last two months. Every fragment of information swirled through me like a storm. *The Weaver wasn't dead.* A bigger part of me than I wanted to admit rejoiced. I wanted only to hate him, to condemn him and find a way to kill him all over again for violating Nora, but I couldn't.

"I tried to tell you the night you came," Nora insisted.

She had, and I made her rest. She tried again the next morning too. That didn't stop the betrayal from fraying the edges of my heart. She could've sent word with Halven—he stopped here as well as the beach—or sent another messenger. Something. *Anything.*

And worse, Kail knew. The nightmare no one should ever trust.

"There's more," she whispered.

"More?" Katie raked her fingers down her cheeks. "What else could there possibly be?"

Halven stepped forward and held out a fist. I stood frozen, staring at the gloved hand. More. There was more. I wasn't sure I could handle it.

"Take it," Halven said in a sympathetic voice.

I held my palm out. A moment later, it was full of red ribbons. "What's this?" I forced myself to ask. None of them answered me. Nora's cheeks flushed, and she kept her eyes on her boots. Even Kail avoided my gaze.

"For crying out loud," Katie huffed. She took a ribbon from me and turned it over. "The Sandman has a Dream Keeper. Baku." Katie frowned. "What does that mean? Baku's a Dream Keeper too?"

"He was spying on you for Rowan," Nora said softly.

I balled the ribbons in my fist. "That's not possible."

"It makes sense." She winced, hesitating. "Rowan knew a lot about me."

"That doesn't mean anything," I said harshly. Baku was my friend long before Nora was born. We were alone in our solitude, bonded by it. The trusted chimera would never turn on me. "What does *he* say about it? That Baku was his spy too?"

Nora looked as if I slapped her but shook her head. "The Weaver didn't know until today."

"I don't believe it." Was it hot in here? Why was it so hot? I tugged at the neck of my shirt. "It's another lie, isn't it?"

Nora flinched. "I didn't lie to you."

"You didn't tell me something as important as the Weaver being alive." It was a near shout edged with panic. Sand inched slowly, cautiously, from my satchel, circling my hand. It sensed my anger and hurt and was ready to strike in my defense. "You know what? Nevermind. I can't talk about this right now. We need to go see the Wish Granter and get the knife so we can put Mare down."

"Sandman." Nora's voice was low as she reached for my arm.

I spun away from her and stalked back past the dog. The artist. The trolls. It was almost a half night's walk to get where we were going. Maybe by then I would be pulled together enough to hold a conversation. *Maybe.*

***

The Green Sea smelled of decaying fish, making me loathe to touch it, but we would need the token to get back from the island, so I couldn't toss it in. I took the gold medallion from inside my vest and ignored the curious stares at my back. I hadn't looked at Nora since we left, though I desperately wanted to. We had to talk. Really talk. I shook my head before thoughts of Nora could cloud it. The chipped token was heavy in my palm.

First, the knife.

With a sigh, I curled my fingers around the token and dunked my fist into the water. The reaction was immediate. Water hissed and rippled as a sail rose from the sea. Barnacles grew along the mast of a great, rotting ship, and Katie gasped at the skeleton crew leering down from the deck. I opted to avoid looking at them.

It only took a few moments for The Spectral to bob on top of the water. I stood, flashing the token that made me their commander, and one of the crew members tossed a rope ladder over the railing. The end dangled into the festering water a few yards from shore. No matter. I spared a pinch of sand to form a dock and strode straight for the waiting vessel.

<h1 style="text-align:center">Chapter Thirteen</h1>

Nora

Every curse word in the English language filled my head. *Repeatedly*. Katie was here in the Nightmare Realm. She was watching me like I had horns and a forked tail. The exact place, the exact look, the exact everything I wanted to avoid. Well, perhaps not the *exact* place. A rickety pirate ship run by a literal skeleton crew never came up in my imagined scenarios.

The first mate hovered nearby, pieces of sinew hanging from his exposed jaw, staring at me with his one good eye. *Good* being objective; the other dangled from its socket, covered with bot flies. It took everything in me to suppress the memory of Natalie with both of her eyes clawed out. The way the blood coated her cheeks. The two black, haunting pits in her beautiful face. I pushed away the image of her dull, lifeless eyes sitting in her hands, not because I didn't want to feel sorrow, but because I was terrified of *not* feeling it.

Your friend died well, the Weaver supplied.

Bile rose. "I hope, whoever this Wish Granter is, she grinds you to dust."

Your threats are so… He made a sharp, disgusted sound. *The Wish Granter isn't a miracle worker. Even* if *she didn't twist wishes around, she can't do anything about us.*

"We'll see about that," I mumbled.

You'll see your secret outed to the entire realm. I wonder what the nightmares will do if they know I'm in here…

"I know what *I* would do."

"Okay." Katie's voice was short and sharp. "You've been talking to yourself for the last half hour."

I gave her a withering look. "Talking to myself would be the preferred alternative, don't you think?"

"There's a lot I'm thinking." My sister pushed away from the mildew-coated railing and pointed at the first mate. "First, that *that thing* is a complete creeper."

"He's…" *Star struck made* it seem like I was full of myself, but it was the Lady they were awed to see. Whether it was the rarity of me leaving home or that I was *made* was anyone's guess. "He's fascinated. It happens sometimes."

"Privacy. It's a thing." She rushed at him, waving her arms wildly.

It reminded me of the day at the mall when she threatened the boys sitting next to us in the food court. They wanted to ask about my boss' death, but after she snapped at them, they bolted out of there, much like the nightmarish first mate did now. My lips tugged up into a smile. It fell the moment my sister turned her wild stare back on me. There was a reason I didn't want her in the Nightmare Realm—a reason other than her safety. I needed to let go of my life in the Day World, of the person I was then, in order to be the person I had to be now. Not forever, I hoped, but long enough to grow here. To let old anger fade away.

"I've got the basics of your situation," Katie started in a voice full of forced calm. "But it's the newest twist I'm struggling with."

"It's only new to everyone else," I said, shrugging.

"So, he's really in there?" She circled the air around my head with a finger.

"Lucky me, I know." I stared at the endless water. Emerald green waves lapped against the hull, appearing quiet and calm, but it was a lie. I felt the anticipation inside me. The waiting. When one of the cackling grey seagulls from above swooped down, red eyes trained on something beneath the surface, a large, frothy hand snapped it out of the air. It was gone so fast it didn't know what hit it. Not that I personally had anything to fear, but not all of us on board had that luxury.

"Nora Jane Gallagher."

I cringed and peeked over at my sister again. A mistake. Sorrow scarred her face. Anger, too. Frustration. "What?" I demanded.

Katie launched herself at me, wrapping me in a tight hug. I stood stiff, but not for long. Slowly, her hug thawed something inside me, and my arms lifted, returning it. "I hate you so much," she sniffled into my hair.

My heart panged. "I know."

"Why didn't you tell me what was going on?"

And that was the end of that. I pulled away. "Katie." I swallowed the bitter laugh but failed to do the same with the razor-sharp disbelief. "I tried to talk to you about it, and you denied anything happened. Repeatedly."

She opened her mouth and snapped it shut again. What could she say? There wasn't a time after my sister left for college that she didn't vehemently insist there was no truth to the Sandman or any of the things she'd seen.

"You destroyed so much when you left," Katie said, brittle.

"I'm sure I did." *My fault.* Everything was, even if it wasn't. "My choices were to lie and leave or tell the truth and leave. Either way, I couldn't stay and lying was obviously the better option. What do you think Mom would've done with the truth?"

"She wouldn't have believed you," Katie admitted.

"Oh, she would have. She would've believed I was ready for an institution."

"Nora…"

"Did you come all the way here to drag me through a guilt-trip?" She could've saved herself the trouble. I already felt guilty…when I managed to feel at all.

They didn't deserve you, the Weaver chimed in.

"I came to make sure you were okay," she said.

Laughable. We all knew I wasn't, and yet, I was. The old Nora was in trouble, but the me now? I chewed my bottom lip. "I'm sure the Sandman kept you updated."

"Seeing is believing." She plucked at the threads near my wrist, and they squirmed away from her touch.

My cheeks warmed, and I tucked my arms behind my back. "I need to check in with Kail."

I spun on my heel, leaving Katie alone at the bow of the ship, before I wasted another minute dwelling on the past. We had to focus on the now. Except my *now* stood like a statue at the bottom of the stairs leading to a raised tier at the center of the ship. The Sandman's violet eyes followed me across the deck, and I forced myself not to meet them. As hard as that was. If I was going to get to Kail, I had to go right past him. However poorly Katie looked at me, I was convinced his gaze would be worse. I lied, then lied again, and now it looked as if I was doing it a third time. I'd learned my lesson though. I had only needed more time. An opportunity to talk uninterrupted...

"Nora?" the Sandman whispered as I passed.

I ignored him.

Until he grabbed my wrist. "We need to talk about this."

"We don't need to do anything." I tried to pull away, but his grip tightened. It felt as if he held my heart instead of my wrist, squeezing, squeezing, squeezing. "I know, okay?" I admitted softly. "We do, I know, but not now."

"*Right now,*" he insisted.

I wanted to use his own training against him, to lay him out flat right there on the slimy, mildew coated wood, but that would create a scene. And if he turned the tables on me, I would look weak in front of all these nightmares, which I couldn't afford. "You want to talk now? Okay. Let's start with how you lead my sister straight to the heart of the Nightmare Realm after you *promised* to keep her away."

"I'm sorry," he said through his teeth. "But she was going to come with or without me. It seemed safer for it to be *with*."

Ah, there it was. The first barb. Yes, it was better to come to the Nightmare Realm with him. For Katie, at least. But was it better for me? Did I not have enough to make up for here without having to make amends to my family at the same time? "Have we learned *nothing*?" I asked in a low voice. "You let me make my own choices, humored me, and look at us now."

His eyes narrowed. "I didn't *let* you do anything, Nora. You're your own person, and I never tried to control you."

"Didn't you, though?" I regretted the words instantly because they weren't true. He urged me one way or another, but he never forced me to take the advice.

"No!" His shout boomed across the ship. I'd never heard that tone from him before, and it held me in place like cement. When he spoke again, the anger was a quiet undertone as he spoke low enough for only me to hear. "We are in this place because of your repeated deceptions."

I opened my mouth, unsure what was going to come out, but he continued without giving me a chance to speak.

"*You* trusted Rowan and Kail. *You* killed the Weaver. *You* snuck into the Nightmare Realm like some sort of outlaw and brought back the only being who knows how to open the Ever Safe. And now? *Now?* You kept the Weaver a secret from everyone who helped you. It's been *two months*. What do you expect from us? From me? Do you expect me to continue forgiving you? You asked if we learned nothing, and the answer is no. *I* learned something though. Ironically, it was the Weaver who taught me to know when enough was enough."

My mouth ran dry. Was he going to bind me too? I wouldn't hurt the Day World. Heck, we were on our way to *save* it. Not that I wanted to go back, but the idea of being chained anywhere rubbed me the wrong way. "What's that supposed to mean?"

"It means, when this is done." He swallowed hard, his throat bobbing. "When Mare is dealt with and the Weaver is…contained elsewhere, I will go back to the Dream Realm and let you self-destruct in whatever world you choose. But, should you decide to stay in the Night World, it will not be the Dream Realm that you call home." He flicked a grim look behind me and let go of my wrist. "We're here."

The crew moved hastily about the ship as a tall structure appeared through the thickening fog, but I didn't care. Not when I finally *felt* something. Really and truly felt it. The pain nearly brought me straight to my knees. *No.* I *had* learned something. A lot of things. But right now, I needed to lean on one of my old truths—pretending to be fine. After Katie was home safe and sound, after we had the knife, I would talk to the Sandman. Would better explain. Make him understand. This couldn't be it between us. We'd come so far together.

Trust lost is the hardest to regain, the Weaver said sympathetically.

"You would know," I seethed.

Unlike the Weaver, I wasn't a homicidal maniac. Plus, I had a literal eternity. The Sandman couldn't stay angry at me *forever*, could he?

"Are you coming, Lady?" Kail called from across the deck.

I rubbed my aching chest, my heart breaking beneath the surface, and urged my heart to be patient, to keep hope alive. Then I raised my chin, threw back my shoulders, and strode across the ship like I owned it.

Chapter Fourteen

Nora

A gargantuan hedge maze towered over us. The dark, muted green shrubbery was both perfectly trimmed and a hot mess. It was as if a landscaper purposely missed an overgrown patch every few feet, the long finger-like vines swaying in an eerie dance. Somewhere inside the tangle of foliage, wind howled. I glanced back at the pirate ship, but the only part visible through the fog was the crow's nest as it sailed away from the island.

Perfect. We're stuck here.

The Sandman can call it back, the Weaver reminded me. Not that it helped ease my fears. *Besides, you're right where you want to be, aren't you?*

I rolled my eyes. *Yes. I want to go into a maze full of who knows what and—*

You're in the best company for it, he said with nonchalance. *Between Halven and myself, you have a map to the center.*

Halven turned his head slowly in what I could only assume was an examination of the outer wall through his eye-less mask. He knew how to get around, to read the clock in the Blood Tower, to pin-point exact locations, but we were technically *at* our destination. Could he see how to get from here to the center? Was the center even where we needed to go?

Relax, Keeper. I'll share a secret with you: all roads lead to the Wish Granter. It's just a matter of how long it takes.

I scowled.

What good is it if the Dreamer never reaches the nightmare? Residual fear is a nice appetizer, but who wants a veggie platter when you could have a nice juicy steak?

Vegetarians, I said, my voice flat. His laugh seemed genuinely amused.

"Hey," Kail said, loudly, in my ear. "Are you going to throw your two cents into this conversation or not?"

Conversation? Were they talking? My face warmed, my ears buzzing. "What was the question?"

"Halven can only see a direct line to the center so we have to find our way through the maze. Are we splitting up?" he asked like he was speaking to a child.

"What?" My eyes popped. "No way. Are you nuts?"

"We would cover more ground," he argued.

I looked at the Sandman, and my heart seized painfully. The muscle in his jaw jumped. "No," I said. "It doesn't matter which way we go. We'll get there without getting permanently lost."

Kail shot Halven an exasperated look. "It would be *faster*—"

"How do you know?" Katie asked me. "That we won't get lost, I mean."

I sighed and trudged toward the entrance without looking back, "because we're steak."

Their confusion and reluctance pulsed against my back, but it didn't stop them from following. Kail was close on my heels, Halven close on his, while the Sandman and Katie kept their distance. The quiet hush of their conversation filled me with emotions I couldn't decipher. Jealousy, perhaps, that my sister spent the last two months at the beach when I couldn't. That *they* could be close. It was stupid, and I had no right to feel that way, but when had that ever stopped someone? Emotions had no master. The only thing a person could control was their outward reactions.

"Listen, about being steak…" Kail eased up beside me and held his hands up questioningly.

"No one's going to eat you," I said, knowing where his train of thought was headed. "Unless you don't shut up."

The moment we were all inside the maze, the walls surrounding us rustled. Branches shook, starting at the far end and racing closer. All the stray pieces sticking out disappeared into the center of the greenery, only to shoot out across the entrance. They tangled together, pulling and twisting, until there was no opening at all. Only perfectly manicured hedges.

"Yeah, okay," Katie said, her voice wavering. "I'm out."

"I don't blame you," I said, part of me wishing I had the same option. Besides, saying *I told you so* wouldn't help anyone and antagonizing her would probably make her tough it out.

"This isn't over," she promised. "I'm coming back."

Before I could tell her not to, that things would only get worse before they got better, my sister woke up, vanishing from the maze. "Anyone else want to chicken out?" I looked at each of them.

"Seems a little late for that," Kail said with a raised brow.

We all knew it wasn't. I could force the maze to open if I needed to, but whatever fed his courage was fine by me. If Kail needed to convince himself this was mandatory in order to keep going, then that's what it was. I cracked my knuckles and focused on the landscape instead.

The maze was silent again now that we were locked in, and I led the way down the straight passageway. It didn't appear to turn anywhere. The longer we walked, the more I began to wonder if this was a maze at all. It felt like we'd walked miles and miles in a straight line. There were no off-shoots, no other ways to turn.

Sure there are, the Weaver interrupted. *It's an illusion. Look for the darker green patches.*

I ran my hand down the thread on my arm, taking comfort in its presence. *Right. Okay. Nice of you to mention that before.* I squinted at the walls, seeing no difference. *Darker green patches, darker green patch…*my gaze swept over the other side of the passage, and I noticed a single protruding leaf. The wall sucked it back in like it knew I noticed the mistake. I stopped and walked up to the spot, licking my lips. It was slightly darker, but not much. I would never have noticed if it weren't for the leaf. *Are you sure about this?* I asked the Weaver. Walking straight into a wall would be completely embarrassing.

Try it, he drawled.

I scowled at the wall, debating whether I should trust him on this one or not. He wouldn't let me get hurt because he needed me, but there was nothing stopping him from torturing me mentally. In fact, I was pretty sure that was his favorite pastime. The ground boomed once beneath our feet. The sharp penetrating sound rung through the air as if someone were using it as a snare drum.

"What possessed you to leave the knife with the Wish Granter?" Kail chided the Sandman.

"She's stationary," he answered, sounding unsure of himself. "I don't remember doing it, but the Dream Keeper..."

He trailed off at the title. *My* title. Before...

"That seems like a rather weak reason," Kail went on. "What if someone wished for it?"

"Why would anyone wish for it?" His frustration cut the air. "They would have to know she had it first."

"Or," Kail dragged the word out, "they could wish for something to kill one of the Night World rulers and ta-da! Knife on a platter."

The Sandman didn't have time to defend himself further because something small and white zipped across the opening. It was too fast to make out a shape, but it left a trail of smoke in its wake. I stumbled backwards into Halven's chest. "You guys saw that, right?"

"Saw what?" Kail asked.

Another one like the first darted by, scampering up the hedge wall. "That."

A flurry of angry chirps traveled from inside the hidden passage. That was our only warning before a scurry of white squirrels launched themselves at us. Streaks of smoke trailed behind them. They pelted into us before we could duck, their little nails and teeth digging in. I gripped the one on my shoulder and screamed as its abdomen scorched my hand. It fell to the ground, lowered itself into a crouch, and chattered loudly. Its body was solid white, its tail formed solely from the smoke drifting off its back. Beady black eyes swirled. My hand throbbed while another squirrel gnawed its way down my back.

"They're made of dry ice," the Sandman said in a rush, plucking the creature from my back. "Don't touch them with your bare hands."

I kicked at the squirrel still snarling in front of me without making contact. It took off, hopping into the hedges, and I shook out my hand. "This is stupid. I'll just change the maze to open a direct path."

Bad plan.

I clenched my fists. *Great plan.*

There are more nightmares separate from the maze living here. Disrupt their home, and you'll be attacked again.

We'll be attacked again anyway. Being the Lady of Nightmares only offered so much protection. Nightmares had to recognize me first, and that took the mindless ones longer to do sometimes.

"What are you waiting for?" Kail asked.

Freaking Weaver. It would be stupid not to listen to him and invite more trouble than necessary. "We're going—"

Halven shoved me straight through the camouflaged opening, and I tumbled head first into the hedge on the other side. Tiny barbs scratched at my face and hands. I hissed at the burning pain.

"What was that for?" I shouted, extracting myself from the shrubbery. But when I turned around, I was alone.

The opening was gone, replaced with a solid hedge wall, spliced through with giant iron spikes. Blades of grass floated, settling on the ground where I stood a moment before. If Halven hadn't pushed me, I would've been crushed. Or impaled. A shiver ran up my back.

"Sandman?" I called. "Kail?"

There was no reply. I eased open my connection to the Sandman and felt his confused terror pulse through me as if it were my own. Maybe some of it was. But he was alive which was enough for now. I stuck my hands carefully between the spikes and felt around the shrub for any way to get it to open again. Leaves wrapped around my hand, grinding bone against bone. I ripped myself free and stared at the wall.

"Screw it." I pushed up my sleeves and reached out to touch the maze, to find its knotted thread. To tear down its walls.

Don't do it, the Weaver warned again. *They know where you're going, and therefore where to find you.*

"I can't do this alone." I pressed my hand to the ground and searched for what I needed.

You aren't alone, Keeper, but even if you were, you'd manage.

Thread. Thread, thread, thread. Where was it?

Keeper, if you don't trust me, at least trust yourself.

I froze. My nerves calmed, settling into place. Didn't I promise myself to do just that when the Weaver was tormenting me from his own body? Hadn't I been trying to prove myself capable since then? I lifted my hand from the grass and stood.

"Fine."

Good. Then turn left.

"We just came from that way."

Did we?

We definitely had. The entrance to the maze was in that direction, but I went left anyway, making sure the threads on my arm were visible in case anything else wanted to try its luck.

You're turning out to be quite the GPS system, I told him.

He ignored the comment in favor of another order. *Chop, chop. This isn't a leisurely stroll.*

I rolled my eyes. "Stick to directions before I change my mind."

***

It only took a few uninterrupted turns before a gentle humming filled the air, the sound as soft as a mother's lullaby. I blinked, instantly charmed, which was always dangerous in the Nightmare Realm. "Is that something good or something I'll need to fight?" I asked in an airy voice.

You don't need to fight anything, the Weaver answered.

"You…" I blinked again as my thoughts turned fuzzy. "You didn't say it was good."

It's the Wish Granter, he said, sounding slightly mystified himself.

"Good," I breathed. Surely, she was *not* good if the Weaver refused to answer the question, but I needed to see her regardless. "That's good."

Very good indeed because my feet were already carrying me toward the warmth and comfort the song promised. My mind conjured up an image of a beautiful woman, curvy and tall, with a welcoming smile. In my mind, she sat in rocking chair with a warm mug of chocolate. She held it out to me, her lap an open invitation, and a bedtime story waited on her lips.

Wrong, the Weaver promised.

It felt right. I wanted it to be right.

I rounded the curve to find a red glow waiting where the path widened into the heart of the maze. The color faded as I approached the source. When I finally stepped into the very center of the maze, I found out how right he was. There was no woman. No human-like nightmare at all.

Instead, a heart twice my height greeted me. Veins clung to the ground like roots and blood sprayed in a fine mist from the artery. The organ contracted, revealing bluish shapes nestled within. Was that…a *squelch?*

"Some warning would've been nice," I told the Weaver as I clutched my churning stomach.

The mist ceased, leaving no trace on the ground or surrounding hedges. For one awful moment, nothing happened. The following second, my definition of *awful* changed drastically. Veins plucked themselves off the grass with sickening pops, and without their support, the heart fell to its side with a wet splat. The organ twitched violently. Flickers of blue and red emanated from its center, and a tiny trickle of white pus dribbled from the artery. The humming resumed, mixed with the mere whisper of a voice. "Lady Nightmare. Why have you come?"

I swallowed bile. It *talked*. Did it have to talk? "I need something from you."

"Do you?" It sounded intrigued. "What can I possibly give you that you could not take?" I opened my mouth to answer. "Hush now. Show me your wish or I cannot grant it."

"Err…" I patted my jacket, hoping I still had my mini sketchbook in one of the pockets. "It's a—"

No, Keeper. Show *her.*

"I didn't know I needed a photo of the thing," I snapped.

"Come now," the Wish Granter beckoned. The veins crept across the grass toward me. "It will only take a moment."

I stared at the heart, willing myself to step back, but I needed the knife if we were going to stop Mara. "Am I…I mean, I can draw it for you? I don't seem to have any paper, but I could…"

The humming hitched into what I assumed was a laugh before falling back into its previous rhythm. In the next second, the veins snapped forward. Sucker-like appendages latched onto my skin, my clothes no barrier to them, and dragged me forward. My own heart pounded frantically in response, and I pulled in air to scream. The Weaver pushed out against it, silencing me.

Now, now, he cooed. *Save the dramatics.*

Before I could even consider shoving him back into submission, the veins hoisted me, head-first, into the oozing artery.

Chapter Fifteen

The Sandman

Halven rammed into Nora, sending her sailing straight through a hidden opening in the maze, just as the hedge snapped shut. Iron spikes skewered the foliage, and I dove sideways. Metal sliced through my calf. My jaw slammed into the ground, making my head ring. The spikes impaled the opposite side of the passageway with a heavy thud.

I rolled over, the large cut on my leg burning, to find two dozen projectiles spanning the space separating me from Kail. He stared, wide-eyed, at the metal, and seemed to be holding his breath whereas mine was too fast. His eyes stilled halfway between red and green.

"Kail?" I asked when he remained motionless. "Are you hurt?"

He snapped out of his stupor at the sound of my voice and moved lightning fast, leaping between spikes. "Halven!"

Halven was on his stomach right next to the hedge, a spike protruding from the back of his shirt near his side. "I'm fine," he rasped and slid himself free. "It's only a scratch."

Kail spun his brother around, frantically checking for wounds, but I simply stared at the newly formed wall. Nora was on the other side of it…had the spikes attacked there as well? I couldn't feel her emotions—I hadn't for a long while now. My heart flew into a crazed rhythm.

"Nora?" It was a croak. I sucked in a breath and rushed to the hedge, digging at the leaves. "Nora! Nora, can you hear me? Are you okay?"

Halven gripped my arm and hauled me away. *"Run."*

I ripped free of him. There was no way I was going to leave Nora. She would heal from any wound, but that didn't mean she wasn't hurt. She could be injured and bleeding or trapped against the opposite hedge. *Impaled.* Something even worse could've happened on her side…

Kail leapt feet-first between the last two spikes. "Nora's more capable than we are," he said in a rush. "We have to move."

And then I saw why. Halfway down the passage, a zombie-like man stood, watching us. His head was bent at an unnatural angle, his eyes blank. Soiled clothes hung from his emaciated body like a sack. A half-groan, half-laugh echoed around me, but more worrisome was the approaching multitude of voices.

I reached for my sand, but Kail grabbed my wrist. "Save it for when we really need it."

"I'd say we need it," I hissed.

"You Lords and your magic." Kail narrowed his eyes. "There's nothing wrong with running away."

"Nora is—"

"We have a long way to the center of the maze. Don't make me abandon you here," he pressed.

The center of the maze? No. We weren't going anywhere except to find Nora. I scooped a handful of sand from my bag and prepared to throw up a barrier between the three of us and the nightmares when the sky turned yellow. Hail fell—small pellets of molten lava. It singed my hair, burned my face, melted holes in my clothes. Kail cursed loudly at my back. I threw the barrier up overhead instead, but the sheet of pellets shifted to fall at a severe angle. The relentless hail flew around my protection at the same time the zombie moved closer. Behind him, dozens just like him emerged.

"Okay. Run," I agreed. If I ran out of sand and was hurt too badly, my magic would pull me to the beach, and there wasn't time for me to travel back here.

Kail and Halven wasted no time, and neither did I. The lava pellets turned their fury toward the easier, unprotected targets, and the howling cries of the zombie-like nightmares were all that chased after us. Kail trailed a hand along the hedge as we ran. The moment his hand passed an empty space, we veered into it. A claw-foot bathtub greeted us in a small alcove. Bubbles foamed high, a few floating ethereally into the air, and rose petals were sprinkled over the grass.

"A dead-end," Kail groaned, running his hands over the walls.

Halven peered into the bubbles with a cocked head. One of the bubbles floated right up to his face and popped, releasing a high, taunting laugh. The faucet turned on by itself with a low creak, topping off the tub and releasing a strong floral scent. Halven leaned even closer, then jerked back as another bubble popped against the brim of his hat. This time the laugh was nothing short of demonic.

"Do you think it's a fear of bubbles, bathing, or outdoor nudity?" Kail asked.

"Does it matter?" I snapped. "Get away from it before something drags you into the water." I flexed my hands. *Nora, Nora, Nora.* Where was she now? Looking for us? Fighting off other creatures? "We have to find her."

"Something here…" Halven struggled to say. "It stirs a memory."

"This isn't the time," I said, too harshly.

"Nora will be fine." Kail didn't tear his curious gaze away from his brother. "You really should step away from that."

Halven did as he was told and rubbed at his throat. "I've smelled this before."

"Forget about the bathtub," I shouted. "Nora—"

Kail blew out a frustrated breath. "She has the literal creator of this maze inside her head, so if you can just focus on *us* getting to the Wish Granter, that would be great."

It was a truth I didn't want to acknowledge and didn't know how to process. The pain, the anger, of it was too fresh. My trust was broken, my heart too. Unfortunately, love wasn't so easy to shatter. I meant what I said to her on the ship—every word of it—but now…now I would take it all back to see her in one piece.

Would the Weaver help her make it to the center of the maze or would he sabotage our plans? Did he want Mare dead? It was more likely he was playing us—playing *me*. We both agreed to create the knife to get rid of Mare, but he took the consequences harder than I had.

Deep down I knew, even if he was reliving any past pain, the Weaver wasn't suicidal. That had to count for something.

Kail hoisted his brother up from a crouched position by the tub. "Put the petals down. What are you doing?"

I shook my head. "Let's move."

***

I threw my back up against the wall, gasping for breath. My satchel was half empty now after saving us from a variety of nightmares. Hair that sprung out of the hedges and attempted to strangle us, disembodied feet that tried to stomp us into the ground, flesh-eating snails. The complicated scientific equations floating around our heads now were more annoying than dangerous, but my patience had long reached its limit.

"Haven't you done this before?" Kail wheezed. "When you hid the knife?"

I swatted at the numbers and letters drifting around my head. "I wasn't attacked then, obviously."

"Why wouldn't—*oh*…"

"Oh?" I repeated.

Kail waved a hand through the air. "Things were chaotic then."

"Yes." I leveled a hard stare. "Which made things *more* violent."

He gave me a withering look. "Rowan wasted no time snapping up the reins. Everyone was too busy either tormenting each other or hiding before her spies could…*recruit* them. They're not going to give up their hiding place to fight a losing battle with you. Rowan needed you to bring Nora back so there were orders not to touch you."

"You're saying I played into Rowan's hands?"

"No," he said, his tone clipped. "Are you always this tiring, Dream Lord? Though, since you brought it up, if you *had* played into Rowan's hands and brought Nora back, we wouldn't have to deal with Mara. Maybe we've been blaming the wrong person this whole time."

I bristled, torn between anger and guilt, but there wasn't time to settle on which. A quick buzzing sounded within the hedge at my back. I eased away from it and turned slowly. "Did you hear that?"

Silver-winged insects burst from the foliage in a swarm large enough to circle all three of us. They bit and stung and bit and stung. "Enough," I shouted. Sand burst from my satchel and turned each bug to ash. "This is ridiculous."

Halven brushed grey powder from the ruffles of his collar. "We're here." Kail and I exchanged a confused look. "Nearly."

"How nearly?" Kail asked.

Halven pointed to a corner of the millionth dead-end we found. "Nearly," he repeated.

Finally, with a direction to aim for, I used my sand to blow a hole in the hedge. The leaves squealed as the exposed brambles burned. "After you," I told the brothers.

Chapter Sixteen

Nora

There was nothing.

No light.

No weight.

No air, though my body didn't seem to miss it.

Panic lurked deep inside, but the humming filled me like air filled a tire. Slow, heavy pressure that churned my insides. I wasn't sure I existed anymore. Everything was too peaceful; too calm. Even the Weaver was utterly silent—not the slightest hint of a grin to be seen.

"What is your wish, Lady Nightmare?" the Wish Granter asked, her voice slightly garbled. I tried to open my mouth to reply, but the cocoon constricted around me. "Shhh. I must look for myself."

That was the last moment of comfort I felt before the warmth of the heart squeezed me to the point of breaking. Bones snapped and cracked. A scream built in my throat, but then I was suddenly in a familiar living room. *My* living room. All traces of pain vanished, and I gasped with relief. The scent of cookies overwhelmed me in the best way, sweet and a little spicy, like gingerbread. I breathed in the sweet air, let it settle in the cracks of my old memories, and turned to see the house I left months ago.

It looked like someone bought out the entire holiday decoration aisle. Garland with red berries circled the banister, fake poinsettia flowers were pinned to the curtains, and the TV stand was covered with sparkly white fabric. Little snowmen figurines sat on every flat surface of the room. A nativity set took up most of the space on the coffee table and Santa throw pillows lined the couch. My jaw dropped. Never in the history of Gallagher family Christmases had my mother gone this overboard with decorating.

"Nora," my mother called. "It's time to lick the spoon!"

I followed her voice to the kitchen and blanched when I found her in a coordinating Christmas apron and Santa hat. "Mom…?"

"Hurry, silly," she said warmly. "Your father will be home soon with the tree."

The walls around me constricted again, dragging me from the home—the mother—I never had. All of it was gone in the blink of an eye, replaced by the Keep. The exterior door leading to the loom swung open and an unseen force pushed me inside before slamming it shut again. The Weaver's gold eyes flared at the sight of me as they had when I met him there that fateful day. Only, when he stood, knocking the bench over, the door flew open again. The Sandman raced in, throwing handfuls of glimmering sand into the air. Hands were on me. Kail's.

"Give me the knife," he pleaded. "Don't listen to Rowan."

My heart slammed into my breastbone. "Take it," I said in a rush and reached for the knife hidden beneath my vest. Only it wasn't there.

The scene paused, the entire room completely still. "What's this?" the Wish Granter asked. I opened my mouth to ask her the exact same thing when she spoke again. "Hello, Lord. I did not expect to find you here."

"No one does," the Weaver answered, only this time, his voice wasn't in my head. It was the real thing standing in front of me. He swatted the sand, frozen in time, away from his path and came to stand in front of me. Dark hair was swept back into a low bun at the back of his neck, highlighting high cheekbones and a strong jaw. "Do they, Keeper?"

"What a predicament," the warm voice said thoughtfully. "Only one body is allowed in at a time, as you know, Lord. As you also know, I can only grant the body one wish."

"Quite the predicament, indeed." His lips curled up in a familiar grin, and my knees shook. "Which of us shall it be, Keeper? You or me?"

"Weaver," I addressed him carefully. He couldn't steal my wish, could he? What would he ask for? Would he wish to have never died? If he wished for that, I wouldn't have become the ruler of the Nightmare Realm. I wouldn't have brought Mara back. The Sandman and I would find our way back to *us*, but…but if I hadn't killed the Weaver, something worse might have happened. Like him torturing the dream out of me and unleashing his nightmares into the Day World. That was a huge *if* that I couldn't risk. "We need the knife."

"You could be you again." He cocked his head, looking at me like it was the first time. Assessing. Quizzical. "I could be me."

I licked my lips. "What's done is done."

"It can be undone." His gaze softened slightly. "I could wish that you never met the Sandman. That way, you'd never have the chance to kill me and your boss, your friends…your dad, they would be alive. You could have a normal life. A mother like you saw a moment ago."

Never meet the Sandman? My blood drained to my feet at the thought. "My mother was *never* like that," I said around my parched tongue. Our problems aside, she wasn't the type to put in more effort than necessary. Especially when it came to her kids. "The Sandman was all I had growing up."

"That's not true. You had your sister."

I choked on a humorless laugh. "Sisters *hate* each other growing up as much as they love each other."

"Is that your wish then?" the Wish Granter asked.

"I wish for the knife," I shouted before the Weaver could say otherwise. "The knife the Sandman gave you. I wish for it."

The Weaver's grin widened, revealing perfectly straight teeth. "She will only grant that which is most wanted."

"You are Lord and Lady, I will not twist the wish as I usually do. I'll give you exactly what you ask for in respect of your titles," she assured me.

"That's what I want the most," I insisted. "To get the knife so I can right my wrong."

"Ah," the Wish Granter said thoughtfully. "Now *that* is the right kind of wish, but, Lord, if I may…knowing you are here, if I must choose sides…"

The Weaver waved a lazy hand. "Your loyalty is appreciated."

No. *No, no, no,* this couldn't be happening. It was *my* body she swallowed up which meant it should be *my* wish she granted. "Please." My voice cracked. "Please, don't. This is all messed up—so, so messed up—but I accept it. I…" I wanted this place—to rule here. I didn't understand that until this very moment, didn't want to accept it, but I was doing something here. Something worthwhile and good. In a strange way, I *belonged.* Even if my old feelings were fading, and I was becoming less. I was also becoming more.

The Weaver closed the space between us so that we breathed the same air. Tears burned at the backs of my eyes, but I refused to back down. I *needed* the knife, and we weren't leaving without it. He lifted his hand, empty of thread, and ran one finger down the side of my face before cupping my cheek. My eyes widened at the gentle touch. This was the Weaver. *Gentle* wasn't part of his vocabulary.

"Keeper," he whispered. A spiteful, predatory sound, as if he were thinking seriously about snapping my neck.

"Tell her you want the knife," I growled.

A brow quirked and his chuckle brushed over my lips, his grin never wavering. "Are we going to play nice with each other?"

"I already told you that we will *never* be friends." I tucked my hands behind my back to keep from punching him. One didn't befriend a murderer, especially when his victims were close friends and family, but I couldn't afford to piss him off at the moment.

The Weaver held my gaze, and my breath caught at what stared out from the depths of his golden eyes. It wasn't a monster. It was a little something like what I saw in the mirror. Different, but the same. Hurt. Regret. Desperation. *Want.* His felt crueler, hardened by countless years. Still, in that lingering moment, I felt a connection to him, a deep understanding. I hated it…but I also didn't.

His eyes fell to my lips, the grin fading. Before I could process what that meant, he was kissing me. His lips were warm and soft, the pressure full of pliant desperation. I forgot how to move, the appalling act stealing my ability to function, but it only lasted for a brief moment before I tore myself away. I wanted to scream at him—*how dare he!* My lips burned with the acrid memory, and I was sure it would take years to scrub away.

"What was that?" I demanded. "You can't just go around kissing people when you *know* they loathe you."

His grin returned, but his eyes remained glossy. Wistful, almost. "Relax. The Sandman seems to like doing that very much, so I wanted to see what the big deal was. Alas, I still don't understand the appeal."

My mouth gaped open and shut. He couldn't be serious. *Rat bastard.*

"You'll forgive me," he said, unworried.

I most certainly would *not.* My cheeks blazed with fury. Who did he think he was? Maybe I *should* let him wish himself back into his body, if only so I could kill him all over again. Stab him a few times instead of the once.

"I wish for the knife the Sandman gave you," the Weaver said in the quietest of voices.

My heart skipped a beat. "You…*what?*"

"Looks like we'll be stuck with each other for a while longer." He tried to grin wider before giving up and it dropped off his face completely. "Maybe now you'll reconsider my offer of friendship."

"Fat chance," I said, but the Weaver's body crumpled to the floor before I finished speaking. His blood seeped around him as it had when I drove the knife into his heart. The frozen image of the Sandman and Kail vanished, and a hard weight dug into the base of my spine. I moved languidly, twisting my arm around to grip what I knew would be cold metal.

The moment my fingers wrapped around the handle of the knife, the entire setting dropped away. The *nothing* was back, only the humming was alarmingly absent, and this time I desperately needed air. Panic overflowed my nervous system. I twisted and turned in an attempt to free myself, only to find I didn't need freeing because grass tickled my skin. When I opened my eyes, I saw the muted blue sky of the Nightmare Realm above me. The giant heart was back in place, the veins holding it in an upright position as a light spray of blood fanned out from the top of the aorta. I scrambled to my feet and clutched the knife—*the knife*—to my chest. "Weaver?" I whispered.

Still here.

I closed my eyes, hating the words I was about to say. Especially after the stunt he pulled. "Thanks. For this."

He was silent for a moment. *You're welcome, Nora.*

I jerked at the sound of his voice forming my name for the first time.

"There!" Kail shouted.

Three sets of feet pounded the ground behind me. I turned slowly to face them, and it took everything I had not to run to the Sandman. It was a jackhammer to my insides knowing I couldn't. At least, not until we figured things out. What he said on the ship…a shallow, pained breath left my lungs.

The Sandman stood beside Kail and Halven, all three of them looking like they braved a war single-handedly. They stared at the knife with matching looks of surprise. A sudden wave of exhaustion hit me, a weariness not of my body but my heart. A fierce battle I didn't know I was fighting, finally won. Or maybe lost.

But over.

I shuffled toward the single path out of the maze's center on wobbly legs. On my way by, I shoved the knife against Kail's blood-soaked chest. The hedges whipped back, creating a clear path to the foggy shore of the Green Sea. I heard the others behind me: slow, hesitant. I was too tired to see if they were actually following or if the maze was working to swallow them back up.

Chapter Seventeen

The Sandman

The ship ride and following trek to Nora's palace was deathly quiet. Tension did the speaking for everyone. Nora's headspace was clear to read—angry, exhausted, and determined. I didn't know what her determination was focused on—Mare or something that happened inside the Wish Granter—but it was impossible to ask after our fight. I didn't know how to fix things, especially when I was still so angry, but the way I felt when the hedge separated us told me we had to speak again. Only, not today.

I held my hand out to Kail. "Knife."

Kail, for once, did as he was asked without commentary. He simply extracted the blade from inside his coat and handed it over. I turned the knife over in my hand, feeling its power throb almost painfully up my arm, before tucking it away in my satchel.

It was time to go back to the Dream Realm to replenish my sand supply, but my feet refused to move.

Nora drew in a steady breath. "Sandman…"

"Don't." My voice was firm, the crack barely held beneath the surface, and I couldn't bring myself to look at her. There was little worse than being at war with yourself. "Not right now."

Luckily, she had enough mercy for me not to push it, though the air still thickened further.

"We'll meet again in a few hours then," Kail said, uneasy. "Get this done."

I nodded once, my head heavy, my heart heavier, but this time my limbs obeyed. They carried me away from Nora. I was halfway to the cattails near the palace when I spun on my heel and walked part of the way back. "You're okay?" I asked, my gaze steadily directed at Nora's boots. "You weren't injured?"

There was a heavy pause before Nora answered, "No. I'm fine."

"Good." I cleared my throat and, this time when I walked away, I didn't look back.

***

Halven waited at the barrier to the Dream Realm. His back was to me, his hands folded carefully behind his back. "You wasted no time." My steps slowed. "What are you doing here?"

Halven's hat tilted as he looked up. "We must speak."

"We could've spoken on the ship ride back." I walked past him and onto a sea of glimmering sand. "Did something else happen since I left?"

He followed me inside. "No."

159

His voice gave nothing away, and there was no telling what his expression was behind the mask. I removed the knife from my empty satchel as I bent to refill it. "What is it?"

Halven fiddled with the voluminous fabric around his neck, saying nothing.

Though he was a man of few words, his words carried weight which meant his silence did too. "Did you think I would run off with the knife?" My eyes narrowed with realization. "They sent you to make sure I came back?"

"You are paranoid." Halven angled his head toward me and pounded on his chest as if he could break up whatever held his voice hostage. "I understand why."

I shifted uncomfortably, turning my attention to the sand beneath my hands. Paranoid wasn't the right word. My trust was broken, along with a certain vital organ, but that accusation was unfounded. Nora distrusted me—she proved that again and again—but thinking I would run off without killing Mare first was too much. I shouldn't have voiced otherwise.

"I came beca—" Halven's swallow was audible. "Becau—" He paused, his agitation radiating around him. "Roses."

My satchel full, I removed my stained shirt while the sand scrubbed the dried blood from my skin. "Roses?"

"The Weaver gave me a key." His words were quickly becoming more and more hoarse.

My eyes snapped up. The key to the Ever Safe was lost, likely destroyed by now, since it was created shortly after the first humans. Even nightmares crumbled with age without proper care. The pavilion now standing in the Dream Realm was the fifth or sixth version. There was no way a metal key almost as old as I was survived the elements this long. "A key to what?"

Halven shook his head. "Never said."

I raised my brows. "I'm not sure I'm following."

He drew a long breath as if readying himself for the pain of speaking. "He told me to lose it so—" A cough wracked his body, and he bent to hold his knees until it passed. When he had, he managed to squeeze out, "I am lost."

"You're lost," I repeated, almost a question. The meaning of his words struck ten seconds later. *He was lost.* "You have it. The key he gave you—you kept it because if it was with you, it wouldn't be found."

Halven nodded.

"Is it…" I pressed my eyes shut. Maybe it was better if I didn't know what the key opened—better if *he* didn't know. If it was for the Ever Safe that meant Mare's prize was within reach this entire time.

Halven touched my arm tentatively. When I opened my eyes, he kicked out a leg and pointed to his boot.

A thousand lifetimes passed since I last saw the key to the Ever Safe, yet I recognized it immediately. The metal was worn, eroding away slowly, though it had clearly been cared for enough to survive this long. "You should have destroyed that," I said, breathless.

"That is different than lost."

Weaver. If I could strangle him for this, I would. I flopped down on the sand and hung my head between my knees. A tired, humorless laugh flowed out of me and I was powerless to stop it.

So many beings would've killed for that key.

Halven wore it like a trinket.

A moment later, he sat beside me, silently waiting for my hysteria to pass. Having a nightmare sit beside me, tainting the sand around him, in a show of support only made it worse. I flopped back and threw an arm over my eyes. The laughter instantly gave way to tears. I let them come, let my sleeve soak up each drop without leaving a trace for Halven to see.

"Sandman?" he asked when my silence stretched on.

"Just go," I pleaded. I needed a few minutes to myself. "Don't tell anyone else about the key until I return to the Keep."

I felt him shift, felt the sand crumble as he stood, but he hadn't made it a single step before a distant boom sounded. It was far enough away that it sounded like nothing more than lumber dropped onto the back a truck, and, based on the way it echoed, it was indeed a long distance off. Nightmares occasionally acted up; loud sounds weren't uncommon and occasional lights flared on the horizon.

However, this didn't feel like something that innocent.

"Should I investigate?" Halven rasped.

I took a moment to gather myself and tuck away my emotions. "No. We should get back to Nora."

Baku burst through the barrier, heading straight for us, and I held up a hand to silence Halven. If Nora was right and Baku was Rowan's spy, it was best not to say anything important in front of him. Why take an unnecessary risk? Rowan might be gone, but my trust was shaken. If he sided with Rowan, what was to say he hadn't sided with someone else since then? Baku pranced closer to me, his eyes shifting side-to-side.

"Baku." I managed to keep the suspicion from my voice. Acting differently could tip him off, but what I would've said under normal circumstances failed me. Would I ask about the sound or have him look into it while I went back to the palace? Whatever it was, I had to say something. "Do you know where that noise came from?"

Halven listened to Baku's silence for a moment, then pointed to our right. "That way."

Baku nudged me with his tusk and pointed his trunk in the opposite direction. His hearing was impeccable, but Halven had his way of *knowing* where nightmares were.

"I thought the same as Halven." I squinted into the distance. Unease settled deeper into my soul. Perhaps it would be best to test Baku's loyalty and settle things once and for all. "We'll check that way, and if there's nothing there, we can double back."

Baku's lips curled up. "We can't both be right," I reasoned. "Halven is going that way anyway." I pointed in the direction Baku gave. "He'll look around while we go this way."

I stared at where Halven's eyes should've been, willing myself to catch some sort of clue to his thoughts, but he simply nodded in agreement.

Baku chuffed, and I barely stopped from wincing.

The sound echoed and *could* have come from either direction, but something felt off. "Did you see anything strange on your way here?" I asked him.

Baku shook his head.

"I can read your dreams," I offered, reaching for my sand. He turned and sauntered back toward the barrier. I stared at Halven, willing him to understand that I didn't like this. Not one bit. "Let them know I'll be there soon."

Halven pressed a hand to his chest and bobbed his head. I watched him leave, aching with uncertainty. Nora. Baku. Even Halven who told me about the key instead of Nora… When would enough be enough?

Baku pounded his tiger paws into the sand, the small thuds drawing my attention. "Coming."

There was no way to know where I needed to go. Landscapes stretched on and on, none appearing to have been disturbed, and it wasn't like sound left a trail. Instead, I turned each way Baku tried to stop me from going. If I veered north, he would urge me east. If I went east, he wanted to go west. Each time I ignored his suggestions, he grew more anxious. His ears twitched, his lips quivering.

"What's gotten into you?" I asked.

Baku unhinged his jaw, stretched it from side to side, and shut it again.

I inhaled and moved into a new landscape. The ground was covered in grey pits with raised ridges of purple and orange, like coral. It crunched slightly beneath my boots but held its shape. The air smelled of salt. A low growl came from Baku, and I scanned the area for any approaching nightmares. There were none that I could see, though I was sure they were around. For the first time, I wondered if it wasn't me Baku was warning, but them.

"Maybe I'm wrong," I said with faked sincerity. "There's no harm looking here first."

Baku's nails raked across the surface, creating a crackling sound as bits of coral broke away. Then he ran, nothing more than a blur of black and orange fur. I stood immobile for two seconds. They felt like twenty because, though Baku couldn't speak, I could sense his annoyance. I didn't know if he expected me to follow him or stay my path. Was he running toward his spy-master, to warn them I was close, or away from them in hopes of keeping me from the truth?

I sent sand after Baku. A bug formed, no larger than a flea, and attached itself to the ridge of his ear. Through it, I saw what he saw. I didn't dare give it my full attention, but I got flashes each time I blinked. The further Baku went, the faster my heart sped. *Ice caves.* He was headed straight for them. The coral ground gradually gave way to snow, a dusting at first, then inches, then feet. Baku moved so quickly he didn't sink into the soft powder. So quickly, in fact, that he was just outside the caves in a matter of minutes.

He wasn't alone.

The second half of the army was there—the one I saw in Baku's dream the day we confronted Rowan. We never found where they went, but Halven had scoured most of the Nightmare Realm and a group this size was hard to hide…we assumed it disbanded without Rowan there to give orders.

We were wrong.

Very wrong.

Chapter Eighteen

Nora

"Ding dong," Kail said, breezing into my art studio.

I didn't bother to look up from my latest drawing. It wasn't clear yet what the finished design would be, but the head was triangular, and tentacles filled half the page. So far, it was strangely elegant.

"No one's home."

"We're supposed to be getting ready to go slash up an Ancient, and you're doodling?"

His beak skimmed my shoulder, and I brought my elbow back into his stomach. "I'm *designing*, and it helps me relax."

Relax and take my mind off things. A lot of things. The Sandman, mainly, but also what happened inside the Wish Granter. I couldn't erase the taste of the Weaver's lips from my own. Bitter. Metallic. Wholly awful. If cutting them from my face would erase what happened, I'd do it.

Come now, the Weaver said. *It wasn't so bad.*

It was worse, I snapped. If *he* was my last kiss, I would invent a way to physically torture him if it took a hundred years. It wasn't like I would move on from the Sandman. Even if I wanted to, my choices as Lady Nightmare were zero, so if he never forgave me…

"Plus," I added with a pointed stare, "as you know, I need to stop things like you from barging into places they shouldn't."

Kail ignored my comment and lifted a paper. He studied the sketch of the new front doors I installed earlier. The once-wooden doors were now strong metal, ten inches thick. There was only one door now instead of two, and the frame was shaped like an old-fashioned keyhole. It wasn't the most aesthetically pleasing with oddly shaped patches bolted together every which way, interior rods exposed in places as if the metal had melted around them. No part of it matched the rest of the palace—it would really only look right in a scrap yard—but if anyone tried breaking in, they wouldn't escape.

Behind each of those different patches was something murderous. A family of sprites was in charge of the inner workings, their home a series of connecting tunnels inside the door. Their skin was soft as velvet but potent pollen fell from them like dandruff, causing anaphylaxis. There were other deadly things waiting too; In case of emergency, the sprites would open the appropriate piece, unleashing anything from poisonous gas to a swarm of hornets that wouldn't stop stinging until their victim was dead. It wasn't my most creative work, but time was short.

"There seems to be a tiny problem," Kail said when it was obvious I wasn't going to ask what he wanted.

I sketched in rough edges of webbed hands. "There are never *tiny* problems here."

"Ah, but there are." He walked the length of the room and tapped the edge of the table with his fingertips. "The east side of the castle is overrun with hedgehogs."

A laugh burst from my mouth. "Nice try. Go away, I'm busy."

"I'm completely serious," he said, horrified. "They're all different colors and smell like dirty feet. Also, they keep *hissing* at me."

"Animal instinct is so spot on, don't you think?" Part of me wanted to race to the far side of the palace and squeal over how cute they were. I'd always wanted a hedgehog, but my mother was worried they would give me salmonella. Dad let us have a dog, but when he left, we weren't even allowed to keep a goldfish. I sighed. The nightmare version of hedgehogs wouldn't be anything like the ones in the Day World anyway. Seeing them harass Kail would be worth the walk though.

Kail's taps became more insistent. "This amuses you?"

"Oh, you have no idea how much." I smiled wide. "How did they get in?"

"I'm assuming they waddled."

The frustration in his voice only brightened my smile, and I set my pencil down to look at him. "Are you really bothering me with this? Get them out of there. Or don't. I don't use that side of the palace."

He scowled. "Because you gave it to *me*."

My amusement bloomed. "Merry Christmas, Kail. You're now a proud pet parent."

"Get rid of them," he said, teeth bared.

"*You* get rid of them."

"Nora—" He paused and took a deep breath, gathering himself. "They shoot their quills. It's very unpleasant."

"That's just a myth." Returning to my drawing, I added long, narrow eyes to the design. Next, I had to decide whether to give it a nose or gills.

"Is it?" He pulled the neck of his shirt down to expose countless little red welts. "Not only that, but they're coated in some sort of…agitator…because, why not?"

I sniffed the air. "Do you smell that?"

"What? Nora. Focus. Hedgehogs—"

"Fear." I abandoned my sketch and stepped up to Kail to inhale the air around him. It was entirely possible I was enjoying this too much. "Ah, yes. Definitely fear."

He leapt away. "I'm not afraid of them. I just want them *gone*."

It's true. He's not afraid of them, the Weaver chimed in like a co-conspirator. *He's afraid of things touching him while he sleeps.*

I shuffled the information around in my head. Had I ever seen him sleep? All those nights he spent training me away from the Blood Tower, I was always the first to pass out. The last to wake. His bedroom in the tower had no door to keep things out—was that something Rowan did on purpose? He had kept to a different cell the night we spent in the prison too. Maybe it was some sort of strange paranoia about his own specialty. He was the unknown to Dreamers, so maybe he hated other nightmares sneaking up on him.

Where do you come up with your theories? He was asleep when I broke him in two, the Weaver explained. *It's that simple.*

It felt as if he splashed cold water against my insides. Any nugget of playfulness—of wanting to use the information against Kail—vanished in an instant. "Come on, ya big baby."

***

Laughter poured from me, an endless well, until I sat on the ground struggling to breathe. When Kail said the east side of the palace was *overrun*, I thought it was an exaggeration. It was more of an understatement, if anything.

"I'm *so* glad you think this is funny," Kail growled.

"I'm sorry," I lied between breaths. "It's just—"

"If you tell me how cute they are one more time, I swear I'll open that door and throw you inside."

"All right, all right." I dabbed the tears from my eyes and stood up. The closed door to Kail's personal quarters was riddled with quills. A few were there before I came, most after I waltzed in like it was no big deal. A point to me for avoiding them. "We need something to use as a shield."

"What? No. Use your Weaver mojo to make them impale each other. Problem solved."

I raised my upper lip in disgust. They were too cute for that. Too cute to be nightmares. The brief look I got when I opened the door revealed a blanket of rainbow hedgehogs covering nearly every surface. Reds and oranges, blues and purples, yellows and greens. I doubted there were two of the exact same shade. They were smaller than the ones people owned as pets. Smaller nearly always meant cuter. They had beady black eyes that shimmered as if they were about to cry and adorably twitchy noses. But those flying quills were definitely an issue.

"I highly doubt you're interested in the cleanup that would leave," I told him.

Kail folded his arms across his chest. "Fine. You like them so much, turn them into stuffed animals and keep them on your bed."

"Alterations hurt, remember? We'll usher them out the same way they got in."

"We don't know *how* they got in." He tilted his head to stare at me as if I had checked out of the conversation. "Besides, that's hardly important."

"If things are slipping inside my safe space, it's extremely important. Now, shield," I repeated. Granted, these were less an issue than the Hours or Mara, but the obvious entrances were covered now. If there was something we missed, I'd have to add it to my growing list of structural changes. When Kail didn't move, I flicked my hands at him. "Unless you want to volunteer yourself for the job?"

You don't need a shield, the Weaver said. *Just tell them to cease.*

I grinned as Kail disappeared around the corner, grumbling under his breath. *I know,* I told him. *But it's more fun this way.*

Poor Kail.

Poor Kail, my rear-end. He locked me in a museum with a very angry monkey.

The Weaver chuckled. *I thought that was rather genius. A test within a test.*

You would.

Kail returned, dragging a piece of driftwood down the hall with one hand, the bottom scraping against the stone floor. It wasn't wide enough to protect one of my arms, let alone my entire body. "Here." He held it out between us. "This should work."

I took it, pretending to examine its worth. I found small notches and areas that appeared to be purposely scraped down. "Where did you find this?"

"We all have our secrets, Lady. Especially me."

"That's exactly what worries me." I dropped the wood to the ground. It hit with a hollow clunk. "Stand over there."

"What happened to needing a shield?" he asked, wary, but moved away from the door where the hedgehogs' projectiles wouldn't reach.

I plucked a quill from the door and flicked it at him. "Stand over there and *shush*," I clarified.

With a deep breath, I reached for the knob. A surge of darkness flowed through my veins. *All taken care of*, the Weaver said, smug. *All you have to do now is shoo them away.*

I didn't ask for your help. I ground my teeth together to keep from speaking out loud. Kail knowing the Weaver talked to me didn't mean it wasn't awkward if I talked back in front of him.

Do friends need to ask? It seemed like a genuine question.

"*You* need to," I snarled. We weren't friends. Our interests might align for the moment, but they wouldn't always. If there wasn't a life-or-death situation, I expected him to stay seated. Even then, if I was about to die, a heads up would be nice. Especially since his idea of *help* included tossing me out of a rusted-out globe.

I wasn't helping you. I was helping the Sandman.

With a quiet *tsk*, I eased open the door to the east side of the castle, half expecting the Weaver to have played a practical joke on me. But, when no quills came flying, I loosened a breath and stepped inside. The hedgehogs sounded almost human when a wave of v*ooshlada*—their way of saying *our lady*—swept through the room and echoed through the hallways.

"You can't be in here. Go out the same way you came in," I ordered.

It took a moment for any of them to move, but slowly they crept away. More hedgehogs filed into the hall from open rooms. Everything about their departure was neat and orderly, the way highway traffic could be if people weren't jerks about merging. I almost hated to see them go, if only for the fact that they bothered Kail. As their numbers thinned, I was happy to see they left…presents behind that were as colorful as they were.

"Are they gone?" Kail called.

"Almost." I picked my way carefully through the excrement. "Come on. We need to follow them."

"I'll do it," he said quickly, popping up beside me. "You can go back to your drawings."

My brows rose at the eagerness in his voice and inched further up my forehead when I saw the edge of panic in his eyes. "What's with the sudden change of attitude?"

"What?" He forced a laugh. "I can manage following them out and overseeing the hole patched up. You were only needed to make them stand down."

"Uh huh," I said slowly. There was no way I was walking away now. Kail should've known that much after all our time together. Curiosity was one of my worst vices.

"It's fine, really," he insisted when I didn't turn away.

"It is," I agreed. It was fine for me to investigate my own palace's weak spots.

I eased inside after the last of the hedgehogs and froze. Rocks, once cemented into place with whatever material the nightmares used, were scattered on the ground. Dust and tiny chunks of stone coated the floor. But it wasn't those things that had my heart racing. It was the hammer and chisel leaning in the corner, and the way the broken stone around the hole pressed slightly outward. As if someone were breaking *out*, not in.

"Nora, I can explain," Kail said quickly. "It's not what you think."

"Not what I think?" I repeated in a whisper. "What is it you think I'm thinking exactly?" Even I wasn't sure.

Kail took wide steps to the side. "That I was letting nightmares in to harm you."

I jerked at the accusation. While I didn't know what to think, it wasn't that. Maybe it needed to be—he had turned on Rowan, and even helped train me to kill her. He still needed me though. He needed me to put him and Halven back together, and to kill Mara. After both those things were accomplished, maybe I would doubt him, but not until then.

"I don't think that," I promised, "but start explaining before I do."

Kail rushed to the hole, jacket flowing, and began stuffing rocks back into the wall. "It's just...you know..."

When he didn't elaborate I said, "no, I don't know."

"Me and all my *hidey holes*," he supplied flippantly, though the carelessness didn't ring true.

That's what I called his escape route out of the Blood Tower. His secret passage to run away from Rowan. My shoulders fell at what that implied. As much as I wasn't completely sure of Kail, I *wanted* to be. And I wanted him to be sure of me too. Sure that I wouldn't blackmail him or hold him here against his will. If Kail didn't trust me, how could I expect any of the others to?

There you were, worried your emotions were fading.

Shut up, Weaver. Not that he was wrong, but he wasn't entirely right either. Apparently, I had only lost my ability to feel guilty about slaughtering things.

For what it's worth, I never stopped caring about personal relationships either, he supplied.

I wasn't sure if that made things better or worse.

"Kail, if you ever want to leave, you're welcome to use the front door," I said in a strained voice.

He nodded.

"You don't have to keep helping me if you don't want to." *That* hurt to say. Because I needed him. Very much. Especially if the Sandman was serious about what he said on the ship. "I appreciate your help—Halven's too—but if you really don't want to be here, you can go. I'll still make good on my promise."

"I know you will," he said quietly, still sifting through rocks to puzzle the wall back together.

I chewed on my bottom lip. "Then what's with all this?"

Without turning around to look at me, he shrugged. "Old habits are hard to break, I suppose, but I'll fix it." His voice was thin and nervous. I hated it, and not in the same way I hated his sarcasm and occasional underhanded tricks.

"Good," I said, whether he meant mending the wall or fixing whatever made him feel as if a secret door was necessary. "We wouldn't want any raccoons to catch wind of today's adventure and pay a visit."

"We can't have that." He lifted another stone and froze. "Nora?" he asked, his voice hard and steady.

His abrupt change in tone raised the hair on my arms. "What?"

There was a long, heavy pause. "Remind me what your sister looks like."

"Katie?" I blinked in surprise. "You know what she looks like; she was just here a day ago."

"Humor me."

"A few inches taller than me, dark hair—" I sucked in a breath, my head cocked. If he didn't care what Katie looked like yesterday, he shouldn't care what she looked like today. Unless…I tried to see past him, outside, but his shoulders were too wide. "What's with the sudden interest?"

"Because I'm pretty sure that's her."

My heart bottomed out. I was across the room in three steps, shoving him away from the hole. Across the lawn, Katie trudged between two nightmares—one a centaur with incredibly long antlers and the other a large blob of clear gel. Bits and pieces of nightmares floated inside its formless torso as if it hadn't finished digesting its last meal. Katie's hands were bound in front of her, a dirty cloth shoved in her mouth, and yet, the closer they got, the more defiance shone on my sister's face.

"This has to be a joke," I half-yelled.

Kail leaned down beside me to peek outside. "It looks rather serious to me."

I growled wordlessly. Of course it was serious—my sister was taken hostage by nightmares. *Again.* The very thing I wanted to avoid. I kicked the rocks loose from the wall, squeezed outside, and bolted straight for them.

"What's this?" I called in my best Lady Nightmare voice.

The blob waited until I was close enough to speak normally. "We wanted her, but she claimed to be under your protection."

My nostrils flared. "Did she?"

"Along with other things," the centaur added.

Katie reached her bound hands up and yanked out the gag, flexing her jaw from side to side. "Are we done with this whole charade yet?"

The centaur stomped an overgrown hoof. "No one said you could speak!"

I held up a hand. "Thank you for bringing her to me. I'll take it from here."

I grabbed Katie's upper arm and led her toward the front of the palace. *Under my protection.* Of course she would come up with something like that. Something that would ultimately hurt my reputation. Protecting Dreamers was the Sandman's signature move.

"What are you doing here?" I hissed the second we were out of earshot.

"I told you this wasn't over," she said calmly. "I came back for the full Nora-version-of-events and promise to listen judgment free."

Like that was possible, but once my sister set her mind to something, that was it. "You're an idiot," I said and hauled her inside.

***

Apparently, it *was* possible for Katie to listen without implying I was off my rocker. Or that I was selfish. Or stupid for trusting people I shouldn't, not trusting people I should, and keeping the Weaver's presence a secret. She didn't say much at all, really. A welcomed surprise.

"Side note," my sister said after a long period of contemplative silence. We were sprawled out together on my bed, staring at the ceiling, our legs tangled together. "I'm seeing your old psychologist now."

"Colleen?"

"Yup. She's really helping me. I can't tell her what's actually going on, of course, but she's ace at picking up on things anyway."

"That's great, Katie," I said, and I meant it. Colleen was sweet. It was me that had been the problem during our sessions, but if she helped Katie despite a laundry list of un-truths, I was glad. "You should try the Italian restaurant down the street from the office. Their bread is to die for."

"Noted."

She picked nervously at a hangnail, and I scrambled to find a topic to break the tension. It was information overload, I knew, but she couldn't keep coming to the Nightmare Realm. Now that she knew about my new reality, she needed to stay away. Let me come to her. Assuming all the nightmares would listen to her claims of protection was foolish when many of them were nothing but horrendous looking wild animals.

But, for now, I wanted to take advantage of this chance to enjoy a few minutes together. And if it stoked the flames of my fading self, all the better.

"Do you know what I miss? Hot apple pie, cheesy lasagna, *chocolate…*" I sighed wistfully.

She turned her head to look at me, thoughts churning behind her eyes. "Come home, and I'll personally make all of that for you."

"Okay, when I said I missed those things, I meant the *good* kind—"

Katie pinched my arm and laughed for the first time. "My cooking has improved."

"Improving charred food isn't difficult. It just means you learned to set the timer on the stove. *Oww,*" I cried as she pinched me again.

"Jen is teaching me," she said, her cheeks pink.

"Jen?" Last I knew, they broke up because Jen wanted something more serious and Katie was seeing that guy… Kevin? Keenan? "Spill," I demanded.

She did. The edge in her voice smoothed as she talked about her ex-girlfriend, or her *ex*-ex girlfriend. I wasn't going to interrupt to ask when her words and body language told me all I needed to know—that they were still crazy about each other. She avoided talking about Mom and Paul while I avoided talking about the Sandman. There was no need to rub salt in old wounds when we were finally having a conversation that didn't leave us at each other's throats. We talked instead about TV shows I missed and new movies that came out. Internet memes. The possibility of Katie dying her hair again—blue this time, or maybe purple.

The conversation went on and on until my cheeks hurt from smiling and my eyelids grew heavy.

Chapter Nineteen

Nora

The bed shifted, rolling me off my side and onto my back. I groaned into the pillow. How long was I out? Two minutes? Three? Not long enough, whatever it was.

"What, Kail?" I grumbled.

"It's me."

I flew up in a tangle of sheets. The Sandman sat on the edge of the mattress, elbows resting on his knees, and my heart flip-flopped. Was he here to talk? Forgive me? Hear me out, at least? A hundred unvoiced thoughts rushed to my tongue, all of them fighting for a chance to go first. Excuses, excuses, and more excuses. They all seemed equally wanting, but I had to say something. Anything.

"Hi," I breathed. Not helpful, but a better greeting than *I swear I was going to tell you everything.*

"You might be right." He stared at the floor, soft brown curls floating around his forehead, and I fought not to reach out to touch them. "About Baku, I mean."

Baku? He came here to talk to me about that good for nothing nightmare eater? That's why the Sandman was in my bedroom: to tell me that I was right about his *"friend"* being a spy. "I might be right…" I repeated, my shoulders slumped.

"Most likely right," he amended.

I pursed my lips. I already knew I was right. It was completely obvious Baku was working against us; Rowan wasn't going to forge her own notes, and it connected a lot of dots. How she knew exactly what to say to manipulate me into killing the Weaver, and how Kail knew I liked to draw when I had never mentioned it.

But…Baku wasn't my friend. He was the Sandman's. This visit wasn't because he forgave me; it was because he needed me. We were each other's safe space. He needed comfort now, and, outside of this moment, it didn't mean anything would change. Not yet anyway.

I exhaled quietly and slid up further in the bed, rubbing my arms though I wasn't cold. "I'm sorry, Sandman," I said, genuinely disappointed on his behalf. "I know you two were close."

He let out a dry laugh. "Well, I suppose I shouldn't be surprised. It was always friends by default for us, right? We were all the other had."

That was how he described Baku to me at first. Enemy of his enemy. His associate. That didn't make the betrayal any less painful, I imagined. "It doesn't matter how you became friends," I whispered.

"Only that it was a lie." His voice was low, broken. "Like so many things are."

I flinched. "Sandman—"

"It doesn't matter." He stood quickly and brushed his palms off on his thighs. The spell was broken. An icy wall slammed down on his desperate grief almost immediately. "Rowan's second army still exists, and Baku knew all this time."

I untangled myself from the covers and slid from the bed. If Baku knew and didn't tell us, that meant he was on their side. The question was, who controlled the army? I thought Kail and I had weeded out the rebels capable of starting an uprising, but we must have missed someone. We couldn't fight Mara *and* someone else with an army at the same time. "What should we do?"

"Take care of Mare." The Sandman kept his gaze anywhere but on me. "Once the immediate danger is gone, you can deal with your nightmares, and I can deal with Baku. If it's true he's betraying us, that is."

If it's true, the Weaver scoffed.

I zeroed in on another part of his words, my insides twisting. This was it then. He wanted to kill Mara and go our separate ways, but he hadn't heard me out yet. He *had* to hear me out first…right?

This is hardly the time to worry about your love life, the Weaver reasoned.

"Have you heard anything from Halven about a key?" he asked suddenly.

"A key? To what?" I spoke quietly, not trusting my voice.

"Nevermind. We'll leave in a few hours for the ice caves," he said, then left without a backward glance.

We aren't waiting until Mara is dead to deal with the army? the Weaver asked.

"There isn't time to deal with it." I stared at the door, hoping the Sandman would come back in, knowing he wouldn't.

You're forgetting the first law of ruling this realm.

I sighed and headed for my wardrobe. "And what would that be?"

The grin lifted. *Delegate.*

***

This isn't the best of ideas, the Weaver told me for the fifth time. *When I said delegate, I meant…really anything other than this.*

"The Hours are motivated."

Motivated to kill you, perhaps.

I chewed my lip, regretting that I told Kail to hang back, and stared up at the clock tower. They would break out eventually. Releasing them meant they would have less reason to be angry, and it would give them a purpose. At least, I hoped.

"I'll have to kill them first, but something tells me they want Mara dead more than me. Besides, the Sandman and I have a solid plan which is what they wanted." Of course, I wasn't about to divulge what the plan was. Betrayal was nearly impossible to see coming, and I already didn't trust the Hours.

The Weaver scoffed. *There are twelve of them, not including the Chime and the Hands. They can handle killing two things at once.*

"You've been in my head too long." I rubbed my sweaty palms together. "The Weaver I know wouldn't worry about some measly *nightmares.* Especially since the Sandman is back at full power. The only thing holding him back is the whole balance thing. And morals."

Don't those hold you back too?

Did they? I supposed so, though I assumed it was my humanity that kept me in check. My morals were greying, but the balance was important. I believed in it enough to follow in the Sandman's footsteps when it came to not blowing up my every problem. Not that I didn't *want* to…

"I should go in there now."

Is there a game plan?

Right. Game plan. "Walk in, walk out?"

Guns-a-blazin' then? Shall we let some darkness out?

It wasn't a horrible idea, actually. The Hours knew I was powerful enough to trap them, but there was no harm in flaunting it. It worked well enough the first time.

Wonderful, the Weaver said buoyantly.

The darkness swirled faster and faster. Leaking out. Snaking around me like a cloak. I forced myself to ignore the tendrils in my peripheral vision and focus on the clock. Everything appeared frozen, the same time as when I left. Maybe that meant they were all dead, and this was a waste of time.

Don't get your hopes up.

Whatever. I dragged my feet up to the sealed door. "Here goes nothing."

The Weaver was silent.

"You could offer a little encouragement, you know."

Why bother? Every time I try, you get angry.

"Jerk." I clenched my jaw and laid a hand on the door. "Open sesame."

I felt the Weaver's eye roll, but he worked his magic much faster than I could have. The door made a small hiss and fell inward. *The fastest route then?* he asked. *Assuming I'll be your tour guide yet again.*

"Can it, Weaver." I stepped into the dark interior of the clock. It smelled of dust, metal, and oil. The only splash of color came from the many golden cogwheels. I hadn't noticed the beauty of it before. The intricately designed gears were interspersed with black, creating wonderfully elaborate patterns on the walls, but not a single one moved. The stillness sent a chill up my spine. "Fine. Yes. Directions."

I wanted to close my eyes and let the Weaver do the walking, but unfortunately my eyes were his. So I endured his carefree instructions. *Turn left. Go straight. Pull this lever.* It was like he didn't even have to try. Maybe he didn't, but how he kept so many landscapes straight was beyond me.

There, he said. *The door to the Chime.*

I paused, my hand on the lever that would open it. The Hours had to know I was inside, but they were nowhere to be seen. Their strange absence could've meant a lot of things, but my money was on an ambush. What better way to hurt me than to wait until I was in the very center of their lair to attack as a unit. My free hand drifted to the threads around my arm.

I would wait to attack. You do want their help, after all.

Sure, I snapped back. *Wait until it's too late for backup. Great plan.*

You die, I die, he cautioned. *Trust me.*

Trust him. *Ha!* I trusted his self-preservation, but what was to say he wouldn't simply transfer himself into the next person? He didn't need me specifically—he only needed a body.

It wasn't easy putting myself here. There's no guarantee it would work a second time, so just go in there.

No wonder he'd stuck around when there were stronger creatures to body snatch. Something mindless, even, where he wouldn't need to share headspace.

Nora, he said in exasperation.

Fine, fine. I pulled the lever. Because I was an idiot. And because the Weaver loved the Sandman in his own way. He wouldn't hurt him by hurting me. *Probably* wouldn't. There was always the chance it was like when Katie and I were growing up. *We* could hurt each other, but no one else was allowed.

As the door lifted, a clatter of metal on metal filled the chamber, and I braced myself for whatever came next: arrows, fists, swords. Something was bound to come flying out. The movement intensified, and shadows filled the gap between the floor and the half-lifted door.

"Don't," someone demanded, and everything fell silent.

This is a good sign, right? I asked.

I hope so.

The door came to a stop with a resounding thud. The Hours stood around the room, their hatred thick and cloying. Their hands held weapons—bows, swords, whips, shining metal objects I didn't know the names of. I held my breath and counted all twelve of them which meant I only had to worry about protecting my front.

The Chime shifted at the center, chains clanking. "Lady Nightmare."

The darkness around me flared. *Play it cool,* I reminded myself. I was in charge. I was in power. Throwing my shoulders back, I strode into the room with a hammering heart. "I'm surprised to find you here," I said as calmly as possible. "No luck breaking out or did you decide to be good nightmares for a change?"

"Lady," the Chime said again, his voice strained. His face was more angelic than I remembered. Or maybe it was a matter of not bothering to notice the first time when I had been under duress. There was a faint bronze shimmer to his skin that matched his clothing, and small bells pierced his ears, six on each side. "We—"

"Save it." I gave an exaggerated sigh. "I have a job for you."

The Chime stared. After a long moment, he took hold of his chain. "I cannot leave the clock."

"They can." I gestured at the Hours. They hadn't moved a muscle since I stepped into the room. "And they will."

"We will never take orders from a Dreamer," Three shouted.

"Won't you?" I quirked an eyebrow and, with a smooth slip of a finger, extracted a thread.

Interesting choice, the Weaver mused.

I flicked the thread, and he pushed magic into it. One second, Three was openly defying me from the center of the clock face. The next, when the puff of sulfuric smoke dissipated, she screamed from inside an iron maiden. Her mask shone behind the rectangular opening, her fingers slipping up to the hole. The inner spikes wouldn't emerge unless she tried to escape, which I anticipated happening any moment now.

"Anyone else?" I asked.

They all stared at Three in awed silence. One by one, their masked faces drifted to the other iron maidens now positioned menacingly at their backs. The contraptions were open, ready to snap them up. Two and Seven shifted. I was sure they would seal their own fate by running, but an agonized cry wiped that notion away. Three's armor crunched, giving beneath the sharp spikes. Her scream faded to a whimper, then the only sound was her rasping breaths.

"What would you have the Hours do?" the Chime asked slowly.

"Rowan sent part of her army to a snowy landscape near some ice caves." I rolled my shoulders and tried to downplay the significance. "I don't know which one exactly. You will find them, and you will kill them all without making a scene."

Eleven cleared his throat. "What of Mara?"

I smirked, annoyed. Questioning my orders, questioning my plans...all of that was over. "Take care of it today. I want them gone before I get there."

Walk out, the Weaver said.

I spun on my heel. My orders were given. There was no other reason to stay. No reason except that they hadn't agreed and leaving without any reassurance made me jittery. What if they decided not to obey? What if they decided to follow me from the clock and exact revenge away from the threat of the iron maidens?

"What of Three?" one of them called. "Release her."

A dreadful laugh came from deep inside me. I spared a single, fleeting look over my shoulder and said, "No."

I flipped the lever on my way out, and the door slammed shut behind me. *Any chance this solves my problems with them?*

They've seen enough of your power, the Weaver said thoughtfully. *But unless you kill Mara, I don't imagine it's enough. Honestly, you should probably kill them too.*

I snorted. *There's still time for that.*

Nora? The Weaver's tone changed. Hardened. *They're at the ice caves.*

That's what the Sandman said.

Find him. Now.

Chapter Twenty

The Sandman

Baku lurked at the edge of the Dream Realm, tail swishing in aggravation. My eyes narrowed as I tracked his movements. The chimera had no idea that I knew he was a spy. If he did, I wouldn't be able to feed him false information, but pretending was difficult when we had worked together for so long. If we had ever truly worked together at all. Were we ever true friends? Maybe Baku only came to see me because someone sent him.

"Hungry?" I called from where I stood beneath the brightest star. *Our* spot—Nora's and mine. Apparently, I enjoyed reminiscing about people that wanted to rip me down to nothing. There were so many lies, so much deceit, that it would surprise me more now if someone told the truth. Myself included since I was currently beginning to weave my own web of untruths. "If you want to go hunting, I'll come along. I promised I would meet Nora shortly anyway."

Baku slowed then nodded, and I followed him through the barrier into the Nightmare Realm.

I couldn't come right out and accuse him of treachery. In truth, Baku was always a spy. He passed important information to me for centuries, but was it always complete? There were times he cut off the dreams I read before I was finished, and others when he refused to let me read his dreams at all. I never thought much of it then because everyone deserved their privacy, but now?

Outside the Dream Realm, Baku went straight for Rowan's second army. I wanted to believe it didn't mean he was controlling them himself. Without being able to speak, he couldn't give orders, but that only proved he was indeed working for someone else.

"Have you seen any sign of Mara?" I asked, careful to keep my tone light.

He gave a small shake of his head.

My fingers twitched nervously against my legs. "Halven mentioned seeing her in the west near the vampire farm. Maybe you could take a look later."

He waved his trunk noncommittally.

"I'm sorry I keep asking you for help. This isn't your fight, but there has to be some sign of her," I ventured. How far would I have pressed him before? "Maybe if I read your dreams, I can pick up on something you missed. A clue or a—"

Baku pounced away, lips curling up in disgust, when he eyed me sticking a hand into my satchel.

"Are you mad at me?" I closed my fist gently around the sand in case I needed to use it for self-defense. Against Baku. A thing I never expected to worry about. "If I've done something to upset you, it wasn't intentional."

We stared at one another other, letting the silence speak for us both. Then he took off at lightning speed. His course altered slightly to the right, away from the army, and straight for the ice caves. It was possible that was a coincidence, but not likely. My doubts vanished in a cloud of smoke. Baku was working against me, Nora, and both worlds. There was only danger in denying the truth.

Chapter Twenty-One

Nora

Kail droned on and on about issues that needed my attention when we returned from killing Mara. I only half-listened from almost the moment he opened his mouth. Minor squabbles from miscreants were the absolute least of my problems. Had the Weaver bothered with this nonsense? I doubted it. He probably ate popcorn while he watched them tear each other apart. Got a problem? Don't worry—the Weaver will let you settle it gladiator style. It wasn't a bad idea, really.

Hmm? the Weaver asked as if thinking his name summoned him from whatever dark pit he hid away in. *I stopped listening a long time ago.*

Ditto. I sighed.

He made a noise like clucking his tongue. *I've been thinking.*

I told you twenty times, I'm not going out to find the Sandman. He'll be here soon, and you can tell him whatever revelation you had then. Unless you want to fill me in? Honestly, it was ridiculous that he wouldn't tell me what relevance the ice caves had until everyone was together.

I've been thinking about something else, he clarified.

Oh? I nodded to Kail, so it looked like I was listening. *That's never good.*

Ha. Ha. How easily you forgot the mention of a key.

I didn't forget. It just didn't seem important enough to worry about, considering. "Okay," I agreed without knowing what Kail suggested.

I want to try something.

Absolute pass.

Hear me out, the Weaver urged. *You've seen my memories before, but what if we found one together?*

That was unexpected and rather unnecessary when he could just tell me whatever he wanted me to know. "Got it," I told Kail absently and rapped my fingers on the table. *What's your angle?*

The Weaver grunted, annoyed. *Must I have one? Honestly, Keeper—*

What happened to Nora?

Nora, he clipped. *I'm not sure what the memory is, but I'm more than happy to watch it myself.*

You have to watch your own memories?

I do now, he grumbled. *This arrangement isn't exactly all sunshine and rainbows for me either.*

"Are we almost done?" I asked Kail.

Kail leveled a hard look at me. "All we're doing is waiting for the Sandman, so we might as well sort this out now."

"Why? You want our ducks in a row in case someone kills me?" I joked, but I knew why he was doing this now. He wanted a plan for later because it made him feel as if there would *be* a later.

The muscle in his jaw twitched. "I didn't say that."

Are you joining me or not?

Fine. I leaned back in my seat and motioned for Kail to continue. *Multitasking for the win.*

Lovely.

Darkness clouded my vision almost instantly. I blinked to be sure my eyes weren't closed, though I wasn't sure which was more terrifying—the Weaver controlling my eyelids or being temporarily blinded. Glowing fissures whizzed by. The Weaver hummed a monotone song that was like a hammer to my head. I rubbed my temples against the growing pain.

This is weird, I thought at him.

Ah. A fissure eased to a stop in front of us. *Here we are. After you…*

Kail's voice felt far away, his help even further. Would he notice if this was the Weaver's way of trapping me in the passenger seat? If not, the Sandman would, and he'd be along any time now. I needed to get this over with before Kail noticed my mind was somewhere else completely and freaked out. *Here goes nothing.* I shoved my head into the fissure as I had the other times a memory appeared and waited.

A landscape spread around me with tunnel-like cobwebs spiraling straight up toward the sky. Rose petals shot out of the tops. They were red at first but quickly blackened before hitting the ground where they disintegrated. Footprints marked the flat, ash-covered ground as if it were snow. One set. The Weaver looked around slowly, and cleared his throat.

"Lord," rasped a familiar voice.

"Halven." The Weaver spun around, and the masked nightmare bowed low. "It took you long enough."

Halven straightened. "Forgive me."

The Weaver stepped closer and spoke in a low whisper. "I need you to do something."

"Anything, Lord."

The Weaver held out a fist, and Halven brought his palm up to meet it. "This needs to be permanently lost."

Kail slammed his palms down on the table in front of me, and the fissure snapped shut. His masked face hovered in front of me, eyes flashing violently through colors. "Did you hear what I just said?"

"No." My voice felt lost somewhere between here and there. What did the Weaver give Halven? Why did he want us both to watch the exchange? "Are we done?" I asked again.

"*Are we done?*" His ever-changing eyes narrowed. "Do you have no opinion on the matter? You have an opinion on *everything.*"

I shrugged and shoved myself out of the chair. "Do what you think is best."

Kail lifted his hands to my face and slapped my cheeks between them. "I don't think you want me to do that."

I leaned away from his palms and rolled my eyes. "Fine. Do whatever you think I would tell you to do."

The key, the Weaver blurted.

Let the key go.

Halven had it. The key to the Ever Safe. We have to make sure it's secure.

Every muscle within my body tensed. To give the key to a nightmare, especially one with a brother at Rowan's mercy, was the stupidest way to dispose of something so important to the safety of both worlds.

Halven had it? I sucked in a breath, willing the frustration to stay within a manageable parameter. For half a second, I succeeded. Then I was on my feet. "That's the key you gave him? Seriously?"

Kail startled. "I didn't—"

"Not you," I snarled. "You gave Halven the key to the Ever Safe, and you didn't think that was something I should know?" I snapped at the Weaver.

Obviously, I thought you should know.

"He's been the front man in the search for Mara for months. What if she caught him and tortured the location out of him?" I shrieked, then whipped around to face Kail. "And you. Did you know? Wait—" I held up my hands. "Don't answer that. Where is the key now?"

Kail straightened. "I wish I did know. It would make this entire…*conversation*…a lot more interesting."

Halven never knew what it was. It was of little importance to him— just another job I asked of him in a long line of tasks.

I struggled for breath. Struggled to see straight. To not punch something. Halven was out there looking for Mara all this time with the key *on him*. Alone. And there I was, feeling like the only one who made mistakes. Because mistakes were for rookies.

Breathe, the Weaver reminded me.

I exhaled through my mouth. In through my nose. "Why am I just hearing about this?"

Kail shifted nervously. "Halven wouldn't tell Mara anything." *Ah…*

"*Ah?* So you did know about this?" I ground out. Kail started to reply, but I closed my fingers together, mimicking a shut mouth. "Not. You."

It's possible that I forgot giving it to him, hence the memory, but I've seen it recently…

Kail paused, obviously hesitant to continue. *Tied on Halven's boot.*

"You forgot." That was completely insane. No way could not one, but *two* people, forget where the key to the Ever Safe was. "What's wrong with you people? You act like it's a bike lock we're dealing with here and not the damn apocalypse."

Do you think after millennia, you'll remember everything that happened this year?

"It's kind of hard to forget!" I screamed. My entire life changed this year. The Sandman turned out to be real, I lost friends and family to horrific murders, I killed the Weaver, became the Weaver, abandoned my family, gained a realm…gained darkness and a parasite. A certain…*fondness* for it all and a spark of hatred for myself. No, I wouldn't forget this year. This was the year Nora died and was reborn.

You would be surprised.

"Okay. Okay." I paced the room, fingers digging into my scalp, while Kail looked on, intrigued. "So, he has the key." A nervous laugh burst from my chest. "We need to get it from him and destroy it."

What a novel idea, the Weaver said in a flat voice.

"It's indestructible," Kail whispered. "If it wasn't, they wouldn't have bothered giving it to Halven. The lords would've blown it up themselves."

Of course it was. I covered my face and screamed, attempting to give my frustration an outlet. "Fine. Great. Then what? We hide it somewhere? That worked so well with the knife you and Rowan gave me."

This time there's no Baku to spy and retrieve the key.

"I have an idea." Kail smiled a plastic smile, and I knew his suggestion was going to be the icing on my cake. "We can give it to your sister."

Forget frosting—that was some baking show level fancy fondant.

I whirled on him. "Want to run that by me again?"

Mara was in the Day World when I gave it to Halven…it makes sense since she can't get back there.

"You *would* be on his side," I retorted.

Kail pursed his lips. "Calm down before the vein in your forehead ruptures."

"Don't tell me to calm down!" My throat burned with the words. I bent over, gripping my sides, and dragged in air like it was in short supply. Right, rational. I had to be rational. I closed my eyes and counted to ten. "I want Mara dead, I want *him* out of my head, and I want things to just be *normal* again. Every time I think things can't possibly get worse, they do."

The Sandman will forgive you, the Weaver said with surety.

"Shut up, shut up, *shut up!*" I covered my ears, hunching over. This had nothing to do with the Sandman.

After a long minute, Kail's hand settled on my shoulder. I stiffened but allowed it to stay. "The key will be safe in the Day World. Mara won't be able to get it, and there aren't any nightmares left on that side."

My hands dropped, and I met his gaze. "First, are you sure there's no one left over there? Because I'm not. Maybe everyone *forgot* about some random evil they tossed over the fence into the neighbor's yard. Second, stop bringing my sister into this mess."

"She doesn't seem like the type that's going to let us keep her out of it," he said.

God, I hated him for being right. "Screw you, Kail."

He rolled his neck with a humorless laugh. "My whole life is one big *screw you*. We're giving it to your sister. End of story."

Chapter Twenty-Two

The Sandman

Seeing Nora made my chest ache only slightly more than not seeing her, and slightly less than knowing Baku was a spy for both Rowan and Mare. I couldn't look at her yet, but I felt her. It was as if the entire room was hyper-sensitive to her presence. The air shifted with her every movement, and the silence waited with bated breath for the sound of her voice. I stood near the door to the empty chamber while Nora paced along the far wall about ten feet away. Halven and Kail stood between us, anxiety rippling off them both. I wanted it to be due to the situation, but I knew better. The tension between Nora and me was nearly unbearable.

"So," Kail ventured. "Is there a purpose to this get-together or are we going to stand around all day?"

Nora's lips moved as if she were talking, but no sound left her. At least not until she bent over, hands digging into her abdomen, and dragged in a shallow breath. "The ice caves." She stood upright again, eyes squeezed shut. "The Weaver said that the Ever Safe is beneath the ice caves."

No one moved. No one breathed.

"No. It was in a jungle." I could still remember how rudimentary it was—one of the Weaver's first full landscapes. He created it just to help lure the Ancients in, either out of curiosity or anger at the *blight* we left in their charred world. There were dense trees, sweeping vines, and the violent screams of cicadas, but not much else.

"Apparently, he thought it would be better after Mara broke out to change things," Nora said, her face ghostly white. "Throw her off the scent."

Kail fell against the wall with a bitter laugh, and Halven reached out to steady him. He swatted his brother's hand away. "Welcome to the end of days."

No one replied. What could any of us say? If the Weaver really had altered the jungle into ice caves—and there was no reason for him to lie about it—then Mare already found what she was looking for. If we didn't get there before she found a way into the Ever Safe, everything we did was for nothing.

"And *you*—" Kail seethed to Halven. "You have the key?"

Halven nodded and bent to untie it from his boot. "I didn't know."

Kail snatched it from his brother's hand. "I'll deal with *this* the way it should've been dealt with before."

I stepped forward, heart thumping wildly at the sight of Kail with the key. "Give it to me."

"What do you think I'm going to do, Sandman? Hand it over to the enemy?" He glowered. "After all I've done to keep us alive?"

"I don't trust anyone," I stated. "Especially not you."

Kail opened his mouth to argue, but Nora grabbed his fist where the key was tucked. "Let me have it," she whispered. "You need to give it to someone who can make your plan happen."

"Fine." Kail barred his teeth and relinquished the key to her.

Nora tucked it away in her pocket. "I'm giving it to Katie."

She *wanted* to involve Katie? I couldn't deny it was a good idea, but hadn't she wanted her sister away from all this?

"What about Mara?" Kail asked.

A plan formed in my head, buried beneath the emotional heaviness that lurked there. "Baku won't let us near the ice caves if he thinks we know Mare's there." He was trying to keep us away regardless, and I didn't want to bait him into an outright attack. "I'll leave a false trail for him to follow."

"Wise," Kail agreed, nodding. "I don't want to be eaten."

Nora groaned. "Kail, be constructive or be quiet."

"You want constructive? Is no one going to talk about what happens to the rest of us if the two of you fail?"

"We know what will happen," Nora muttered.

Halven cleared his throat and spoke in a low voice. "If the Ever Safe is opened, nightmares will perish first."

He wasn't incorrect, but it didn't matter who died first. If the safe opened, nightmares died, the realm crumbled, taking the Dream Realm with it, and finally, the Day World. Without night, there could be no day. Without darkness, no light. Each piece of our worlds was a support beam—lose one, and they all fell. There wasn't an alternative sequence of events, unless…I sucked in a shallow breath. Unless there was a contingency plan.

Would it be worth it? If Nora and I couldn't keep the safe closed, would anyone else be able to shut it? After all it took from the Weaver and me the first time…I looked at the threads around Nora's arm as the pieces of my plan coalesced. It was worth a try.

"Give them an army," I said, hardly believing my own suggestion.

Nora took half a step toward me. "Give *who* an army?"

"Them." I motioned to Kail and Halven. "Give them a chance to go down fighting in case we fail."

Halven stiffened while Kail didn't move a muscle. It was a risk, I knew. Giving nightmares an army that they could march against Nora later, against me, was asking for trouble, but it could also get us *out* of trouble. If either of them wanted Nora dead, they had enough opportunity already. Besides, they both seemed to care about Nora, in their own way.

"That's absolutely the *worst* advice I've ever heard," Nora said. "Kail had the Blood Army and look what he did with it."

Kail whirled on her and, suddenly, our tension wasn't the only source of discomfort in the room. "*Rowan* had an army. Not me."

I stared at her chin, not daring to look higher. It seemed like she wouldn't say anything for the longest time, but then she nodded. "Right. You're right." Her fingers drifted to the thread at her wrist. "I'll do it if you promise to get us out of the ice caves should we need assistance."

"Of course," Halven agreed quickly.

If we were stuck in the ice caves, it would be because things went poorly, but if it made her feel better…I only hoped I wasn't setting us up for bigger problems in the future—should we *have* a future. "It's settled then," I said quietly.

Nora sighed. "As long as the Hours are doing what I told them to, Mara's force shouldn't be a problem."

"Sure," Kail said nervously. "As long as they are…"

Nora pulled her hair back and twisted it into a severe bun. "They will, or I'll do a lot worse than locking them in a clock."

A chill ran through me at the easily tossed out implication. I didn't doubt she meant it. How much of that was the Weaver's doing? She had to rule the nightmares with an iron fist, but not around us. Not around *me*.

"There are giant trees full of nests that overlook the ice caves. Meet me there as soon as you can," I said, looking to Nora's boots.

***

When I got back, I found Baku curled up like a cat just outside of the waters' reach. His elephant ears were relaxed against his body and his trunk was snugly tucked between his tiger paws. *Even traitors needed sleep.*

I paused a few feet away and stared. It would be easy enough to end him now if Nora were with me. The knife suddenly weighed a million pounds. Even if it worked without nightmare magic, I couldn't do it. Baku wasn't who I thought he was, but that didn't erase all those years together. He was the only thing that had kept me from crushing loneliness. I wasn't sure I could ever kill him, but if I did, it wouldn't be like this. He would see it coming, and he would understand why.

Now however, it was time for my performance.

"Baku," I called, forcing my voice to sound strained.

The chimera rolled from his side, ears perked, and sand fell from one side of his face. His innocent, dazed expression was a blow.

"Halven thinks Mare moved again." I bent to my knees to refill my satchel. No matter how much I tried, I couldn't remember if he was around when I learned about the ice caves. "He saw her near the ant hill, but soon lost sight of her. She must be hiding inside the colony."

It made sense to hide there. Giant ants could be troublesome, but there were endless places to hide within their tunnels. Baku launched to his feet, uncertainty flashing in his eyes. *Ah, yes.* The first phase of betrayal. Only, it had to be Mare's loyalty he was contemplating. Wheels visibly turned in his head, and it wasn't hard for me to guess his thoughts. Why would she move without telling him? Did something happen in the caves?

"We have a plan," I admitted. The key to a successful lie was keeping to the truth as much as possible. "Nora's making an army to search the tunnels for Mare, and I'll meet her at the palace. Can you stake out the hill? If she leaves, we need to know which direction she goes."

Baku shook the sand from his brindle coat and studied me as if deciding what to do.

I stood, the satchel bursting with sand at my hip, and injected near-panic into my voice. "Please, Baku. I promised to meet Nora, but there's only one way out of that ant hill. We can't lose our best chance."

He nodded slowly but didn't move until I did. I felt his sharp gaze at my back as I raced in the direction of Nora's palace. I caught glimpses of him as he followed me part of the way, running parallel to my path when he should have veered right a long time ago.

As I neared the outskirts of a landscape that bordered the palace, Baku finally turned away. Using as little sand as I could, I used the same technique that lured the Blood Army away from the Rowan trees. *Just in case.* A replica of myself continued forward, carrying the name of Baku's spymaster, while I slunk away in the opposite direction. I held my breath, waiting to hear the sound of Baku's footfalls behind me, but after none came, I bolted.

Chapter Twenty-Three

Nora

Thread flowed through my fingers so fast, it burned. Treadles clacked against one another. My breath was shallow. Baku was working with Mara. *Mara.* Each time the thought passed through my mind, it was like a fresh slice of a knife. It made sense, I supposed, seeing as both he and Mara were *other* in a world of dreams and nightmares, but it didn't excuse him. Weaseling his way into the Sandman's affections only to turn around and use that closeness, that trust, to spy…

You're taking this rather personally.

"It *is* personal." I jerked the loom too hard, fraying the thread. "If you betray the Sandman, you betray me."

You betrayed him.

I winced. It was true twice over, but it hadn't been intentional. Or maybe it was intentional, but I never set out with that goal. It just…*happened*. I felt cornered. I shoved away from the loom. "No one asked you, Weaver."

"These private conversations with your predecessor make me extremely uncomfortable," Kail said.

"No one asked you either," I shot at him where he stood against the wall.

He rolled his eyes. "I don't know why you're so surprised about Baku. Keep your enemy close and whatnot."

"What does that say about you?"

Kail simply smirked.

Should we not be asking Baku's motives?

My breath stuck for a moment. It felt different now that the Sandman acknowledged it as the truth. I couldn't pretend it might all be in my head, or that I was making something out of nothing. "His motives are that he's a heathen nightmare, obviously," I said in a huff. "Evil and calculating and eager to mess with everyone."

You make it sound like those are bad things.

"You…" Before I could take the bait, a thought hit me—*really* hit me—and I spun to look at Kail. "Baku isn't a nightmare."

Kail scoffed. "You think the Weaver would create something that ate the rest of us?"

I stared at him, my face stoic. "Yes."

You wound me, Keeper.

"The Weaver wasn't always…" Kail pinched his lips tight together in a grimace. "Nevermind. He doesn't need me inflating his ego."

"Definitely not," I agreed.

"You know how you feel about your nightmares," he continued. "Would you create something like Baku?"

He knew I wouldn't. "He's an Ancient too? That would explain why he's working with Mara." There was another creature like him now, so he wasn't alone, and if he helped Mara open the Ever Safe, he never would be again.

"Figuring that out just now, eh? Anyway, I think you can stop now." Kail waved a hand at the loom. "You'll never be able to create this many nightmares without passing out, and the Sandman said to meet him in a few hours. It's been at least seven."

I stared at the pile of threads heaped in front of me. The newest additions to my growing army. Undoubtedly loyal and ready to go in case Kail needed them to pull our sorry butts out of whatever predicament we found ourselves in. Ice caves didn't exactly scream prime fighting conditions when Mara could corner us as easily as we could corner her.

When the Sandman suggested letting Kail have command over a nightmare army, I thought I entered the twilight zone. I mean, it was *Kail,* for one, and a huge risk regardless. If Kail was waiting for the perfect moment to strike, this would be it. He'd have the manpower and, after fighting with Mara, weakened prey. With enough power, he could try forcing me to reunite him with Halven even though I promised…*keep your enemies close.* Baku had played his cards well enough to fool everyone, and Kail was undoubtedly more conniving.

Did I have enough nightmares? Yes; but I had to delay the inevitable somehow.

"Right." I slipped from the bench and gathered the threads in my arms.

It was time. We needed to meet the Sandman west of the Ever Safe doors, far from where our enemy made camp. While the Hours kept them distracted, we would sneak into the caves. Before that, I had to deliver the key to the Dream Realm.

"Chin up, Lady. You'll stop her," Kail said with certainty.

That was probably the best motivational speech I was going to get, but I appreciated him trying. I hugged the unborn nightmares to my chest. "Guess we should get this show on the road."

Kail nodded solemnly and took the pile of thread from my arms.

"Chivalry isn't dead after all," I said with a forced smile. There were so many nightmares to make, so many pieces of myself—of the Weaver—to give away. But this was a long-term plan. A failsafe for the realm and, in turn, both worlds.

A long-term plan with short-term deadlines, the Weaver commented.

That's why I have you, I quipped. He didn't get to second guess the plan in the final hour when he hadn't bothered to come up with an alternative before now, and he could've. I was positive he had more devious plots left in him than cheetahs had spots.

I followed Kail down the Keep's outer staircase and through the courtyard surrounding the Keep. My bottom lip was raw from where I anxiously gnawed on it, but I couldn't stop as I exited the palace. The sound of the pixies sliding bolts into place reverberated in my ears. It wasn't exactly *home,* but it was the closest thing I had.

Which is why we must defend it.

I blew out a breath. *Stop being so…*

Contrary? the Weaver offered. *It's called being realistic. Very few things are ever all or nothing.*

"Lady." Halven stepped up from behind me and inclined his head.

I quickly patted the secret pocket sewn inside my shirt to feel the press of the key. It was like carrying air, an impossibility if one didn't consider magic, but the shape of it still dug into my skin beneath my new clothes.

Each layer of fabric the Doll Maker used for my battle outfit was as thin as paper. The darkest of blues pressed against my skin with the lightest blue—nearly white—over all eight varying shades. Despite the whimsical feel, the cut was fiercer than I was. Jagged, rough lines, raw edges, and decorative, studded gold buttons. The left sleeve wrapped around my arm like a bandage, the fabric darkening back to the deepest shade at my wrist, while my right arm was bare, save for my threads. The ends of them thrummed against my pulse points on my wrist and at the soft hollow of my neck where they laid like a choker. It paired perfectly with shimmering black pants made of thick, flexible fabric. I had returned these clothes back when they were first sent, or I thought I had before Kail produced them this morning. *They should fit you now,* he had told me as he sauntered away.

They always *fit.* But that wasn't what Kail meant.

I drew from his confidence in me, and it brushed up against the budding kernel of my own. *Okay, Nora. You're doing okay.* The Sandman and I were going to do this. We were going to kill Mara.

You two are quite the dynamic duo. Maybe now that you're both on the same page, you won't screw this up.

Seriously?

His sigh breezed through me. *I'm tired, Keeper.*

Yeah, but that's the gloomiest encouragement I've ever heard. Do you even want me to succeed?

Take it or leave it, he said, grumpier than I'd ever heard him. For that reason alone, I would take it.

Someone had already moved the other threads from my art room—most likely Halven given they were separated into neat piles. I scooped up the end of one, letting the rest trail on the ground. This was too many…*what was I thinking?* Though some were future landscapes which needed to be stored for later use…

Kail shifted in front of me and caught my gaze. In his, I saw conflict. Each flickering color said something different. Sorrow, worry, eagerness, determination, affection. I looked away before any of it could rock my decisions. Kail needed to think I would make it back for me to believe it, as ridiculous as that felt. Apparently, I still had more work to do on trusting myself.

"You might want to move," I told him, and he stepped back to stand beside Halven.

I coaxed the first nightmare free and snapped the thread. An iron rhinoceros emerged, held together with shifting panels, her nostrils steaming. The scent of burning wool filled the courtyard as another nightmare followed. And another and another. The sky darkened with sulfuric smoke, and my muscles begged for a break.

Nora, came the Weaver's voice. Gentle. Wary. *Let me finish for you.*

"No way." I wasn't going to give him permission to wear my body like a costume.

I don't need your permission, he hedged.

"Don't even think about it."

I can only help so much this way.

It will have to be enough, I snapped.

Then I waited.

Waited for the swooping sensation of him ignoring my wishes. The fading. The loss of control. I made as many nightmares as I could in those few precious moments, but when nothing happened—when nothing even *tried* to happen—my arms dropped heavily to my sides.

What? he asked, unamused. *Did you* want *me to force my way to the surface? I daresay that it isn't fun for either of us.*

For either of us? It sucked for me, but it seemed like he enjoyed it enough. Especially when he was firmly in control.

It's rather like forcing myself into a latex suit two sizes too small, but let's stay on task, yes? Do you want me to do it or not?

I looked out at the array of newly created nightmares—the birds of prey, the hobgoblins, the possessed farm equipment, and things with no known names—then down to the remaining piles of thread. The Sandman expected us soon, and there was still my side quest with the key to take care of.

"Fine," I said reluctantly. "Do it."

There was an immediate pull at my center. Brisk and painful.

Are you sure?

"I said so, didn't I?"

Then relax. When I didn't, the Weaver added a withering, *Please.*

I took a deep breath and let it out through my mouth. Kail and Halven were moving about the crowd, organizing the new nightmares into formation. Would they notice if the Weaver tried anything sketchy? He already attacked Kail once…

A moment later, my concerns didn't matter. The Weaver was pushing too hard for me to concentrate on *what ifs,* so I exhaled again, letting it knock down my defenses. The Weaver slithered by them and right up to the surface with a slimy feeling that made me shudder. He didn't bother to comment on my repulsion, nor did he try to sabotage anything. No, the Weaver simply took up where I left off, and I watched my body move in response to his commands.

Magic bubbled. Fizzled. Stretched. I felt myself drifting further back the longer he worked. As he strained. We were nearly finished with the usable threads, but what strength would we have left over? The Sandman said we were of equal strength, but it depended on where we allocated our power. I was giving mine to the nightmares—they would fight for me while I regained the depleted magic—but *I* needed to fight Mara. Not them.

Weaver, I called weakly. *We have enough.* My thoughts slammed into something solid, and I spun around with a gasp. A clear box brimming with black swirling tendrils burned through the darkness. *What is this?*

"That, Nora dear, is why I continued to call you *Keeper* after the dream was gone."

It shook me to hear him speak with my voice. *What?* I assumed he called me Keeper out of habit, or maybe because I 'kept' him. *Explain.*

"I couldn't let you play with *all* our magic before you learned to control yourself."

My lips parted, and I pressed up against the box. *So much.* There was so much. What I used all this time was a mere raindrop in a thunderstorm. If I had access to this much power, we could've stopped Mara the first time. The Sandman had an equal amount? He was holding back way more than I had ever imagined, all in the name of maintaining balance.

"The power you used in the globe is not the same power that's in there," he said with a sense of glee.

Then he let go. The sudden, unexpected control of my body hit like a tidal wave, and I fell to my knees into the grass. "Jerk," I croaked.

"Nora!" Kail flew to my side and skidded across the lawn to grip my shoulders. "What happened?"

Give yourself a few moments. You won't feel tired for long.

"Nothing," I breathed. Then, to the Weaver, *you're not getting out of an explanation.*

"But—"

"No *buts*." I forced myself to my feet. "Get Halven over here."

He hesitated. "Right. You have to take the key to the—"

"No." Taking the key to Katie wasn't all I had to do before I left. I fought back a smirk. "I'm going to give you what you asked for."

His chest expanded with a deep, silent breath. "Now?"

"Well, I am walking off to potential doom and all that, but if you'd rather wait—"

"Halven!" he screamed.

I laughed a real, true laugh. There was enough magic left inside me, box or no box, to make good on my promise. Kail deserved it. As did Halven. Sure, I wasn't exactly happy about the army thing, but they'd already done plenty for me.

Halven appeared next to me. "Lady?"

"You still want to be put back together, right?" I placed my hand on his shoulder. "This might be our last shot."

Halven stiffened beneath my touch. "No, Lady."

"No?" My brows shot up. "But I thought…"

"It won't be our last chance."

Kail shoved between us. "What are you talking about, brother?"

"I meant to be reassuring," Halven clarified.

"Yes, yes," Kail gripped his brother's hand and tugged him closer. "All is fine and dandy. Let's do this."

Eager, aren't they, the Weaver thought.

Why wouldn't they be? They were kept apart and in pain for years. "It…might hurt," I said because I had no idea if the process would be painless. It had hurt them coming apart, and I *hoped* it hurt Rowan when I put her back into her tree.

"It's worth it," Kail insisted

I reached out to them with closed eyes. Their knots, different yet the same, throbbed inside their chests. Unlike with Rowan, I saw everything perfectly. The frayed edges, hanging limp and grey, and the spark that traveled through each one until those decaying ends flared to life. The threads reached for each other. Tugged and stretched along the bridge I created until, with one final, blinding flash of gold, there was only one knot.

I stepped back, my body aching as if I had a fever deep in my bones and cracked my eyes open. One pair of boots stood before me. Matte black. *It worked.* I beamed. *It worked!* My eyes were fixed on those boots so unlike Kail's worn pair or Halven's ridiculous, court jester style shoes. What were they…or was he…now?

My eyes trailed up fitted black pants, the flare of Kail's trench coat missing. Bare hands, the same warm brown tone I was used to, tugged the bottom of a red shirt up. Crimson lines snaked over his skin in the same irregular pattern that decorated Halven's coat, the same pattern that seemed to scar Kail's abdomen before. The astonished laugh was half Kail, half Halven's rasp. No longer a strained sound, but rougher, more masculine.

Finally, I gathered the courage to look at his face. The long beak was no more. The mask now hugged his nose with a gentle curve . Instead of white, the half mask was decorated with the same black and red design from Halven's Venetian mask. Only it wasn't black and red for long. The red quickly morphed to purple, then blue, yellow, green, while his eyes were two orbs absent of any color but black. On his head, sat a large black hat. The brim was smaller than Halven's, less ostentatious, but more mysterious.

I didn't know how to react or what to think. Maybe it was because I had gotten used to them, but he was a hundred times more intimidating like this…more…*nightmarish*. Until he smiled. It was a beautiful thing full of Halven's kindness and Kail's swagger. "Hello," I said, matching his smile. "And you are?"

"Kail," he said quickly. "We were always Kail."

I folded my arms and pretended to study him. "I suppose this body will do."

Kail held his arms out as if to ask *'what's wrong with it?'* "It's my natural form."

"Yes," I agreed. "It's yours. Unless you betray me."

"Lady—"

I held up a hand. "I'll trust the Halven part of you not to use *an army* against me."

"Only to save you," he promised with more sincerity than I expected.

"Good." I patted him on the shoulder and turned on my heel. "Then you know what to do."

When I was almost out of earshot, Kail whispered. "Good luck, Nora."

***

"Please be here," I whispered at the edge of the Sandman's domed barrier. If Katie wasn't asleep, we would need a lightning-fast backup plan because the Sandman was too occupied to Day

Walk and find her. I hesitated outside of the barrier. The magic emanated from it, tingling against my skin in warning. The Weaver wasn't meant to be in the Dream Realm, but how I longed for it. The stars, the sand, the luminescent water. Memories that made up so much of the last five years, but I wanted the beach to be here tomorrow so today, I had to do my job.

My hand slipped past the glowing barrier, the magic zap-zap-zapping like tiny electrical currents. I jumped the rest of the way through and was instantly surrounded by the familiar scent of lilac and fresh air. It was almost cloying, but I still gulped it down. The scent was game boards drawn in the sand and fantastical tales of legends, known and unknown. Math homework gone unfinished when the Sandman said he had no idea what x equaled and *why were there letters in math anyway?* A thousand dancing, swirling, twisting dreams given life. Seeing the Sandman's face for the first time. Leaving this place for the last time. All of that and more.

My gaze automatically drifted up to the sky to find the brightest star. It pulled me forward as if my feet weren't my own. Slowly, slowly, I inched across the beach from the far side until the water became visible. It was every bit as majestic as I remembered, but my focus unexpectedly zeroed in on something else. A tall, sand-made sunflower stood in our spot, staring up at the sky, petals gleaming, and my heart shattered right there on the beach.

"Hey, Nora," Katie said from behind me. "What are you doing here? I thought you couldn't come because you messed up the beach or whatever?"

I jumped and spun around, hand over my racing heart. "How long has that been here?"

"What? The flower? As long as I've been coming. Why?"

"No reason." *Every reason.* It was still there which meant either the Sandman still cared about me or he hadn't bothered to get rid of it yet. A pit formed in my stomach. "You're right. I shouldn't be here, so I'll get right to it. I need you to take something back to the Day World to keep safe."

"What is it this time?" she asked, curious.

I opened my mouth to tell her about the key, but the words stuck as I contemplated her question. "What do you mean *this time?*"

"First the dream, now this. I'm not a safety deposit box."

My world spun. *She couldn't mean…* "*You're* the new Dream Keeper?" I blurted.

Her hands rose between us in surrender. "Calm down there, killer. Didn't the Sandman tell you?"

"Does it *sound* like he told me?" I asked with dismay. "He's supposed to be *protecting* you. He promised to keep you out of all of this."

"Right." Katie rolled her eyes. "I'm pretty sure the one he's protecting is you. The rest of the world comes second."

That was a lie—the balance came first—but he had promised me. *He promised.* Katie wasn't supposed to get involved in any Night World business. Instead, the Sandman walked her right to my door and had the audacity to get upset with me for holding back information? At least I tried to tell him about the Weaver.

You're about to involve your sister with the key, the Weaver chimed in.

That's different, I shot back. *I didn't put anything in her head. All she has to do is stick the key in a drawer or melt it down.*

"Everything okay?" Katie touched my arm. "You look a little pale."

"I'm peachy," I answered through my teeth. I dug the key from my pocket and held it out to her. "Take this key back with you and hide it somewhere. Anywhere."

She plucked it from my outstretched hand and turned it over. "What's it for?"

"I'm going to err on the side of caution and say *don't ask, don't tell.* Just keep it on your side of the barrier."

"But—"

"Please," I begged.

Katie drew in a slow breath, closed her fingers around the key, and lunged at me. I didn't have time to move before her arms wrapped around me in a tight hug. "I love you."

"I love you too." I gingerly returned the hug. Katie was a lot of things, but most importantly, she was my sister. "I'm really sorry about all of this."

She squeezed a little harder. "I know you are."

"I can't come home again," I said carefully. "Ever."

Katie swallowed hard. "Lucky for me, I know where you live so you'll never get rid of me."

Except one day, Katie would grow old and die. Decades from now, hopefully, but what was that to someone like me? We would have to make every day count. And if I didn't make it back from killing Mara, she had to stay away. From here *and* the Nightmare Realm, for as long as they stood.

"Don't just waltz into the Nightmare Realm, okay? I never want you to get hurt because of me again." The sand shifted beneath my boots, disintegrating from the prolonged contact. "I have to go, but I'll see you soon."

Katie pulled away and held up the key. "I'll take care of this."

"Thank you."

I gave my sister a small smile and spared another glimpse at the sunflower before leaving them both behind.

Chapter Twenty-Four

The Sandman

The Hours were methodical. I watched them work from the giant eagle's nest on the other side of the ice caves, pleased they were taking their assignment seriously. A death cry carried across the landscapes followed by a shifting of the army. They moved in a confused, frantic fashion, rallying around the death, or so it appeared from this distance. The Hours kept the panic at a slow burn—a benefit of the nightmares' mindless nature—so I doubted Mare knew anything was wrong yet.

I expected Nora to be here by now, but I was confident she would come. Soon, I hoped, before the Ancient grew suspicious. Or Baku. Kail's army would stay far enough away that I wouldn't be able to see it, even from this height. Instead, I kept my eyes peeled for a single figure. Nora would be coming from the direction where cut logs gave way into towering trees.

One of the green and black speckled eggs in the nest rolled up against my leg. I shoved it away and moved a few of the loose sticks to form a barrier between the two unhatched nightmares. I doubted they were ever meant to hatch, but still, the way the other eagles watched me from their own nearby nests let me know they wouldn't hesitate to protect them. The only thing likely holding them back was the fact that I vaporized the owner of this one.

A shadow wove between neatly stacked, chopped logs below. I leaned over the edge of the nest and squinted. My heart ricocheted against my chest. *Nora.* She shone as bright as the sun, as dark as pitch, and my anger burned away like a flame to paper. The Lady of Nightmares never seemed so fitting a title as it did in this moment.

Nora was an enigma—a being made of Day and Night, of light and dark, and she glowed with them both. She moved languidly, unafraid of any nightmares lurking nearby, and it finally hit me. *Rule by fear,* Kail taught her.

And she did.

She could walk as fearlessly as she did. At the palace, hearing her threaten the Hours worried me, but now I understood. She had indeed become a lady with kindness in her heart and steel in her soul. I had to make things right with her before we took on Mare.

I slid down the tree, guided by sand. Nora must've seen me because when I landed on the pine-covered ground, she was waiting. "Any trouble?" I asked at the sight of her pinched expression.

She shrugged silently and refused to look at me. Was it because I hadn't looked at her in the palace? My brows lowered. No, she wasn't that petty—but there was something bothering her. Judging by the severe clenching of her jaw, it was anger fueling whatever this was.

"Nora?" I asked. "What happened? Did Kail—"

She huffed. "Kail? What would Kail do?"

"Well…" Confusion settled in. "You gave him an army, right?"

"It was your idea," she snapped, stepping closer. Her gold eyes blazed when she finally looked up. "But, no. Kail hasn't done anything. You on the other hand…"

I sucked in a breath. "Me?"

"I asked you to leave Katie *out of this world*." She jabbed a finger into my chest. "And you made her the new *Dream Keeper*?"

Oh. That. Given everything else that happened, I'd almost forgotten Nora didn't know. "Nora, I—"

"You had the audacity to get mad at me, to walk away from *us*, because I didn't have a chance to tell you about the Weaver—even though I tried to tell you and I would have—when you did this? To my *sister*? You broke your promise to keep her safe twice, but somehow *I'm* the bad guy?" Scarlet colored her cheeks, tears brimmed at her eyes, and she took a ragged breath. "I've done a lot of things I shouldn't have, and you always forgave me. I would've forgiven you too."

"Would have?" I asked desperately.

"It doesn't matter." Her shoulders jerked in a shrug. "When we're done here, you can leave me to my own destruction."

Suddenly, I was two inches tall. I was in shock on the ship, allowing my emotions to rule me, when I said those things. They were words of anger, nothing more, and I had every right to be mad. It would've taken me time to process Nora's revelation, well-deserved time, but I loved her more than I loved anything.

"You're right," I croaked. "We kept things from each other, both of us."

Nora's lip quivered. "She's my *sister*."

"I know." Before I had time to worry that she would push me away, I crushed her to my chest. "I'm sorry, Nora. She was the safest choice, but I'll move it to someone else. I swear I will."

"Forget it. This isn't the time," she mumbled into my shirt. "Let's call a truce until Mara is dead."

She was right. This was absolutely the worst time, but it could be our last if anything went wrong. I lifted her chin and wiped escaped tears off each cheek. "Can I kiss you?"

Nora leaned up on her toes and pressed her lips to mine. It said all the things we didn't have time to say, most importantly that we were sorry and still loved each other. The kiss didn't last long—*couldn't* last long—but it was enough to put me at ease. Nora set her forehead on my chest with a relieved sigh before stepping back.

"Ready?" she asked.

I took the knife from my belt and turned it over in my hand, feeling its capacity for destruction. It scared me. The last time I used it, worlds were cleaved in two. "As I'll ever be," I admitted.

***

Gusts of frigid air cut through my clothes. It swirled out of the round opening to the ice caves, whistling in a way that seemed to speak. *Come inside*, it beckoned. *Bask in my splendor.*

It was beautiful in a way that only made it more dangerous. The grotesque nightmares held no surprise when they released their fearsome attacks, but the pretty ones? The landscapes, the creatures, that calmed Dreamers before snapping them up with hidden horrors…those were the ones to look out for because you never knew what to expect.

Nora inched closer until our arms brushed. I ran a finger along her jaw, memorizing her profile. "We can do this," I whispered.

She nodded, but her focus remained on the dark opening. Up close, the ice was a brilliant aquamarine with ripples just beneath the surface. It was as smooth as glass up close and, from a distance, as reflective as a mirror. Deep inside the opening, the ice appeared to glow from within, but from where we stood, it was cloaked in shadow. I took the first step, knowing it was that or stand at the opening all day, but I didn't mind. Let me be the one to step into a trap.

When nothing jumped out at us or scurried off to spread the news of our arrival, it only felt more wrong. We crept further and further toward the glowing interior, our steps nearly silent on the icy ground. I scanned the ceiling to be sure nothing hung over our heads, and that the dips and curves of the tunnel were clear of danger—at least, any visible danger. Beside me, Nora took in our surroundings as if in slow motion, her luminous eyes absorbing the entirety of the cave mouth. I was too afraid to speak and have my words travel to Mare's ears, so when her eyes finally landed on me, I offered a reassuring smile. She returned it and silently pointed forward.

On and on we went, slowly choosing which branches to take. Right, right, left, right, straight…on and on the system went with nothing noticeably amiss. The glow of the caves stayed in front of and behind us, trapping us in a bubble of semi-darkness. Another left. Straight again. It was quickly becoming clear this was going to take too long, and we needed to reassess. I slowed to a stop and ran a hand down my face.

Unfortunately, Nora must not have noticed because she slammed into my back a moment later. Her loud gasp filled the tunnel as her feet flew out from under her. She landed on the slippery ice and slid a few feet away. The soft *thump* of the impact echoed around us. And echoed and echoed. I winced, not daring to move, and waited. Nora stared at me, wide-eyed, not breathing.

Seconds ticked by, minutes perhaps, but nothing happened. Nora eased to her feet and mouthed *sorry*. I wasn't convinced we were in the clear yet and gave her a terse smile. Something had heard that, without doubt. Nora took small steps back to my side and rubbed at what had to be sore palms from trying to catch her fall.

She wasn't the only thing to move. Within the glossy surface of the walls, at the edge of the lit area, there was a flutter of white fabric. I sucked in a breath, pulse racing, just as Mare materialized behind Nora.

"There you are, darlings."

Chapter Twenty-Five

Nora

My entire body quivered at the sound of Mara's voice. She sounded stronger with the way her voice bounced off the walls. When I spun around, my chest heaved at the sight of her. Her hair was matted and the shift she wore a tattered mess, but everything else about her seemed fiercer than when I last saw her. The bones of her legs were visible still, but now muscle surrounded them, her face was now full, and eyes no longer sunken. *How?* It wasn't that long ago I saw her in the clock tower.

The Ever Safe, the Weaver said cautiously. *She must be feeding off its energy somehow.*

My eyes widened. *Can she do that?*

"When you began picking off the nightmares outside, I knew it would only be a matter of time before you came yourselves." Mara trailed her sharp nails along the ice, leaving white trails across the glossy surface. "We can do this a number of ways. You could give me the key—"

The Sandman let out a harsh growl. "You're *not* opening the gates."

"Or I can kill you and take it," she finished.

"Yeah, okay," I said before either of them could squeeze in another word. "We aren't doing the whole threatening conversation bit. You're not going to give up, we're not going to give up, so let's just get this over with."

Mara snarled wordlessly. "Eager to die, Lady? I can get back in without the key. It's just more difficult."

"The key is in the only place you'll never get it, so all this—" I motioned between us, ignoring the second half of her proclamation, "is pointless."

"I was wrong. You aren't useful to me," she roared, launching herself at us before she finished speaking.

Her blows were fueled by rage, but they were no less precise. It was only thanks to the Sandman's quick reflexes that we both managed to avoid her nails swiping toward our faces. He blasted her back with a sand-made bowling ball to the chest and unsheathed the knife.

The power slammed into me like a wrecking ball, and I stumbled back into the wall. A giant fish stared out of the ice beside my head with red eyes and rows upon rows of needle-like teeth. A small scream fell from my lips before I realized it was frozen solid. Mara's hiss drew my attention away.

Sand circled the Ancient. Stabbing, cutting, gripping, but Mara continued to lash out. The Sandman slashed with the knife, but never quickly enough. He needed help. If I could immobilize her, this would be over in seconds.

Delegate! the Weaver screamed as I flew forward. *Delegate!*

I drew a thread from my wrist and created a large Venus fly trap. Its roots scrambled to find a patch of dirt to dig into, and it flexed a giant blue and green mouth. A lock of Mara's hair must've touched one of the hair triggers when she leapt away from the sand, and the trap slammed shut on her shoulder, the rest of her body dangling between its blades.

Stupid plant, the Weaver grumbled.

Mara shrieked, and the Sandman drove the knife toward her chest. I held my breath and braced for the impact. But the flytrap instinctively flung its head upward and attempted to suck Mara in further. The knife hit empty air.

Terrible choice.

"If you have a better plan, be my guest," I fumed.

Mara's hand emerged from one side of the leathery plant, clear liquid dripping to the floor. The nightmare opened its mouth, dropping its prey, and flailed until it lay still on the ground. The Sandman spun, trying to take out our enemy before she regained her footing. I took a single step with a new thread ready between my fingers.

Don't you dare go over there with him swinging that knife around, the Weaver said in a hard voice.

He was right. The Sandman was acting like a man possessed. His movements were panic-driven and messy, while Mara's were made of pure determination. If I got in the way, or if Mara threw me in his path, I was a goner. We needed to use the knife together, so I wasn't doing much good over here by myself.

I tossed a nightmare out as a distraction. A ten-foot yeti covered in white fur hunched over to keep his head from scraping against the ceiling. Thick spittle rained down on both Mara and the Sandman, and there was a split second of terror when I wasn't sure who the yeti would attack—the Sandman or

Mara. If the Sandman was too badly injured, he would disappear to his realm, leaving me here alone. A huge *hell no.*

I had to do my part. I placed my palms on the wall and tracked the knot belonging to the ice caves. My breath was ragged, my palms sweating. I had to be exact. And Mara had to stop moving. *Oh God, oh God.* I was going to miss. I was going to—

There, the Weaver barked. *Hurry.*

I plucked at the piece of thread he indicated without a second thought and launched myself at the frozen wall now blocking the middle of the tunnel. Inside, Mara was frozen mid-attack. Nails out. Teeth bared. Behind her, the yeti pounded against the thick ice with little effect.

"Nice move," the Sandman wheezed. He stretched his back, fists pressing into his lower vertebrae. "Ready?"

Did he even have to ask? "Ready."

He held the knife with his left hand and wrapped my right around his. Quickly, he placed the knife just above Mara's heart, then positioned his other palm at the end of the knife. "I'll use sand to push it through the ice," he informed me. Sand swirled around his hand a moment later, glowing blue. He brought it away, readying to slam the blade straight though to its target when something body slammed the yeti into the wall. Blood streaked across the clear surface as he slid to the ground, lifeless.

The Sandman's hand hovered, and my heart nearly gave out. "Do it," I urged.

His hand moved in what felt like slow motion. Closer. Closer. The tip dug into the ice. One more second and—

The ice exploded.

Baku's tusks tore through the wall, sending us both flying back amid hunks of ice. The knife clattered out of the Sandman's hand. It slid down the tunnel along with us. Baku dug his claws deep into the ice floor and snarled. I knew he was strong—no one would fear him if he wasn't and the Weaver would've ended him a long time ago.

Fifty-fifty shot back then, he glowered. *But now? End him.*

I wasn't sure if *could* kill him. He had burst through a three-foot-thick wall of ice like it was a banner at the start of a football game. Mara now stood behind him, shaking clumps of ice from her hair.

"Sandman?" I breathed.

He stared at Baku as if he'd never truly seen him before. I supposed he hadn't. "Baku, what are you doing?" It wasn't a question, but a plea. "If she lets the Ancients out, they'll destroy everything."

Baku's lips curled in disgust.

"That's the point," Mara stated with an air of superiority. "To end the worlds and get back to *my* version. When things were dark and violent, and everyone *liked* it that way. When *we* were the only living things to walk a dead, scorched earth."

Worse than the nightmares who needed fear to survive, worse than the Weaver who killed with warped purpose, the Ancients wanted to destroy for the fun of it. Something told me it wouldn't be a quick, painless death for anyone.

Least of all us, the Weaver chimed in.

The last thing on my mind was *us.* It was Katie. It was my mom and Paul. Kail. The people depending on us, even though not all of them knew it. I scrambled to my feet and scurried for the knife. Without it, this was over. All of it.

"No!" the Sandman cried.

His yell echoed off the smooth walls, echoed down to my bones, but I didn't dare look back. Instead, I dove for the knife, hard pebbles of ice digging into my stomach and chest, and my fingers closed around the handle a second before Mara's foot came down. I ground my teeth against the pain of what was surely five broken knuckles.

With my free hand, I pulled a thread from my wrist, quick as lightning, and flicked it without bringing the nightmare out. Then I drove the needle-sharp thread into the top of her foot. It went straight through, protruding from her calloused sole, and into my hand trapped underneath. I swallowed a cry when she shrieked and lost her balance on the ice, toppling over, taking the thread with her.

The Sandman dragged me to my feet. Blood flowed into one of his eyes from a gash in his forehead.

"Baku?" I asked.

"Gone."

I wasn't sure if he meant gone as in *gone* or gone as in dead, but I had little time to dwell on it. The Sandman held a hand out and sand shot from his satchel. With a snap of his fingers, the sand circled Mara and turned to thick, white glue. She clawed at it, unable to tear it apart. Unable to escape. I fought the urge to cry. It would be done. *Done.*

The Sandman covered my broken hand with his and together, we slammed the knife straight into Mara's chest. She gasped, eyes bulging. Blood bubbled from between her lips, and she writhed against the hilt of the knife. We withdrew the blade. The Sandman slid it back into its sheath, and I fell to me knees to watch her die.

The sand fell away from Mara's body, leaving her sprawled and bleeding on the ice. Each breath was tattered and wet. Her eyes…they were as bright as ever. Not dull. Not near death. I shifted back to my feet and leaned toward the Sandman.

"We should stab her again," I suggested.

A few times, perhaps, the Weaver added.

"Fools." The blood garbled Mara's voice. "I was made from the world, and it will take the world to end me."

No. No, no, no. This wasn't right. This was supposed to *work.*

"Quickly," the Sandman said, grabbing Mara's wrist. "We'll take her to the Day World while she's weak. She won't be able to heal there."

Yes. It was better than nothing. I lunged at the idea, at Mara—but my hand met ice. The Sandman fell forward at the sudden disappearance of Mara's body. Her laugh echoed behind us, chilling me more than the ice caves ever could.

"Hurry!" I shouted. Mara was wounded—she had to be easier to catch while weakened. "We can still—"

The tunnel collapsed with a mighty roar right over the yeti's corpse. The ice fell in sheets. Jagged shards splintered up from the ground and icicles dangled precariously overhead.

Like hell, I growled to myself. Mara wasn't going to trap us in here and run off. I placed my uninjured hand on the nearest wall and snatched the knotted thread. All it would take was the squeeze of my fist and the entire landscape would die.

I wouldn't.

Why not? I snapped back.

It's ice, Nora. When it dies, it will either, A: melt. There's miles of it, so getting washed away is actually counterproductive. Or, B: it will collapse on your pretty little head.

"Crap," I groaned.

The Sandman held the knife out in front of him as if he'd never seen it before.

I stormed back to where the red-eyed fish stared out at us and placed my palm over the thin veneer of ice that separated us.

It was a quick fix, turning its body temperature up until the ice melted around it. It twitched inside its own personal bubble of water. "Follow Mara," I told it, then turned back to the Sandman. "Please tell me we have another backup plan."

His violet eyes churned as he looked helplessly at me. "I do."

Chapter Twenty-Six

Nora

The Sandman's voice went through me like an electric shock. I knew…I *knew* whatever he said next wouldn't be good. "Nevermind," I said and held up my hands to silence him. "I'll come up with something. Just give me a minute."

"Nora." This time his voice didn't tremble. "It's not enough. Us—you and me—we aren't enough like this."

We had to be enough. If we weren't, who was? There was a way to stop Mara—there was always a way. No problem was unsolvable. "We'll make it work," I said, pacing. "We'll…find where she snuck out of the Ever Safe, shove her back inside, and seal it off."

"It's already sealed," the Sandman said quietly. "Why do you think she hasn't used it again?"

Okay. I scowled and twisted my hands together. "Then we'll chop her up and put the pieces in different corners of the Night World."

The Sandman eased up to my side and placed one hand over my swollen knuckles. "The Weaver and I were never fully good or bad, dream or nightmare, before we banished Mare. We weren't balanced by one another, but together we had equal parts of both realms. He and I…we needed each other. Cleaving our worlds in two took something from us that we shouldn't have gambled with."

"Right, right. The balance righted itself," I said quickly, the words all blending together. This wasn't the time for a history lesson. So what if they used to be sixty-forty good and evil or whatever; I'd come to learn it was all relative. Good people did bad things all the time. Both worlds had their monsters. "You were right. We should try to get her back to the Day World. It's worth a try, though my vote is still for dismemberment."

"Nora."

"Of course, if we go with your plan, we'd probably have to stay for a while to make sure she wasn't a threat. She does look stronger now," I mused. "We'll need to get the key back from Katie."

My muscles shivered, the thought of extended Day Walking enough to send me running for the hills. We wouldn't have to stay as long this time though, and we could always take shifts. A few days here, a few days there. It wouldn't be like before—it couldn't. And when Mara was weak enough, we could leave her to rot.

"*Nora.*"

I froze at the Sandman's harsh tone. *Definitely, definitely wasn't going to like this.*

He gently lifted my chin, forcing me to look at him, and I instantly wished with everything inside me that I hadn't. A full year hadn't passed since I saw his face for the first time. This was an expression I'd yet to encounter. One I never wanted to again. There were elements I recognized—determination, resignation, adoration. Sorrow, even. What it lacked, I realized with a bolt of terror, was hope.

Oh no. The Weaver's words breezed through me, echoing my own thoughts.

"What?" I squeaked.

"I love you," he said, truth dripping from every syllable.

He did, yes, but that wasn't what he was saying. Not really. I backed out of his grip. "*What?*" I repeated.

"Nora, listen to me." He spoke slowly and moved even slower, his palms cupping my face. The knife was still in his right hand and now pressed gently against my cheek. "Mare said *world.* The *world* created her."

Whatever that meant.

It means, the Weaver paused, seemingly at a loss for words. *He better not be taking this where I think he is...*

"Okay." I struggled to inhale. "I'm not following."

"The world," he said again, his gaze piercing me.

I placed my hands over his. "Sandman, you're scaring me."

"You're going to be fine. Everyone's going to be fine," he said, broken. His eyes glazed over with a thin layer of unshed tears, and suddenly, I was broken too.

"Explain before I completely lose it," I begged.

The world, the Weaver supplied, *created the Ancients. They were made from the violence of the world coming together, whereas the Sandman and I were made from magic afterwards.*

"Spell it out for me!" I shouted to them.

The Sandman flinched. "If we can restore balance in the Night World, it should balance *both* worlds."

A single, completely balanced being could destroy her, the Weaver agreed bitterly.

"How *exactly* does that happen?" I asked warily.

"The Weaver's magic taints my beach, and my magic inside a nightmare will kill it. Can something like that truly work together?" His throat bobbed as he swallowed hard. "It's not cohesive enough."

My body went cold. If our magic couldn't work together, taking her to the Day World was our only option. Why did it feel like that wasn't his pending suggestion? "And?" I urged. "Do you want to use the knife to rip open the barrier between Day and Night again? Is it even possible?"

"If it were, that information died along with the Dream Keeper I used to hold it." The Sandman's hands fell from my face, and he pulled the knife from its sheath, the blade still coated black with Mara's blood. "You killed the Weaver with this."

Don't you dare say another word! the Weaver raged.

"Stop," I said, breathless, the Weaver's panic sparking my own.

"You have his power in you," he said, ignoring me.

"I have *him* in me," I corrected. "And that's only because he put himself there. It's not an automatic transfer."

He ran a hand through his hair. "If you had both dark and light powers—"

"No," I said before he could finish. "Did you hear me? That's not how it works."

"I could put myself there too," he insisted.

I leapt away from him and the knife. If my pulse was any faster, my heart would explode. Everything around me faded, my focus sharpening on the man before me. "I'm not killing you. Are you crazy?"

He took a step toward me and I took another back. "I wouldn't be dead," he said patiently.

I had *major* opinions on that, but it didn't matter because I wasn't going to do it. Even if it worked, even if the Sandman claimed another pocket inside my head and we successfully killed Mara, there was absolutely no chance I would be able to drive a knife into his chest. Stabbing the Weaver had been traumatic enough. If I killed the person I loved most, what did that make me?

"I don't need a third voice in my head—especially when you two would be fighting with each other twenty-four-seven. Besides, what's to say the magic would combine inside me? Maybe they would eat at the other until all three of us were dead. *Really* dead."

"They wouldn't." The Sandman held up the knife. Black and gold, blue and silver. A patchwork of both magics, held together with the blood of two Night Lords. "It worked before."

"Yes. *Before you changed things.*" I took a deep breath to keep myself from falling apart. Even if there was a guarantee that killing him wouldn't change things again, make them worse, it wasn't an option. "It's not going to happen, Sandman."

He darted forward and crushed me to him before I could flee. "You had me long before any of this happened, and you'll have me long after it ends."

"Not if you're dead, I won't." My throat constricted, my words coming out choked.

"If the worlds end, it won't matter. We'll be gone. All of us. Me, you, Kail. Katie…" He pulled away and his star-flecked eyes bored into me. "Do it, Nora. I've lived a long time, and I've made an eternity's worth of mistakes. Let me fix them. Later we can work on getting the Weaver and me into separate bodies."

Tears burned the backs of my eyes. "You're clearly having a moment—"

"We'll put him in a hamster or something, of course," he said, the joke not quite reaching its mark.

A hamster? the Weaver growled. *Do not do this, Nora. There's a strong chance all of us will die.*

He didn't need to convince me. Not even a little. "I love you. That's why I'm saying no. We'll find another way."

The Sandman backed out of our embrace, taking my hands, and wrapped them around the knife's handle. The Weaver exploded into a wordless shriek that mirrored my own feelings. Just touching the knife made my entire body go numb. I tried to yank myself from his grip, but he was stronger. It felt as if my brain was about to short circuit. My back hit the side of an icy tunnel, and I felt the frigid temperature with every molecule.

"Stop," I begged.

Gently, the Sandman aimed the tip of the knife between his ribs, resting it against the skin underneath. "Here."

"No!" I flexed my fingers to drop the knife, but he squeezed harder.

"It's okay," he promised.

Enough, the Weaver roared and, in the blink of an eye, rammed himself forward, taking control of my body.

The Sandman's eyes widened. Warm liquid flowed over my hand, and I screamed. Only the sound didn't come out because the Weaver held fast.

"Forgive me, old friend," he rasped in that voice that was only partially mine. "This wasn't your wrong to set right."

There was a groan then. From me. *Me.*

The world spun ever-so-slowly. As I fell to my knees, I noticed the distinct lack of a weapon protruding from the Sandman's chest. Because it was in mine.

Hold onto the darkness, Nora, the Weaver instructed. *Hold it tight.*

"What?" I breathed to the Weaver and slumped to the side.

The Sandman caught me. His lips were moving. His beautiful lips. I lifted my hand to touch them—or at least, I tried. Darkness stole them away. It stole everything. My vision. Sound. Feeling. It didn't even hurt, being stabbed in the heart.

Chapter Twenty-Seven

Keeper, called a familiar voice. *Nora.*

The blackest black surrounded me, but I knew I wasn't alone. A golden orb emerged out of nowhere, surrounded by a mass of dark spirals. The faint glow shone through strands of swirling darkness and peeked out from tiny holes. I drifted toward it as it called my name again. The swirls reached toward me. Beckoned. I stretched out a hand. The threads on my arm slid down, the ends fraying out as if eager.

Hold tight, the voice said again. How many times had it repeated those words now? A thousand? How long had I been like…this? Here? Where was I?

The spirals brushed over my fingertips, and I gasped. Pure, unfiltered power burst through my body. The spirals pulled me in. Cradled me until I was cocooned in their golden light. I gripped the coils as hard as I could.

Now, listen.

Listen? I was listening. Hanging onto every word. Grasping onto them for life itself.

"Nora!" cried another voice. It was the sound of breaking. Of a window shattering. A million little pieces of pebbled glass cascading over cement. But it was also the sound of warmth, of dreams and promises. Memories. Reality filtered in. The knife…it was imbedded in my chest. A dull, throbbing pain pounded around it. Faintly. So faintly. Fading, fading, fading.

Do not let go, the Weaver urged.

You killed me. It wasn't an accusation, merely a statement. I didn't have it in me to feel angry or betrayed. *You saved him.*

I saved us all, the Weaver said, terse. *Unless you let go.*

A part of me, distant and tired, wanted to loosen my grip. To let go and drift away. *Why save everyone? What do you get out of it?*

I get to live, he stated as if it were obvious. *It was your hand that held the knife. Where could my power escape to if we're in a closed loop? I can't let you die because I can't get out of your body. So, if you don't listen to me, if you don't hang on, you die. I die. He dies.*

If I killed myself, there would be no more Weaver. Without the Weaver, there would be no more balance. He acted out of self-preservation, but that wasn't the only reason. I felt him in this space, whatever it was. Where I would've expected him to feel like a bed of nails, the Weaver's essence wrapped around me like a warm blanket. A bit of a coarse blanket, perhaps, and made of the itchiest wool, but if I was going to die, I would take it over the alternative.

The balance always rights itself, the Weaver said, slightly smug. *Follow the Sandman's voice. Wake us up and let's find out what our new existence looks like.*

New existence. Did I want to see what that looked like? Changing the first time was brutal enough. What if it was worse this time? What if I lost more of myself until nothing was left? The numbness couldn't extend much more if I wanted to keep my humanity, but perhaps living without it was better than not living at all. I stared into the swirling darkness. I had to make a choice: live as the Weaver or die as Nora.

But...maybe I wouldn't have to choose. A new existence had potential.

"Nora, please," the Sandman called.

The sound was far away. Reaching it felt impossible, but I had to try. I forced myself to move, pushing my way through time and space, dragging the bundle of light behind me like a ball and chain.

"Not again," he whispered repeatedly. "Open your eyes, Nora."

Regret filled me. I stabbed the Weaver, and now the Weaver had stabbed me in return. Both times, the Sandman was there, thinking me either dead or dying. I was glad I didn't experience this part the first time. It had been like a dreamless sleep then— one moment I was awake, the next I was waking.

Now it was more like clawing my way out of a coffin buried six-feet underground. Freedom was there above me, and I scratched my way toward it with lungs ready to burst.

Hold tight, the Weaver reminded me when my grip loosened.

So I did. I held so tight that it hurt.

Blue caves glistened overhead. I gasped for breath and rolled onto my hands and knees. Ice bit into my palms as I coughed and coughed, drawing ragged breaths between each painful heave.

Relax, the Weaver droned. *We're alive. Try to remember that requires breathing.*

Hot tears flowed down my cheeks. They dripped to the ground and melted small divots into the ice. My fingers curled over the smooth ground. Without warning, blood spurted from my mouth, over and over until I thought I would die all over again, the coughing picking up it where it had left off. The Sandman rubbed my back in slow circles until it slowed to a stop. I focused on his touch. Let it pull me back.

I wiped my mouth on the back of my hand and fought the urge to collapse. "I'm okay," I lied. My chest felt exactly like one would expect after being stabbed. "Help me sit?"

The Sandman eased me back off my shaky arms to sit against the tunnel wall. Tear tracks stained his face, and his shoulders were slumped. In pain, in relief. "Why did you do that?" he croaked.

"It wasn't me. It was—" I gasped. Threads of gold broke through his violet irises, weaving neatly between the silver specks, and bled into the whites of his eyes. Or, what used to be the whites, but were now black as pitch.

"Nora?"

I flew to my feet, woozy and nauseous, and patted at my chest. The hole remained in my shirt, but the knife itself was gone, as was the pain…and the wound. "Where is it? The knife, where is it?"

I pulled the magic out to save us. It's gone.

"We need it," I rasped. "To kill Mara, we need it."

The Sandman gave me a gentle *shh* and ran his fingers through my hair. "It didn't kill her, remember? It won't help us."

My mind was blank except for pain and shock. Mostly shock. Without the knife, without us being a single, completely balanced being, what were we supposed to do?

"What do I look like?" the Sandman asked quietly.

"Like…you?"

He shook his head and inched closer to me, inches from my face. "What do I look like? Your eyes. They're gold from corner to corner, except for the very center. It's dark blue with…" His lips parted with an awed gasp. "With silver flecks."

We are remade, the Weaver said in wonder.

I met his gaze, a smile creeping over my face. *It worked.* "Yours too. Are different, I mean."

The Sandman crushed me in his arms. "I love you. I love you, I love you, I love you," he repeated in a single breath.

"I'm sorry," I said, returning the embrace with every ounce of strength I had left. "The Weaver—"

"I know." He tightened his grip and placed a kiss on my shoulder. "I'm going to kill him a thousand times for this."

Tell him I said good luck.

I'm not telling him that, I replied.

His breathing was uneven against my neck. "I will never forget what he did."

Tough crowd, the Weaver said with a sigh. *At least ask him which part.*

"He wants to know which part," I relayed.

The Sandman pulled back and cracked a smile—a thing I hadn't seen in what felt like forever. "Weaver," he paused as if unsure he could speak to me to reach him. "I'm not sure if I'll be able to forgive all that you've done. You've acted rashly and put people in danger for as long as I can remember, but…it's always gone as you planned."

Except that once, he grumbled.

"What you did was reckless," the Sandman continued. Then he stopped, though I could tell there was more he wanted to say by the way he paused.

You're welcome.

"We're alive," I said slowly.

"We're new," he corrected. "And old."

I shrugged one shoulder. "New or old, we're *both* alive."

"Yes." The Sandman rubbed his chin thoughtfully. "His heinous plan worked."

He'll be grateful one day when he recovers from seeing you dead. Again.

Not sure he'll ever get over that, I said tersely. If our roles were reversed, I never would.

"Do you feel it?" he asked, almost reverently. "My power alongside yours?"

I tilted my head and looked inward. There was the darkness I became so accustomed to, but above it, propped up like a new bud on a dying stem, was a cloud of silver. "I feel it," I said quietly. "It's small, but I feel it."

You are aware Mara's likely banging away at the safe by now, yes?

"Crap." I leapt to my feet. "Mara."

The Sandman stood, his movements achingly slow. He probably *did* ache—the stabbing wound wasn't my only source of pain. The Dream magic inside me was heavy, as I'm sure the Nightmare magic was to him. He flexed his hands carefully as if testing their new strength, or, perhaps, fearing the sand wouldn't respond to him anymore. I waited silently next to him as the worry drained ever-so-slowly from his expression. Then with a flick of his wrist, the blocked passage shattered outward. "After you."

I looked down the icy tunnel and shivered, though not from the cold. Mara was so close, and there wasn't time to waste exploring empty passages. I placed a hand on the wall and felt for the fish's thread. "That way," I said, pointing to the tunnel that tilted down at the fork in front of us.

***

We followed the fish down, up, and down again until we were only a few steps away. It swam in a horseshoe around the opening to another tunnel. Mara had to be down there, if not because of the fish leading us this way, then because of the repetitive thuds coming from inside. I shooed the fish away, so it wouldn't inadvertently rat us out. It took off like a rocket, the water pocket refreezing.

"What do you think she's doing in there?" I whispered.

The Sandman tapped the flat side of an exposed sand-made blade against his palm. "I don't know."

"You're going to cut yourself," I said, placing a hand on his forearm to still his nervous movements.

"If it doesn't work this time…" He winced.

"Don't make me be the optimistic one."

There wasn't anything else we could do except try. Most of me still belonged to the Nightmare Realm which made me feel less balanced instead of more, but maybe Mara needed that chaos to kill her. Not two halves of a whole, but jagged pieces to a puzzle.

I really didn't want to have magic twist me up and spit me out a third time, so if this didn't work, it was the Day World or bust. Taking the Sandman's hand, I led the way without another word. If he came out with another doubtful sentence, I'd probably crumble anyway.

We followed the tunnel where it veered off, filled with skeletal remains. A mammoth's skull took up the entire space and more, the ice partially swallowing the bone. The tusks were twice as long as the Sandman was tall, two jutting up into the ceiling and another two down into the ground. There were three sets of eye sockets on each side—the largest near the top, another slightly smaller toward the front, and an even smaller one in between. Behind the skull, the ribcage acted as support for the tunnel.

The Sandman slipped through a gap between the top and bottom jaw, and I eased through behind him. A large blue scorpion shifted near the top of the skull, tail clicking. I glared at it, daring it to make a move, and tugged the Sandman away. We proceeded slowly beneath the spinal cord. We came to the end of the ribcage to find a long tail with a spiked harness for drilling tunnels, perhaps, or battle, chained to the tip.

On it was Baku.

He lifted his lips in a silent growl and slunk down from his perch with more grace than I would have thought possible. The chimera lowered into a crawl-like stance, prowling toward us. *Crap.* I glanced at the Sandman. Baku dead would be fine with me, but it was still his call. His face gave nothing away other than the pain of seeing his friend prepared to attack.

"He's going to give us away," I whispered.

"I know."

I clenched my jaw. "Do something."

"I can't..." he admitted reluctantly.

But I could. I was so close to the wall that all I had to do was tilt my hand to make contact. It was harder finding the cave's

thread with only the tip of my pinky finger, but not impossible.
I didn't dare move more than that and risk Baku noticing. My
hands trembled as the nightmare eater got closer and closer. If I
had another few seconds, I could easily—

Excuse me, the Weaver said, slipping forward and waiting. I
wrinkled my nose and let him do the work. It was over in a
second. The ice beneath Baku melted, the water sucking him
under, the ice immediately reforming around him. I stared in
horror at the frozen form a few feet away. Looking at the
Sandman was too hard.

"Come on," I whispered.

We didn't have far to go because Mara stood in the shadows,
watching. Something long and curved spun in her hands. At her
back a hole was gouged into the ice. I didn't know what she
hoped to accomplish by unearthing the doors when she had no
key, but it didn't make a difference.

She ran at us, her scream vibrating against my eardrums. A
glint of metal was the only warning of her weapon swiping out.
It sliced just above my kneecap, and I fell with a strangled scream
of my own. The Sandman wasted no time hurling sand-made
weapons at her. He parried her thrusts with a pipe and used it to
knock her feet out from under her. She leapt up with ease. I
stopped watching then and scanned our surroundings.

Think, Nora, think, I told myself. We had to get the advantage,
even if it was only for a moment. The Sandman slammed back
into one of the skeleton's ribs with a resounding crack, and an
idea formed.

Do it. Do something, the Weaver urged.

I took a thread from my wrist and produced a four-foot, 3D
diamond puzzle made of the same stone. It held its shape until I
climbed to my feet and hobbled two steps, then it collapsed into

a heap that no Dreamer would ever be able to piece back together.

That's what you chose? the Weaver yelled. *Why not the heavy-weight boxer or the—*

"Shut up," I growled and picked up one of the L-shaped pieces.

Mara swooped in front of me, and I swung at her head. The puzzle piece connected, snapping her neck sideways. The Sandman followed as she slid down the tunnel toward the spiked ball. I took the moment to hook the puzzle piece around one of the exposed ribs and pulled. I could sense the bone giving—getting ready to snap, but it just needed a little more strength. Swallowing a scream, I lifted my injured leg up, leveraged my foot on the icy wall, and shoved my whole body back. The bone splintered. Sweat beaded on my forehead as I readjusted myself and did it again.

This time the bone snapped in two, splinters flying. I landed hard and stopped sliding backward when my head cracked against the opposite wall. There was no time to clear the ringing from my ears. I grasped another thread. This time a large, ivory-toned creature with four arms covered in suction cups emerged, somewhere between a starfish and an octopus. It barreled into the fight, knocking the Sandman back. He landed in front of me, a deep cut from ear to collar bone bleeding freely.

"We have to get her on the bone," I urged and climbed to my feet. "She won't be able to get free without ripping herself apart."

The new nightmare fell backward with Mara wrapped against its chest. The suction cups pulsed, and dark veins popped up along its rubbery arms. The Sandman cursed and lifted his knife.

"Wait!" I cried.

But it was too late. He swung down at the same time Mara flipped the nightmare over, shielding herself from the blade. The nightmare shuddered and, one-by-one, the suction cups turned black and still. I grunted wordlessly. My plan was *going to work*. The Sandman leapt onto the nightmare's back, pressing them both into the ice. Mara wriggled and squirmed, nearly toppling him.

"Screw this." I grabbed a long piece of the diamond puzzle from the floor. The sharp edge ripped open my palm, but I barely felt the sting. There was only the briefest of moments where I paused to consider my plan. Too brief for the Weaver to tell me not to do it. For *me* to talk myself out of it. I drove the puzzle piece through the Sandman's shoulder, bones grinding against gemstone. It slid effortlessly into the boneless nightmare beneath, and then into Mara like a pick into stone. It wasn't clear who screamed first. Me or one of them.

"I'm so sorry." I took the knife from the floor where the Sandman had dropped it before it turned into a pile of sand. "So, so, so sorry."

Hurry, the Weaver urged. *It won't hold her for long.*

The pile of impaled bodies was already shifting as Mara scrambled to escape. My heart was a hummingbird ready to flit away, taking me with it. My entire body shook as I ignored the Sandman's face, pinched in pain, and the nightmare's ever-blackening form. My body flowed through the motions as if it were nothing but a dream. A bad, *bad* dream.

The knife slammed into the side of Mara's head with a dull, wet *thunk.*

I froze, hand still wrapped around the handle, waiting. *Waiting.* Waiting.

For her to move.

For her to speak.

For something, anything to happen.

It felt like days but couldn't have been more than twenty seconds.

The Sandman lifted himself up, tearing the diamond shard the rest of the way through his body. He grunted and clutched at the wound. Blood flowed down onto the decaying nightmare. I fixated on that. On his hand, slick with thick red blood. It leaked between his fingers. Ran down his forearm to his elbow.

"I'm sorry," I croaked, the words not even close to enough.

"Don't be sorry," he rasped. "I'll heal."

I nodded. *Right.* Heal. He would heal. But he was still in a lot of pain. It was a miracle he wasn't swept back to the beach, but nothing vital was hit. He could still fight if he absolutely needed to.

How about a little less gloom and doom, and a little more 'yay, mission accomplished'?

"Is it?" I asked aloud.

"Is what?" The Sandman rolled the nightmare off Mara's body with his good arm. "Nora?"

"Is it mission accomplished?" I blinked a dozen times until my vision cleared. "She's dead, right?"

He offered me a smile, as pained as it was. "Yes. She's dead."

She didn't look dead. Not like other things looked dead, and I would know. Mara looked more like a photograph—a moment frozen in time. Her palms still pressed to the ground and one leg bent upward, foot planted as if she were about to shove herself up and make a run for it. If it weren't for the knife still sticking out of her skull…

"You're sure?" I squeaked.

How much more dead do you want her to be? the Weaver asked, annoyed. *You used the blood of two lords. It's the closest you'll get to how the world used to be.*

The Sandman ran a hand from my cheek down to my shoulder, and gave it a reassuring squeeze. "I promise."

I let out a breath and leaned back onto my heels. My leg screamed all over again with the motion, and I hissed. "I'm fine," I said when I saw the Sandman open his mouth to ask. The blood of two lords. I wiped the sticky blood from the backs of my hands onto my pants. Was that what did it? Our blood? Mine on the knife, his on the diamond shard? Did it matter? It took less than a heartbeat to answer my own question. *No.* It didn't. "What should we do with the body?" I asked.

"I don't think it matters." The Sandman ripped the blade from Mara's head, globs of brain matter showering the area, and slipped the filthy knife back into its sheath. I cringed. Did he have to keep it?

"I don't feel comfortable leaving it here." I studied the chiseled part of the ice cave and did a quick patch job. Whatever Mara was after was going to stay hidden.

"We could burn it."

I nodded. "But not in here."

The Sandman rolled Mara onto her side. "We could…" He paused, blushing.

"What?" I pried open my hand to assess the cut and nearly blacked out when the cold air hit the wound. It was deep enough to see bone.

"Nevermind," he faltered. "It's a bad idea."

Oh? the Weaver said curiously.

I clenched my fist shut again—it felt marginally better that way—and pressed it against my chest. "What's a bad idea?"

"I…" He took a deep breath, unable to meet my eyes. "I don't want to leave him like that."

"Wh—" *Oh,* was right. I looked toward the chimera frozen a few yards away. "Baku."

"It's a bad idea," he said again.

It was. It was a horrible idea. He was a spy. An enemy. Still, he had been a friend once which deserved some level of respect. Just as the Sandman didn't punish the Weaver more harshly than he could have, he couldn't punish Baku to an eternity in frozen terror. I understood. I didn't agree, but I understood.

"Okay." The word was sour. "I'll let him out, but he has to stay caged."

Not here, the Weaver added. *If you're going to be stupid about this, at least make sure he's far away from this place.*

I couldn't argue with that. With my jaw clenched so hard my teeth ached, I found the thread yet again and cut the ice around the chimera, leaving him completely frozen, but easily transportable with the right equipment.

"Consider it my *sorry for stabbing you* gift," I said with a half-smile. "I'll go get Kail to help with the heavy lifting."

"I've got him," the Sandman said quietly.

I gave a terse laugh and stood. "And miss out on the chance for Kail to do more work? I would never."

"Thank you," he said so quietly I barely heard.

He didn't have to thank me. It wasn't any less than he would do for me. I kissed him on top of the head, sparing a long moment to breathe him in. The lilac scent I knew so well blended with the harsh, cold scent of ice and the metallic tang of blood, but underneath was something else. Something new, something old. Something…*us.* I kissed his hair again. "Wait here," I said softly, and left.

***

When I finally limped my way to where Kail waited with the nightmare army, it was everything I could do not to collapse. He would've caught me, I was sure, as long as I waited until he was close enough to manage it. That wasn't the problem. The problem was my image. I still really, *really* didn't want another revolt on my hands.

Smart, the Weaver said.

Please stop talking, I snapped, too exhausted to deal with him. Or anyone, really.

"Nora!" Kail shoved his way out of the formation and gripped my arms painfully tight. "Are you okay? What happened? Where's the Sandman? Is Mara—"

"Dead." I patted his chest with the edge of my fist. *We did it,* I wanted to shout. Now that I was out of the caves, the gravity of that sunk in, but as much as I'd come to love Kail, I wanted to celebrate with the Sandman first. "Send three of the strongest nightmares in. There are a couple of…things to carry out, and then I need you to help the Sandman with something. I sort of stabbed him so…"

Kail's eyes blew wide. "Repeat that."

"I stabbed him." I scanned the nightmares and leaned closer to whisper in his ear. "Before you go, bring me the Hours."

He pulled away and tilted his head. "Why?"

They were traitors. Though they obeyed me this once, it didn't mean they always would. I was finished looking over my shoulder. There was one chance for loyalty, and they blew it before I even sat at the loom.

Yes. I would avoid a revolt.

Today.
Tomorrow.
Always.
The Hours would be my latest example.
"*Why?*" I met his gaze. "I'm not as forgiving as the Dream Lord."
Understanding filled Kail's expression and he bowed, the gesture his brother's influence. "Of course, Lady."

Chapter Twenty-Eight

The Sandman

Long, tattered ribbons in all shades of yellow and blue hung from overhead coils. Some brushed against the dirt while others floated obnoxiously in my face. I wasn't sure what fear the landscape was supposed to instill in Dreamers, but it was far from the ice caves and I was tired down to my very core. Dragging a frozen solid Baku across the Nightmare Realm—assisted by the new Kail or not—wasn't easy when my shoulder still oozed blood. A few inches over and the shard would've hit my heart, sending me straight back to the beach.

"This works for now," I said and leaned against one of the coil supports.

Kail lifted the rope of a sand-made sled and bent over, gasping. "He's heavier than he looks."

"It's his diet," I said with a small smile.

Kail glared at me, his new appearance jarring. It was the eyes—black orbs didn't exactly inspire confidence in someone's benevolence. I wish Nora had waited until after we took care of Mare to put him back together with Halven so she wouldn't be completely alone right now. I sighed. It didn't matter. She sent Kail with me specifically, claiming she had something to take care of. I'd ask what later.

"Nora should've stabbed you a couple more times when she had the chance," Kail griped.

I pinched my lips. *She should've stabbed me* first. But then I would be gone, and Nora would be what? Playing host to two warring Night Lords? The Weaver made the right decision, even if it was irresponsible. I'd make him pay for it one day, regardless. When he was out of Nora's head and locked away somewhere. When we no longer had to worry about fighting for our survival. But that was the distant future. There were too many uncertainties, mainly what would happen to Nora without the Weaver, but one day…

One day, we *would* have to fight to survive again. The threat could come from nowhere or it could bloom closer to home, but it would come. Eventually. By then, Nora would undoubtedly be able to fight without help. She'd come so far in such a short amount of time that I could only imagine the powerhouse she would be in a few hundred years.

"You should probably kill him," Kail said, interrupting my musing, and motioned to Baku.

"Probably," I agreed. Unlike with the Weaver, I would reinforce his binding and often, but his prison wasn't what worried me. There was no caging an idea. Baku's ideas, his desire to help Mare open the Ever Safe, were a danger to everyone. I studied my former companion through the thick layer of ice. "He betrayed me."

"Everyone seems to betray the ones they love at some point," Kail said sincerely.

"Yes." I winced. "We didn't all try to release ancient monsters and destroy the world though."

Kail shrugged.

"What about you?" I asked quietly. "Who have you betrayed?"

"Me?" He laughed mirthlessly. "I think the question should be who *haven't* I betrayed. A nightmare of the unknown wouldn't live up to his name otherwise."

I narrowed my eyes at his admission. "Then how many have you loved?"

The amusement drained from Kail's face, and he fiddled with a worn yellow ribbon. "Ah, you have me there, Dream Lord. I've never betrayed a loved one."

"Right, because you've never loved anyone but yourself." It sounded cruel, perhaps, but Kail had always been nothing if not self-centered.

"That's not true. Or..." One side of his mouth quirked into a rueful grin. "I guess it is seeing as Halven was my other half."

I rolled my eyes and backtracked the way we came. My shoulder itched where it slowly mended and screamed where it hadn't yet started. A day or two from now, when it was nothing but a pink mark, I was going to think more on the fact that Nora ran me through without a second thought. It was smart—unexpected from Mare's point-of-view—but...she didn't even flinch until after the job was done.

"I know what you're thinking," Kail called, running after me. "That I can't love."

"Am I so transparent?" I asked.

Outside the ribbons, I turned to Baku and began the painstaking process of creating a prison large enough, *strong* enough, to hold him. It would have to allow other nightmares to wander in; I couldn't starve him. Though I knew nothing I did would make him forget he was locked up, I hoped there was something salvageable between us. At the very least, maybe we would stop hating each other one day.

"I can, you know," Kail continued as I worked.

I lifted a brow at him. Was he still fixated on this? This was what I got for trying to confide in a nightmare. "You're taking this rather seriously when I only asked for personal reasons."

He groaned and folded his arms across his chest. "This is harder than I thought it would be. Halven was the one that knew how to talk to people while I was the one left with the ability to be articulate. He learned, sort of, but…I guess I'm out of practice."

"Kail." I paused with a handful of sand resting in my hand and shifted uncomfortably. "This new attitude of yours is putting me on edge. Say what you want to say so I can focus on my work."

His cheeks flushed. "I won't betray Nora. That's where you were going with your questions, right?"

"No." I dragged out the syllable. It was entirely about my situation with Baku. "I'm not worried about that because if you do, I'll personally hunt you down, and you know that."

Kail gave me a half-hearted salute.

I shook my head and put the finishing touches on Baku's cell. The walls glowed a faint blue with flecks of gold where the light hit. I liberally threw another layer of magic at it to be safe, then turned to Kail. "You probably don't want to be here for the next part."

He wasted no time leaving me there alone. Maybe it was the awkwardness that sent him sprinting toward the palace, or that he was as worried about Nora's solo plan as I was. It wasn't that she was incapable—she had proved otherwise over and over—but her choices weren't always the wisest. Killing the Weaver, taking Mare's advice on traveling back to the Night World…the consequences should've deterred her from future rash decisions, but with the Weaver in her head doing things like making Nora stab herself in the heart…I pressed my eyes shut and shook the thought from my mind. It was over and done, but Baku wasn't.

As I added the final layer of sand to the underground slab, I allowed myself a final moment to rein in my emotions. Then it was time. I dumped the remaining sand from my satchel and ushered it through. It coated Baku's body, eroding the ice from head to toe. It took longer than I anticipated, and I refused to look as he made a variety of grunts and groans. Being half frozen had to be uncomfortable, but it would pass. Unlike the pain in my chest. Baku might as well have run me through like Nora had, one tusk at a time.

I waited patiently when it was over for Baku to stop throwing himself against the walls. He dug pits in the soft dirt and climbed the coils to scratch at the ceiling until he swayed with exhaustion. Finally, when he fell to the ground with a sorrowful huff, I approached and removed the pouch from around my neck to read his dreams. I had to know why he did it. The sand fell from between my fingers and spun into an empty plateau, then, when the sand was almost gone, it twisted up in the center. A tiny Baku sat at the center. Alone.

"You were lonely," I said in a hoarse whisper. "Did you want to open the door because you wanted to see others like you?"

Baku flopped his ears over his face.

"I'm sorry I never realized how you felt," I choked. *I'm sorry that I wasn't enough of a friend for you.* We were never really friends like the Weaver and I once were. Baku and I spent time together because we were both completely alone, and while that turned into something like affection, it wasn't what either of us needed.

When Nora started coming to the beach, I should've put two and two together. She was more like me than Baku was and with every passing night, we grew closer. I asked Baku not to come to the beach when she was expected without considering his feelings. He thought I traded him in for a different type of friendship, and I supposed I had. If I included him from the beginning, maybe we wouldn't be in our current situation. Or, maybe, it still wouldn't have filled his void.

"I'm sorry," I said again, a mere whisper.

I walked away. One heavy, heartbreaking step at a time.

Chapter Twenty-Nine

Nora

Three months later

The Hours' masks were stark against the black marble of the Keep. Kail leaned over the edge of the roof, holding the final one—number six—in place. The masks circled the open half of the building starting with one, ending with twelve, staring out in almost every direction, yet visible no matter where one looked.

"A little to the left," I yelled from my place in the courtyard. He slid the numbered mask over an inch. "There. That's perfect."

His string of curses blurred together as he struggled to attach one of the heavy-duty command strips Katie brought from the Day World. She loved the idea of hanging the masks as a warning, though I couldn't say the same for anyone else.

"Make sure the hook is straight," I shouted.

"So you've told me," he called back. "At least a hundred times."

I chuckled. He was a different nightmare lately. More helpful, less snarky. *More* meaning he asked fewer questions when I told him to do something like hang the Hours' masks. *Less* meaning I got a sincere *good morning* out of him now before he switched off the polite, Halven-side of his personality.

You would be bored if he were polite, the Weaver said.

It was true enough. It was one of the only things that still felt normal. The Dream magic left me feeling diluted, weaker, and there was a constant vibrating itch that seemed to travel through my bones. But that same sense of dilution made me stronger in another way. The blackness swirling inside my head was more of a dark grey now. My thoughts were clearer, though still void of guilt over killing random nightmares.

The Hours deserved what they got, just like the nightmares that killed my friends. Mara most of all. If the nightmares that killed Natalie and Emery deserved the horrible deaths I gave them, what did that mean the Weaver deserved? He was the one that had given the orders. I didn't regret killing those creatures, nor would I regret torturing the Weaver should we ever discover a way to extract him.

I closed my eyes and counted to ten. Calm…I had to be calm. If things became too much, if I let the anger overwhelm me, that little box of power the Weaver stashed away threatened to crack open.

I deserve a lot of things, the Weaver breezed. *But until you figure things out, we've decided to play nice, remember?*

I remembered. The decisions at uncomfortably, but he was right. We were forced to deal with each other for now, and that could be as hard or as easy as we wanted to make it. So, despite the fact that he murdered me, we would be…on friendly terms.

I didn't do anything to you that you didn't do to me.

Yes, yes, I snapped. *Truce.*

"What's going on here?" the Sandman asked as he stepped up behind me.

A smile cracked my face, and I leaned back against him. "A little redecorating. I didn't hear you come in."

"I know." He snaked his arms around me in a hug. "Are you ready to go?"

Just like that, my smile fell. Was I ready? Would I ever be? I left home months ago and used Detective Bell to spin the lie about Nevada. My mother and Paul probably hated me now, but I promised I would visit today. Katie stood beside me in this place—she would stand by me there too.

Suddenly, I regretted not seeing my sister since giving her the key to the Ever Safe. The Sandman kept her in the loop, passed messages between us, and delivered gifts, but I'd been so busy culling nightmares that there wasn't time. So, when the invitation came for today, I felt obligated to accept.

"Fine." I let out a harsh breath. "Let's get this over with."

"Good luck," Kail called from the top of Keep. He stood, straightening his clothes, the final mask in place. "You'll need it."

"That one's crooked," I shouted and took the Sandman's hand. "Fix it."

"What? Which one?" he cried in outrage.

I suppressed my giggle just long enough to dart out of the courtyard. "None of them," I whispered conspiratorially. The Sandman's answering laugh warmed me. "Are you sure you want to come?"

"Of course," he said, giving my hand a squeeze. "I'll wait at the end of the street like we discussed in case you need me."

***

I knocked. On my own door. *No.* It *wasn't* my door anymore. Discomfort twisted my insides. What was I supposed to say? How was I supposed to act? I wasn't the Nora they knew anymore—if you could say they ever truly knew me at all. I was a killer, a ruler, a creator. I was fearsome.

Say the opposite of what you want to say, the Weaver suggested.

"I'm not taking advice from you today," I said under my breath.

The door swung open, and for a moment, my mother stared at me like a deer caught in oncoming headlights. Did Katie not tell them I was coming? Oh, I was going to strangle her the next time she fell asleep. The joke was on her. I'd bring clowns. Lots and lots of clowns.

Right now however, one of us had to do something. Speak. Move. *Breathe.*

"Hi, Mom," I blurted, surprising myself.

She flung herself at me, crushing me in a hug. Tears splashed my neck a moment before her sob broke. I froze and stared over her shoulder at Katie, unsure what to do next. My sister stood in the middle of the living room with a smug grin. *Hug her,* she urged, mimicking the act with both arms.

That's the logical response, the Weaver added.

How would you know? Have you ever hugged anyone?

Ouch, he droned. *No need to be spiteful.*

I'll give you spiteful, you s—

"I missed you so much," my mother cried. "Oh, my baby girl."

My arms raised slowly as if they were no longer part of my body. I didn't know what to do. To think or say. Nothing would be enough to make up for the hurt I caused.

"Mom," Katie said, stepping up and resting one hand on her shoulder. "Let her inside."

"Right." My mother sniffled and pulled back. "Right, of course."

There wasn't any hesitation from my mother after that. She led me into the house without breaking physical contact. Her nails dug into my arm so I hard I thought she would draw blood, but I said nothing. The thud of the door behind us felt like the closing of a tomb.

If you can survive the Nightmare Realm, you can survive a single afternoon here, the Weaver said.

Like he would know. This *was* a nightmare. Mine. I had to look my family in the face and take responsibility for a lot that wasn't true. All while they pretended the things that *were* my reality didn't exist. Not that I was still bitter or anything…

You're the absolute worst at pep talks, Weaver. Seriously. Shut up.

First you want them, now you don't. Make up your mind.

Paul came in from the backyard and nearly dropped the plate of ribs in his hands. "Nora." He quickly slid the food onto the counter and rushed around the counter to hug me. It was less invasive, more welcoming, than the one my mom greeted me with. "It's so good to see you. When did you get here?"

"Right now," I said, numb.

"I made your favorites for dinner." He motioned to the table. "I hope you're hungry."

I nodded, though I wasn't. Not even a little. The nightmares kept me well satisfied.

My mother pulled out a chair and patted the seat. "Come sit next to me. I want to hear all about Nevada." She moved with a frantic energy, touching everything, turning plates just so, adjusting silverware.

"You didn't have to do all this," I said, taking in the extensive spread. "I…I can't stay long."

My mother's eyes widened. "You just got here."

I'm fairly certain you're going to regret coming at all, the Weaver whispered.

I already do, I thought back at him. But, at the same time, it was good being here. I hated to admit that even if it was only to myself. I didn't *want* to think of this place as a comfort zone. It was too…I suppressed a cringe. Too soft. Smelling the familiar smells, *feeling* the memories. Not all of them were good, but all of them were like the sun on a winter day. If I took any of this place back with me, it would get me killed.

"Where are you staying? You could stay here." My mom hesitated before she continued. "Ben, too, if he's with you."

"Mom," Katie warned. "You promised not to grill her."

"I'm not. I was only asking a question," she insisted.

I eased up to the table and into the chair. "I can't stay long," I said again.

"Why?" my mom asked. "Why did you leave?"

Ah, here we go.

"Mom," Katie said at the same time Paul said, "Val."

Her eyes bored into me. "I want to understand. Were you in trouble? Do you need help?"

I looked at Katie, begging her to step in. She took the hint without missing a beat. "You're going to scare her off," she warned. "Let's have a nice dinner, okay?"

Cancel the clowns, the Weaver said, enjoying himself far too much.

"Yes," Paul agreed. "We all have a lot to say, I'm sure, but we should go into this slowly and enjoy what time we have together."

"But—" My mother sucked in a breath and sat beside me. "Okay. Okay."

And just like that, she was piling my plate with ribs, corn on the cob, and macaroni salad, none of which were my favorites. But today they were. For them.

***

Three hours later, after a forced second helping because I *looked too thin,* and a giant slice of belated birthday cake, I said goodbye. For the tenth time.

"I really have to go," I repeated. "I'll be back, okay? I promise."

"What's your number, at least?" My mother grabbed a pad of paper and searched frantically for a pen. "At least give us that. Or your address."

"I have her number," Katie said quickly and gave me a subtle wink as if to say *I've got you.*

I like her, the Weaver said. *She's got a flare for extensive planning. Would you like to bet that she has a second phone stashed somewhere so she can message them under your name?*

I studied my older sister. My brave sister. My too-stubborn-for-her-own-good sister. And I smiled. *Sorry, I don't take bets I know I'll lose.*

Hugs followed. More hugs. So many hugs. I took a deep breath and endured it because it was the least I could do. Then I left. They watched—I knew they did. Their gazes clung to me like leeches. I shoved my hands into the pocket of my hooded sweater as I stepped onto the sidewalk and breathed in air heavy with the promise of rain. My steps were brisk, nearly a run.

He'll be there, the Weaver promised.

It wasn't a question of whether the Sandman was waiting or not. He promised he would, so he would, but that didn't mean my heart didn't flutter in anticipation of seeing him. Or that my skin didn't tingle in want of his touch. After all that had happened, he was still my addiction. The thing that kept my world spinning.

Hate to interrupt the internal love fest but would now be a good time to ask for a favor? the Weaver asked slowly.

"For you? Every time is a bad time for that," I said under my breath.

He paused. *Permission is overrated. I'd like for you to hold off on getting me out of here.*

I barked out a laugh. "Are you serious? Not a chance."

What if I'm quiet…er? Quieter.

As if that were possible. It still amazed me he was silent for a solid five months. "Why would you *possibly* want that?"

Because.

He fell silent when the Sandman came into view, and a sense of yearning filled the silence. Mine. And his. *Ah*, I thought bitterly. *You want to use me to get in his good graces before he has a chance to knock you into the next millennium.*

No. The Weaver huffed. *Fine, yes, but that's not the only reason. If I'm not…you know, you… Then I'm nothing to him.*

My heart skipped a beat as I flung my arms around the Sandman. This was where I belonged. With him. Things were better between us lately—the events in the ice cave seemed to have reset more than our magic. We hadn't talked about our fights, but somehow, we didn't need to.

"Hey." His smile was brighter than any star in the sky. "How was it?"

I winced. "Ugh."

"That good, huh?" he asked with a small laugh.

"Even better." I pressed my cheek against his chest, reveling in the steady *thump, thump, thump* of his heartbeat.

Then, to the Weaver, *You're wrong. You're not nothing to him.* He was a thorn in both our sides. A weed to rip out by its roots. The Weaver was our enemy, but it was never that cut and dry. History was fixed. The future was not. Ahead was a road shrouded in dense fog, and the only way we would know what it hid, was to travel through it.

I was not forgiving—I couldn't afford to be—but the Sandman was. All it took was one person to believe in you for change to happen.

"Let's go home," I breathed into the Sandman's chest.

Let's go home.

Chapter Thirty

The Sandman

Home.

The beach stretched out around us, and Nora didn't relinquish her hold on me as we snuggled into the pillows covering the pavilion.

Yes, we were home. *Our* home, now that Nora's magic didn't taint the beach. No nightmares, no fear, no death…those stayed in the Nightmare Realm where they belonged.

Not everything changed. We had, but the realms were largely the same. The Weaver and I cleaved the world apart—Nora and I put it back together. Not completely, but it was a start. I could feel the scratch of the Weaver's magic inside me now. It was a manageable enough sensation that I hoped to get used to it.

"I've been thinking." Nora propped her chin on my chest, and a small smile played on her lips. The stars reflected in her eyes, on her face, and in my heart. "Specifically, about you not having a name…"

"Oh?" I chuckled at the reminder of her past suggestions. "This should be good."

She *tsked* playfully, her nose wrinkling. "I've actually come up with a good one this time. Or, at least, I hope it is."

"I'm intrigued."

She pulled back slightly and toyed with the ties on my vest. "Do you remember how I was really into astronomy?"

I remembered her crying the night she threw her books away, but that wasn't a memory worth having. "I do, yes."

"For the record, there are *a lot* of stupid star names, so my options were limited." Her cheeks burned bright red. "There are two stars nicknamed *'the twins'* so I thought with the balance and everything that it sort of fit, but now that I'm saying it, it sounds dumb."

"It doesn't," I assured her. "Go on."

"Obviously I'm not going to suggest calling you Pollux." She gave a nervous laugh and lightly drummed her fingers against my abdomen. "Castor is weird too, but—and be honest if you hate it—what about Cas?"

"Cas," I repeated, testing the name. It felt strangely…good. I wasn't sure I needed a name, and I wouldn't want anyone but Nora using it, but I liked the idea. The thought of having a role outside of the Lord of Dreams as Nora's equal, not only in magic, but in life. My chest swelled with pride, with love and adoration. "I love it," I whispered and leaned in to kiss her. "I love *you*."

"I love you too," she vowed and leaned up on the pile of pillows until we were nose-to-nose. Every trace of her uncertainty melted away beneath my lips. The kiss was slow and tender, a promise of forever.

I hadn't dared hope for a future like this for us—one where we were together and safe. We had become the guardians of two worlds, rulers of one, as Lord and Lady of Night. There was a lot we needed to figure out, but one thing was always certain: I loved Nora more than anyone could love another living thing.

She and I were twin fires burning bright and eternal. I would fill her darkest moments with hope, and I knew without question, she would fill mine. Because, after all, for every light there was a shadow, for every dream, a nightmare.

Acknowledgements

Most of all, I want all of the readers who stuck with this trilogy and shown it so much love! Your enthusiasm gave me the motivation to keep going on days when I had doubts.

The best CPs in the world: Lauren, Kalyn, Loretta, and Candace.

As always, my Saltmates!

Lindsay & Judy.

Priscilla, Katie, Elle, Melissa, Stacy.

My family: Dan, Ian, Ryan, Nonny, Kathy, Mom, Dad, Heather, and my Georgia family.

I love you all!

Also by Amber R. Duell

Young Adult

The Dark Dreamer Trilogy:
Dream Keeper
Dark Consort
Night Warden

When Stars Are Bright

New Adult
Fragile Chaos

The Prince's Wing

Faeries of Oz series (co-written with Candace Robinson):
Lion (ebook prequel short story)
Tin
Crow
Ozma
Tik-Tok

Vampires in Wonderland (co-written with Candace Robinson):
Rav (ebook prequel short story)
Maddie
Chess
Knave

Once Upon A Wicked Villain (co-written with Candace Robinson):
Spindle of Sin
Tower of Shadows

About the Author

Amber R. Duell was born and raised in a small town in Central New York. She does her best writing in the middle of the night, surviving the daylight hours with massive amounts of caffeine. Her favorite stories are dark with a touch of romance and a villain you either love to hate or hate to love.

When not reading or writing, she enjoys snowboarding, embroidering, snuggling with her cat, and staying up way too late to research genealogy. She loves to travel and has visited more countries than states. Kissing the Blarney Stone and hand-feeding monkeys in the mountains of France will be hard to beat, but that doesn't stop her from trying to find the next real-life adventure.

www.ingramcontent.com/pod-product-compliance
Lightning Source LLC
Chambersburg PA
CBHW051137190726
48290CB00006B/1890